I0344397

The Businessman

OTHER BOOKS BY
THOMAS M. DISCH

NOVELS

The Genocides
The Puppies of Terra
Echo Round His Bones
Black Alice *(with John Sladek)*
Camp Concentration
334
Clara Reeve *(as Leonie Hargrave)*
On Wings of Song
Neighboring Lives *(with Charles Naylor)*

STORY COLLECTIONS

102 H-Bombs & other stories
Fun with Your New Head
Getting into Death
Fundamental Disch
The Man Who Had No Idea

FOR CHILDREN

The Brave Little Toaster

POETRY

The Right Way to Figure Plumbing
ABCDEFG HIJKLM NPOQRST UVWXYZ
Burn This & other essays in criticism
Orders of the Retina
Here I Am, There You Are, Where Were We
Poems of Duty and Responsibility *(forthcoming)*

The Businessman
A TALE OF TERROR

THOMAS M. DISCH

1817

HARPER & ROW, PUBLISHERS, New York
Cambridge, Philadelphia, San Francisco,
London, Mexico City, São Paulo, Sydney

Grateful acknowledgment is made for permission to reprint:

Excerpt from "The Assault on Immortality Begins" from *Henry's Fate* by John Berryman. Copyright © 1969 by John Berryman. Copyright © 1975, 1976, 1977 by Kate Berryman. Reprinted by permission of Farrar, Straus and Giroux, Inc.

FIRST EDITION

Designer: Jane Weinberger

Library of Congress Cataloging in Publication Data

Disch, Thomas M.
   The businessman.

   I. Title.
PS3554.I8B85   1984   813'.54   83-48811
ISBN 0-06-015292-3

84 85 86 87 88 10 9 8 7 6 5 4 3 2 1

The issue always and at bottom is spiritual.
—Dwight D. Eisenhower

The Businessman

CHAPTER

1

When she awoke she did not realize for some time where she was. Then it sank in—she was dead and buried in a grave. How she knew this, by what sense informed, she could not tell. Not by the sight of her eyes, or by any spiritual analog of sight, for how can there be sight where no light enters? Nor was there any tingle of fleshy consciousness in limbs or loins, in heart or mouth. Her body was here in the coffin *with* her, and in some way she was still linked to its disintegrating proteins, but it wasn't through her body's senses she knew these things. There was only this suspended sphere of self-awareness beyond which she could discern certain dim essentials of the earth immuring her—a dense, moist, intricated mass pierced with constella-

1

tions of forward-inching hungers, nodules of intensity against a milky radiance of calm bacterial transformation. *The worms crawl in*—she remembered the rhyme from childhood. *The worms crawl out. The worms play pinochle on your snout.* How long would this go on? The question framed itself coolly, without triggering alarms. Ghosts—such ghosts as she had ever heard of—were supposed to be free to range where they would. Were said to flit. Whereas she remained attached, by some sort of psychic gravity, to this inert carcass, in which even the process of decay was impeded by the chemicals that had been pumped into it.

Almost as the question was formed, the answer existed within her sphere of sentience. Her thinking self would go on thinking . . . indefinitely. Not "forever." Forever remained as unfathomable and foggy an idea as it had been when she was alive. She knew, too, that she would not always be confined to her corpse's coffin, that a time would come when she'd be able to slip loose from the clinging raiment of flesh to flit at liberty like other ghosts.

But that time was not now. Now she was dead, and she had that to think about.

CHAPTER
2

On Tuesdays on his lunch hour Glandier drove to The Bicentennial Sauna on Lake Street and got his ashes hauled by whoever was available. He wasn't choosy. The important thing was to get back to his desk by two o'clock. Not that anyone would have cared if he'd been half an hour late. But *he* cared. He liked to parcel his time into neat whole-hour bundles, a habit he'd carried over from school, where the bells demarcating the hours also signaled a shift of mental gears.

He did, naturally, have his favorites. For a blow job he liked Libby, who was the youngest girl at the sauna and sort of thin and frail. She never got down on her knees in front of him without a little wince of disgust. This had such an immediate positive effect on Glandier that he'd scarcely got his cock down her throat before he'd shot his load. In some ways that seemed a waste of $25, but while it lasted it was great, and for the next ten or fifteen minutes too. Also, it left more time for lunch.

His other favorite must have been the oldest of the lot. Sacajawea she was known as among the clientele of the Bicentennial. A real squaw with a fat ass and big sagging tits and lots of makeup around her eyes. She had a way of drooping her eyelashes down and lifting them up that was sexy as hell though probably just as phony as the lashes. He liked the idea of her having to act like she thought his performance was really hot shit, the way when he was screwing her she'd croon encouraging obscenities, or gasp them if he'd reached that rate of delivery; the way he knew she was grateful for his regular patronage and $5 tips, she being nothing to look at; the way, after he'd got his breath back, she'd start sucking him off again, gratis. Not to much purpose, usually. He could get it up again; that wasn't the problem. But usually he couldn't shoot his load a second time in the forty-five minutes he allotted himself.

The weekly visit to the Bicentennial was a substitute for his former weekly visit to the downtown St. Paul office of Dr. Helbron, a psychiatrist who specialized in combating the depressions and anxieties of upper-echelon executives at 3-M, Honeywell, and other Twin Cities–based multinational corporations. Dr. Helbron had suggested the Bicentennial himself, claiming that all Glandier needed to start feeling like his old self was a little pussy on a regular basis. How could he refuse the experiment with his own doctor promoting the idea?

And it had worked. While he was not precisely his old self again, he couldn't complain any longer of disabling depressions or sudden insane bursts of anger. Those had been the symptoms that had sent him to the doctor's office originally, on the advice of the company's personnel director, Jerry Petersen. Back at that time—the summer of '79—Glandier had done all he could to act like his old self-confident self, smiling a lot and cracking jokes, but while he might disguise his depressions, the anger, when it came, was not so controllable. Before he could think about it, he would flip out and find himself making a scene in a restaurant or berating one of the girls in the office for something probably not her fault. There was a kind of demon of righteousness in him that leapt out like a rattlesnake and with no more warning. After a few such scenes had come to be witnessed by his associates, it had been suggested to him by Jerry Petersen (who was not only the personnel director but a close friend as well) that he should seek professional advice.

A polite way of saying he was crazy. But then he was crazy, it could not be denied. Only a crazy man would murder his wife, and that was what Glandier had done.

CHAPTER

3

At the age of only forty-eight, Joy-Ann Anker was dying of cancer. She'd become violently ill in the second week of a diet that had been, up to that point, a great success. At the hospital they'd done an exploratory operation and discovered a large malignant tumor in her lower colon. It had already spread through her body beyond the point where surgery could hold out any hope. The hospital put her on a course of chemotherapy, which made her almost constantly nauseated, and sent her home. Ironically, the cancer, the operation, and the chemotherapy combined had had the effect of a completely successful diet. For only the second time in her life she was down to her supposedly ideal weight of 114 pounds and could fit into clothes she hadn't worn for

fourteen years. Most of her old clothes, however, she'd giv-
en to her daughter three years ago, at a time when she'd lost
faith in diets. Joy-Ann had cried, after Giselle had gone off
with the boxes of clothes, at her vision of the life that lay
ahead of her, a life of boredom, booze, and loneliness. She
cried now at the thought that even that life wasn't to be
allowed her. Sometimes she could even laugh about the
whole thing. God, obviously, was playing a practical joke.

Officially, she wasn't supposed to know she was dying.
The doctor and the priest had both told her that though the
odds were against her there was still hope. They didn't say
hope for how long, not to her. But during one of Bob's visits
to the hospital, she'd pretended to be asleep, so as not to
have to talk to him (if there was anything worse than visiting
someone in a hospital, it was being visited), and Dr. Wandke
had painted a very different picture for her son-in-law. Six
months. At most. That had been toward the end of January,
which gave her to the end of July if she was lucky.

There was some comfort in being able to pretend she
didn't know. When Father Rommel visited she could just be
her usual self and wasn't under pressure to go to confession.
Whereas if her prognosis were out in the open, she'd have
had to go through the motions of making a confession, and it
would have been a bad confession, since she was still, in her
heart of hearts, holding onto one sin she couldn't or
wouldn't repent of. From a strictly Catholic point of view it
might not be a sin at all—just the opposite, in fact—but it
wasn't something she wanted to discuss with a priest. It had
been bad enough all those years she'd had to confess once a
year to using birth control, but this. . . . In any case, she'd
stopped believing in a lot of things since the children had
left home and she didn't have to be responsible for *their*
religious beliefs.

It occurred to Joy-Ann that she might be able to get back
the clothes she'd given Giselle. Even better, she might ask

for Giselle's own clothes, if Bob hadn't given them away to Goodwill Industries as he'd said he meant to. She called Bob at work and his secretary said he was at a meeting, which naturally she didn't believe. Bob was a good enough son-in-law, especially considering what had happened, but his weekly visits sprang from a sense of duty, not because they enjoyed each other's company. Giselle was all they had in common, and the less said about that the better.

Dutifully he returned her call that evening, and she only had to hint at what she wanted before he volunteered to bring over Giselle's whole wardrobe tomorrow on his way to the office. There were eight cardboard boxes, which seemed a lot at first, but considering how many boxes would be needed to pack up all her clothes when she passed on, it wasn't an especially large wardrobe. She wondered whether he'd brought back Giselle's clothes from Las Vegas. At the time, with the tragedy still uppermost in everyone's mind, she'd known better than to ask, but now, unpacking the eight boxes, she couldn't help but be curious.

There were several casual outfits she couldn't remember Giselle ever wearing, jeans and cotton shirts and such, but only one that provably, by its label, originated in Las Vegas: an orange pants suit made out of a slinky polyester. It fit to perfection and looked, to Mrs. Anker's orthodox eye, just a little obscene. It might be possible to have the pants suit dyed, but she doubted it. What sort of life had Giselle been leading out there? She would never understand what had possessed her daughter to run off like that. It couldn't have been gambling. Giselle was the only one of them immune to that. It must have been madness, pure and simple.

In the end the only items she kept, besides the pants suit, were the things she'd outgrown and given Giselle: the belted suit from Dayton's, the black dress she'd worn to her own mother's funeral and scarcely ever again, and several flowery prints too lightweight for winter. She put them on and

took them off in front of the big bedroom mirror, weeping
sometimes at the thought that she might never live to wear
any of them out on the street, but sometimes smiling too,
because she had undeniably never looked sexier in her life.

CHAPTER

4

There was another world off at an angle from the world she'd known till now, that world six feet above her full of its cars and its houses. Sometimes this other world seemed to be inside her, but when she would reverse her attention inward and try to approach the threshold to that dimly sensed world within, it would go out of focus or fade, though never did it disappear entirely. It was always there, as real as the furniture one stumbles over in a dark room.

Her first clear view of it came in a flash. She saw, across the threshold, a field of pure geometry and color, like a painting that was simultaneously flat on the ground and covering every wall. It bore a general resemblance to a red gingham tablecloth, except that it wavered and the bands of red were just as bright, in their way, as the patches of white, which in fact weren't really white but some other, indefinable color. It seemed incredibly beautiful and important, but before she could grasp why, it was gone.

Afterward she speculated a great deal as to what it was that she had seen, but always, though she could recall quite clearly the look of it, its *sense* eluded her. Patience: that was the first lesson of the afterlife. Patience unmeasured by calendar or clock, or even by the cadences of articulated thought. Most of her subjective time went by in flows of low-level sentience, such as one slips into, in life, only at the edge of sleep. No telling how long these periods of spiritual sleep had lasted. They might be ten-minute dozes; just as likely she might have slept away an entire winter like a seed in frozen ground. Sometimes the ‛constellations of hungers creeping in the soil above her would have completely altered when she awakened, or the liquifying tissues of her dead body would have entered upon some new and more drastic stage of disintegration.

Impossible, even as a spirit divorced from flesh, not to regard these transformations without aversion. Impossible not to strain against that still unbroken linkage that kept her here, sealed in this coffin like a genie in a jug. Not, however, with any sense of dread; rather, she regarded her corpse as she would, in the world above, have reacted to some derelict on Hennepin Avenue, who smells and whose clothes are in rags and whom no one can help even if help had been asked for.

Once it seemed that she had actually won free. A tendon of the corpse's flesh, drying, had tugged a bone out of its socket: it was that sudden popping out she'd thought to be the breaking of the lock. And perhaps it did signal, in a small way, the beginning of her liberation, for afterward the horizon of her awareness seemed greatly enlarged. She came to have an almost panoramic sense of the cemetery grounds—

11

not just the sphere of earth immediately about her but beyond that, to where the other corpses lay and decayed. All of them dead, all inert and without consciousness. She alone, in all that cemetery, lived in the afterlife.

No, that wasn't so. She alone had failed to cross that inner threshold into the realm of the endless gingham cloth. It wasn't just her body she was trapped in, it was the whole world.

CHAPTER
5

The source of grace has its favorite bloodlines, for which there is no accounting. Grace runs in families; it has no relation to merit. Entire generations of sons-of-bitches may enjoy the most infamous good luck, while the wise, the virtuous, and the deserving suffer and sink beneath insupportable burdens. It is perfectly unfair, yet there is nothing religiously inclined people so long for as the assurance that they and theirs belong to a chosen people.

The Ankers were such a family. Joy-Ann, who was doubly an Anker, having been born an Anker and married an Anker cousin, would have denied this emphatically, but those who are so chosen seldom suspect it till quite late in life. She was still too young, at forty-eight, to recognize the marks of grace in what she considered a string of tragic misfortunes. For the source of grace—let us be honest and call it God—is also an ironist and a dweller in paradoxes; He produces good from evil as a matter of course. The Ankers were not notably wicked as a family. They were, admittedly, layabouts and drifters, by and large (even, in a few instances, bums and drunks), but not evil in large, oppressive ways; victims, not victimizers; the sort of people, mournful, meek, and poor in spirit, to whom the Beatitudes have promised, not without irony, heaven and earth. Joy-Ann, for instance, in the fifteen years since her husband's death, had been exempted from the common curse of having to work for a living by an insurance policy her husband had purchased for a quarter at the airport in Las Vegas. He had left Vegas ruined and was buried two weeks later in the Minnesota Veterans' Cemetery by a widow with enough money not only to rescue the mortgage from foreclosure but to purchase an annuity that paid out $8,000 a year! That, together with Dewey's Social Security survivor benefits, had seen the surviving Ankers through the rest of the '60s in comfortable indigence. Bing had gone to Cretin, Giselle to Our Lady of Mercy. Joy-Ann had stayed home and cooked quick, starchy meals from recipes in *Family Circle*. Each year she became a little fatter, a little more querulous, but in her soul she was as happy as a pig in mud. She was getting exactly what she wanted out of life, a free ride.

Now the ride was coming to an end just as inflation had whittled her annuity and benefits down to the point where grocery shopping was once again a source of anxiety. She had been faced with the necessity of having to sell the house. Two real estate agents, independently of each other, had valued it at $80,000, maybe more: four times what she and Dewey could have got for it in 1954 when it had passed to them on the death of her father-in-law, the senior Mr. Anker. A gold mine! All these years she'd lived in it she'd put it in the category of water, air, and sunlight—something necessary but omnipresent. With its shabby back yard and ancient wallpaper, who'd have supposed it wasn't the residential equivalent of the secondhand clothes at the Salvation Army? Eighty thousand dollars for a corner lot on Calumet Avenue? Money was becoming meaningless!

The neighborhood around Calumet had been one of Joy-Ann's longest-standing grievances. First it had got decrepit, then blacks moved in. Then, without her ever noticing, that process had gone into reverse. Houses were painted (except her own) and lawns tidied. Children reappeared on the sidewalks. Though some of them were black, they did set a general tone of prosperity as they pedaled their tricycles and pulled their wagonloads of symbolic sand, since one knew that not even automobiles require as large and constant a cash outlay as children. The Roman matron who said that her children were her jewels was not exaggerating.

Eighty thousand dollars: to be sitting on top of a pile of money like that and to know that it would all go to waste— that was no happy thought. Not literally to waste, of course. Literally it would go to her son-in-law, Robert Glandier. Joy-Ann didn't like him, but he'd always been a dutiful rememberer of Christmases and birthdays. After the tragedy of Giselle, and even more after her own spell in the hospital, he'd been as thoughtful as anyone who was basically inconsiderate could be expected to be. He phoned a couple of times a week and came around on Sunday mornings to take her to church if she felt up to it. Or, more usually, to join her in a Sunday brunch of waffles and bacon. Joy-Ann loved waffles. It didn't make any difference that a few minutes after she ate them she'd have to go into the bathroom to throw up; waffles remained a major satisfaction.

"Are you sure," he had asked her one such Sunday morning, "you don't want to go to eleven o'clock mass? It wouldn't be any trouble."

"No, really. Do you want another waffle?"

"Mmf," he said, nodding his head.

She poured batter onto the two grills and covered them. "The thing is, it doesn't seem so important to me any more. I mean, I don't see any reason why God should be there in church any more than somewhere else. Do you?"

"No. But then I don't believe in God."

Joy-Ann pursed her lips and shook her head, as though to say, *Naughty, naughty.* She was of the widely held opinion that at bottom everyone believed what she believed, if only they'd be honest with themselves.

"I still go to bingo on Tuesday nights," she continued thoughtfully. "Alice Hoffman drives me over. Would you believe I am actually *lucky* at bingo? That's weird, isn't it? I'm consistently lucky at bingo, though sometimes it's a little ironic. I mean, last week I won a turkey. What am I going to do with a turkey?"

"What did you do with it?"

"Well, I could see Alice definitely had her eye on it, but I didn't see any point giving it to *her.* I mean, she isn't exactly starving to death, is she. So I gave it to the sisters. And I got the nicest letter from Sister Rita thanking me. I wish they'd wear habits though, like they used to. And do the mass in Latin again. It just isn't the same."

Joy-Ann started quietly to cry. Latin made her think of requiem masses, and that reminded her that she was dying at the age of only forty-eight. Through her tears she watched the steam rising from the waffle iron.

Glandier watched the waffle iron too, so as not to have to look at his mother-in-law. He resented displays of emotion. He knew, from watching such moments on TV, that he was expected to say something comforting, or else to hug her. But all he could think to say was, "That's all right," which didn't seem much of a comfort, while the idea of physical contact with Joy-Ann was slightly repellant. Not because she

16

didn't still have her looks. Now that she'd slimmed down, she looked all right, especially for a gal of forty-eight. But she was dying, and Glandier had never given any thought before to the inevitability of death, to cancer and what it must do to stomachs, livers, lungs, and all the other spaghetti a person has got wrapped up inside his skin. He wished, fervently, that Joy-Ann would hurry up with her dying.

"They're done," she said, drying her eyes with a napkin, then opening both halves of the waffle iron. The waffles dropped from the upper grills like ripe fruit. She speared her own with a syrup-sticky fork and began to butter it. Lyrically, the butter melted from a solid yellow to a liquid, amber gleam, as though the brown grid of the waffle had been encased in Fabulon.

CHAPTER
6

After he'd got married, in '69—he was thirty then—Glandier's body had started going to pot. At regular intervals all through the '70s he would panic and start dieting and lifting weights in the workshop at the back of the garage. But the diet made him foul-tempered, and he got bored with the weights, so eventually he would return to his original attitude, which was, Fuck it. If that was the way it was going to be, there was no point fighting it.

He let his paunch sprawl over his belt. His jaw softened from Dick Tracy to Porky Pig. Even his arms and shoulders, which used to be beefy if not rock-solid, turned to flab. He didn't get sloppy about what he wore; that would have been a mistake, since his company was particular about its execu-

18

tives' dress code. He bought new shirts and suits as his bulk demanded and, in general, surrendered to the inevitable. A businessman: that was the image he liked to think he presented. A businessman who played golf and smoked dollar cigars and spent a lot of money on drab clothes. A big, fat businessman eating boozy lunches and boozier dinners and leading his peer-group into the life-styles appropriate to middle age.

Not all his peers were prepared to follow him down this path. As the '70s advanced, the serious jocks got more serious. You could see them out jogging on the winding lanes of Willowville, where there'd never been pedestrians before, their styled hair bouncing on their shoulders, their jogging suits stained dark with sweat, their faces locked into defiant grins. Not for Glandier. For him it was the back yard, the lawn chair, a daquiri, a magazine. When old college buddies kidded him about it, he made Falstaff-like jokes at his own expense and filed away his resentment for later revenge. The older executives at work became friendlier. They liked to see a young man in such a hurry to join them in their decrepitude.

Once, drunk and soaking complacently in the bathtub, it dawned on Glandier that *every* businessman at some point in his life must have come to this same decision—to *become* a businessman and leave his youth behind. Now, at forty-one, the transformation was complete, but the bottom had dropped out of the image. Without a wife to show for himself, a wife such as Giselle had been—pretty, deferential, and thirteen years younger than he—there was no longer that important announcement being broadcast to the world concerning his undiminished vitality in the physical department that mattered most of all, the department of sex. He had entered upon a new and scarier stage of disintegration. His figure was ballooning from the slack-muscled grossness allowable in a Brando or an Elvis to the blimpy, sexless softness of an out-and-out fatso. Even the shape and meaning of his face was altering.

He knew he looked terrible, that people made remarks about him, even the secretaries (*especially* the secretaries), that he was regarded, in some quarters, as a man who was coming apart at the seams (as his suits were, once again). But he couldn't help himself. He would get home at night after a hefty dinner at a downtown restaurant and immediately start swilling Heinekens and Dorito Tortilla Chips in front of the TV. The beer made him put on weight faster than hard liquor would have, but it moderated his tendency to get stinking drunk every weekday night. This way at least he could keep his wits about him, and when there wasn't anything worth watching after the news, which was usually the case, he could beaver away at the dining-room table, compiling or inventing statistics to stuff in reports. The work was the thing that kept him going. The work and the idea that somehow things were going to change, that he was on the verge of something important. Even if that importance was a negative factor, Glandier needed it in order to maintain a balance between himself and the universe, one in which the latter did not too much preponderate.

He figured that people supposed he was becoming so fat as a result of the shock of his wife's death in such unsavory circumstances. Maybe there was even something to be said for that idea. Maybe he was feeling some kind of buried guilt (it was possible), and that guilt triggered this terrible craving he felt whenever he resisted the least doughnut. If so, he was glad that the symptom offered no clue to the crime. There was no M chalked on the back of his jacket for everyone but himself to see.

CHAPTER
7

All the bodies were arranged in a pattern that resembled the neatest of suburbs, a checkerboard, a gigantic crossword puzzle. Above the dead, like clues to the puzzle, their names would be cut into the stones. The bodies she was aware of, quite as though she were in a room with them; the names and stones she had to imagine. All that lay above the ground was denied to her perception as much as that which loomed beyond the red-checked veil—heaven, she supposed.

As a girl, she'd been troubled by the pictures she'd seen of heaven—the saints and angels going to church in the clouds—until Sister Rita had explained to her that it would surely be more exciting than that, that it just wasn't possible from our point of view here below to imagine the splendor of looking straight at God's face.

She still couldn't imagine it, though she could, almost at will now, approach that crisscrossed whatever-it-was that separated her from . . .

Then she remembered.

Remembered, in the first instance, only the checked potholder clinging mysteriously to the white enamel face of the Frigidaire.

Then floods of remembrance. Not the small change the mind yields up by pressing associative buttons, such as that little homily Sister Rita had delivered in fifth grade; instead, a *whoosh* of awareness that she was a complete, unique person with her own identity and a past life and a name that had always made her uncomfortable: Giselle. After the singer, Giselle McKenzie. One day in the middle of that life (or what ought to have been the middle of it) she'd realized, in just such a flash of clarity as this, that perfection existed and she was part of it. She had been standing in the kitchen and *zing*, it had come to her with sudden, sweet inevitability, like the punch line of a joke.

Like (which it was) the gift of grace. She hadn't understood then, or for a long while afterward, that *she* had been changed, only that the kitchen didn't quite seem itself. It was breathtaking, a fairy kingdom, lovely, inexplicable, hilarious.

And *mild*.

She could see it all again and hear, here in the stillness of the grave, the Frigidaire and the clock above the stove humming their old electric song. The clock face, which was contained, like a large fried egg with numbers on it, in a walnut skillet, gave the time to be 3:06. She had watched (and she watched again now) the thin red hand sweep graciously around the face. Its motion soothed her quite as though it were a human hand, stroking away all pain, all memories, every thought. She could have watched it go around all day, forever, mindless as the moon, but then as though to demonstrate that in fact she could not, that time and consciousness march on, there was a knock on the door and she had gone to answer it.

CHAPTER
8

Joy-Ann was searching, in Monday's puzzle, for the last three flowers beginning with B: bloodroot, bluet, and bridal wreath. She'd find a B and then trace the upward diagonals through the grid of scrambled letters. There was a knock on the door, and she put the paper aside with a little huff of impatience. The puzzle was always the nicest part of the morning, and anyone calling at this hour was bound to be unwelcome. A salesman, probably, or a bill collector. Ever since she'd started dying she'd stopped bothering with most of the bills.

Instead, and more dismaying, it was Sister Rita from Our Lady of Mercy.

"Sister!" she exclaimed, and Sister Rita's thick black eyebrows flew up like two alarmed crows. She was wearing a knitted cap and a dowdy dark-green winter coat. A stranger would never have known she was a nun.

"Sister, my goodness, I certainly wasn't *expecting* . . . I mean, the house is a *mess*. But come in."

"Just for a minute, if I may. I only stopped by to thank you again for that lovely turkey."

Sister Rita followed Joy-Ann into the littered living room. The couch was covered with yesterday's papers, the nearer of two easy chairs with unsorted clothes from the drier. Capacious ashtrays scented the air.

"Actually," said Sister Rita, setting down her two paper shopping bags and removing her bright striped mittens, "that is a white lie. Thanking you isn't the *only* reason I dropped by. Though the turkey has been appreciated. It served as the basis for four meals and a great deal of nibbling besides."

"Four meals? They must have been small."

"There are only five of us in the convent, now that Sister Terence has departed."

"Rest her soul," said Joy-Ann, without a tremor of her usual dread before the naming of death. Somehow it seemed appropriate for nuns to die, as it did for them to teach music.

"May I?" With an air of comfortable authority, Sister Rita seated herself in the wooden rocker.

Joy-Ann cleared space at the end of the couch next the rocker and sat down with the oddest sense of expectancy, as though she was about to be given a present.

And so she was. Sister Rita reached into one of the shopping bags and took out a present wrapped in obviously recycled wrappings. "This is—" She handed it to Joy-Ann, whose spirits sank as soon as she knew, by the heft of it, that it was a book. "—a token of our appreciation."

"Thank you, Sister, that's very thoughtful. But there's no need—"

"Go ahead, open it, see what it is."

It was a paperback she'd never heard of—some sort of religious book. For the sister's benefit she read the big cerise title aloud: "*And These Thy Gifts* by Claire Cullen. Oh, isn't that nice."

"It doesn't *look* like much, I realize, Mrs. Anker, but it's provided inspiration for thousands of individuals in the same situation as you."

Joy-Ann could feel, at the back of her throat, the first premonition of tears, but she resisted it. Sister Rita had no right to involve her in a serious discussion of her situation, even indirectly.

"Would you like some coffee?" Joy-Ann suggested defensively.

"No, thank you." She unbuttoned her coat to expose a wooden cross hanging on a leather thong, clear warning that she meant to stay and talk. But then, as though she could read Joy-Ann's mind, Sister Rita said she *couldn't* stay, that anything she might have had to say was said much better in Claire Cullen's beautiful book.

Joy-Ann promised to start reading it that very morning. A lie—she had no intention of reading it, ever.

"There *is* one other matter, but I really don't know how to bring it up, Mrs. Anker. I understand that you've been receiving . . . chemotherapy?"

Joy-Ann nodded guardedly.

"Sometimes with chemotherapy there can be undesirable side-effects. Nausea, especially. Sister Terence had weeks, I remember, when she couldn't hold down so much as a glass of milk. But there is, as Sister Terence learned through one of the nurses at the hospital, a way to avoid all that. Did anyone at the hospital discuss this with you, Mrs. Anker?"

Joy-Ann shook her head, not even trying now to hold back the tears. Only an hour earlier she'd thrown up every bite she'd eaten for breakfast, and now she felt a hunger worse than the hunger of any diet.

"I thought they might not have. You see, it's . . . a sensitive matter. It *seems* that anyone can overcome the nausea associated with chemotherapy by using the drug marijuana. In fact, it's quite certain. It works. It worked for Sister Terence quite wonderfully. Of course, she had to learn to inhale the smoke, but once she did she never had any problem keeping down her food."

"Really? But if that's so"—in a tone of incredulity—"why didn't they tell me at the hospital?"

"Because marijuana isn't legal. It will probably be made legal one day, at least for chemotherapy patients, but it isn't yet, not here in Minnesota. That's why I feel a little funny telling you. You may feel it would be wrong to take the law into your own hands."

"You mean, if I smoked marijuana, I wouldn't lose what I ate? As simple as that?"

Sister Rita's heavy eyebrows lifted in confirmation. "Yes, as simple as that."

"How can I get some?"

"I really can't answer that question, Mrs. Anker. It's been some time now since Sister Terence passed on. Do you know any young people who might . . . experiment with drugs?"

Joy-Ann tried to think if she knew any young people at all. "There's the delivery boy. But I haven't paid him for four weeks, and anyhow he's only twelve or thirteen. By young you mean college age, I suppose. No, I really can't think of anyone."

"A relative?" Sister Rita prompted.

"There's my son-in-law, but he's not exactly a young man. I could *ask* him. Marijuana. For heaven's sake. Thank you, Sister. Thank you very much."

CHAPTER
9

"Good morning," said the boy on the other side of the
screen door, with a bright, tight, vacant-eyed smile. "If you
could spare me just five minutes or less of your time, there's
something I'd like to show you that I know you'd like to
see." His hand dug into a cardboard box that rested on the
concrete step. "Now you've probably already seen through
me, ha ha. And if you've guessed that I've come here to sell
you something you wouldn't be too far wrong. Would you
mind telling me, please, the color scheme of your kitchen."

The color scheme of her kitchen. It was like a question
from one of the tests she'd taken in high school. Name the
five causes of the Civil War. Petroleum is the basis of our
industrial strength: discuss. You had to say what they want-

ed to hear. Without thinking, without peeking into the kitchen or the book.

"Blue," Giselle said, without thinking.

Blue, an immensity of blue, rested above Willowville, a message from heaven straight to her heart. All that was not rooted in these level lawns—houses, garages, trees, clothesline poles—was blue.

"Blue," the boy repeated, pleased. Presto, he took a square of blue cloth out of the box and held it up to the screen. Such assurance: as though for any word she might have spoken he could have matched it with something from the box. "Blue it is," he said, and let go of the square of cloth, which fell, with delicate logic, to the concrete step.

She laughed, delighted.

The boy frowned. "Is it an aluminum screen?" He ran a fingernail over the silvery mesh. "They won't hold to aluminum, you know."

"No. I mean, no, I don't know."

"Do you suppose I could come into your kitchen? Otherwise I can't show you what I've got here."

Giselle unfastened the screen, and the boy, after scooping up his fallen square of cloth, came in. He seemed, in his brisk, bright way, immediately at home. His red hair matched the trim on the curtains. His shirt was the watery, washed-out gold of the Formica tabletop. The tan pants blended into the linoleum. A tiger prowling through the jungle couldn't have been better camouflaged.

"Look!" he said. He threw the square of blue cloth—its reverse side was a blue-and-white check—against the side of the stove, to which, with a muffled click, it adhered. He turned to Giselle, demanding an appropriate reaction.

"Beautiful," she said, "just beautiful."

When she said no more, he became uneasy. Blue flames licked up from his orange hair. But surely, she told herself, it was an illusion, part of this change that had come over things

29

so suddenly and so wonderfully. They were beautiful flames.

"I mean," she said, touching a finger to the calico, "it's such a beautiful blue."

"Uh," said the boy, uncertainly. Then, plunging on: "What you're holding in your hand is a Magnapad. But you could almost call it a Magic-pad, couldn't you. The Magnapad is a magnetic potholder. Perhaps you've read about them. Now with Magnapads you don't have to go hunting around for those lost or misplaced potholders when you have to take something off the stove in a hurry. The Magnapad is always right on hand, when it's needed, where it's needed. Magnapads come in four decorator colors—blue, green, red, and yellow, but I'm out of green today. And you don't have to worry about washing them, did I say that? You'll wear out the potholder itself long before the magnet inside has lost its magic touch. You might suppose that just a single one would cost three or even four dollars, but as a matter of fact I'm selling them at the manufacturer's wholesale price of one dollar each, three for two-fifty. You could get three blue Magnapads to match the color scheme of your kitchen. Or—"

He looked about him. In all her kitchen there was nothing blue but the Magnapad clinging to the stove and the flames springing from his head.

"Or—" The flames leaped up, as though a gas jet had been opened to its widest aperture. "—perhaps you'd prefer the Rainbow Assortment." He hung a red Magnapad on the Frigidaire, a yellow one on the oven door, then stared up at her with resolute pathos, like the leanest and least able of predators. "You never have to worry about washing them, did I say that?"

He wanted her to buy one of his potholders. If she did, he would go.

"A dollar, you say," she said.

"Or three for two-fifty."

"Let me look in my purse."

There it stood on the counter by the sink, a bulging black plastic purse. At a glance she knew she wanted nothing to do with it. She would as soon have put her hand into a steel trap as into that purse. Yet, to be rid of him, she defied her forebodings and opened the purse. As though of their own volition, its contents spilled out onto the Formica counter. Now, in the grave, she saw it all spread out again, as clearly as if a store had put it in a window on display: the loose Kleenexes, the keys, the Excedrin bottle, the Frigidaire's warranty, the various matchbooks, the billfold thick with photographs, the half-peeled package of Spearmint Life Savers.

None of this clutter registered as hers. When had she ever been in a restaurant called the Oak Grill? She opened the billfold and looked at a snapshot. Without a mirror she couldn't have said if it was a picture of herself or of someone else. It was as though the brightness of these present moments had made the past invisible, as the brightness of the sun blots out the stars behind it. As though by comparison to Now the past simply didn't exist. Even in this later, so much less brilliant Now of the grave, the only memories she felt to be truly hers were these pertaining to the time, nearly a year, between the day of her awakening and the night of her murder. Like a teenager endlessly replaying her stock of hit singles, she returned to these memories again and again. It was her one recourse from the somber contemplation of the eventless darkness around her.

Time past passed the time—but not at a steady tempo. A day of remembered life might slip by, subjectively, in moments, while moments of remembered life could bring her mind to a standstill, as though she were to stop and stare at a vase of flowers decorating one of the graves above.

Just so had she stood then, bemused, not by the contents of her purse as such but by their seeming lack of content; by their aura, barely perceptible even to her keener sense, of latent evil, evil that wriggled up from the keys and match-books like little black noodles of smoke.

"Something wrong, lady?"

Yes, certainly, there was. She was insane. What she could see coming out of her purse and out of the boy's head, these emanations, were not real, could not be real. And the proof that she was crazy was that even in the midst of these hallucinations she refused to *believe* she was crazy. She knew she was seeing things, suddenly, as they really were: she *knew* it.

"Nothing is wrong," she said at last.

"Did you want the Magnapads. Or not?"

"Yes."

What she had to do, and what she did, was to open the billfold again (ignoring the snapshots and the black emissions) and then to take out the five-dollar bill that she kept, folded in four, in reserve for an emergency.

She unfolded the bill. Abraham Lincoln's face was speckled with dots and scarred with lines, like an aborigine's. Looking at it another way, you could see that the lines and dots *were* his face. He seemed well-intentioned but uncommunicative. She would have preferred the banknote to the Magnapads, as being on the whole more magical. Leaves, laces, letters, lines curled about its four corners in a jumble of arcane significances. There was the bold universality of THE UNITED STATES OF AMERICA, the modest uniqueness of L52894197A, the little stories latent in "Dorothy Andrews Elston, Treasurer of the United States" and "David M. Kennedy, Secretary of the Treasury."

The reverse side was more verdantly green. It showed a temple of some sort, proportioned like the bill. Over the long rectangle of the temple, on a long ribbon: IN GOD WE TRUST.

Yes. Of all possible messages this was surely the most urgent. But so immense, so manifold, so terrible, especially from the new vantage point of the grave.

Yet for all its weight and complexity there was a countervailing simplicity, a gospel as gentle as the water of baptism, in that TRUST. Trusting meant she didn't need to think of it. He would come, in His own time. He was there now, smiling over the cradle of her awakening, addressing her in the baby talk of five-dollar bills and potholders, making her laugh.

"You don't have anything smaller?" the boy asked, when she handed him the lovely Federal Reserve note.

"Is it too large?" she asked surprised. She had supposed it was the same as any other bill, to look at.

The boy flushed red, and the corolla of flame about his head was tinged with a complementary green. "I haven't sold any others so far today," he explained. "I can't change a five."

"Oh."

"Unless—"

"Yes?"

"Magnapads also make startling gifts to give to your friends."

"I'm sure that's so." She smiled.

"Tell you what. If you took three blues ones *and* a Rainbow Assortment I'll throw in a seventh one for free! Would red do? It's what I've got most of."

"Red is fine."

He took a red Magnapad from the box and hung it on the door of the oven.

"Thank you," she said, reaching out to touch his shoulder.

The flames leapt up to an alarming height, then shrank as suddenly to a little necklace of blue diamonds above the collar of his shirt. "Thank *you*, madam!" And he was out the door without a backward look or a word of goodbye.

Alone, she made a pattern on the door of the Frigidaire with the seven Magnapads. The single yellow Magnapad went in the middle, with a brace of blue Magnapads above and below. Then she hung the two red Magnapads to form a double diamond pattern, so:

R

B B

Y

B B

R

For a moment, gazing into the uppermost red Magnapad, it seemed quite certain that if she were to open the door of the Frigidaire she could have stepped directly into eternity. But then, instead, she heard another door open, the front door of the house. It was her husband coming home from work.

CHAPTER

10

The damned are forever blaming other people for the situation they are in. Rapists blame their victims, tax defaulters blame accountants, and gluttons blame bakers, all on the adamic theory that temptation isn't fair play. Glandier blamed his wife for having put him in the completely false position of becoming a murderer; false, because he had never intended to murder her, richly as she may have deserved murdering. It had happened. He had found her, and the impulse overmastered him, surprising him quite as much as it must have her. Admittedly there'd been moments in the months following her disappearance when he'd *imagined* murdering her, but that had been in compensation for his helplessness. Surely when one's wife has run off without warning, without even leaving a note stating her reasons, one is entitled to a few imaginings.

What a year it had been! The pressure, at first, to pretend that nothing was wrong, and then, when his neighbors could no longer be fobbed off with the first set of lies (Giselle was visiting friends, she was nursing her sick mother), the humiliation of having to invent a second line of defense (Giselle was sick and getting treatment out of state), which he knew very well that no one believed. Why does a beautiful twenty-six-year-old wife leave a fat thirty-nine-year-old husband? Having put the question in those terms, Glandier never doubted the answer. It was the punch line of every joke he'd ever told: sex, dirty sex. She'd been fooling around while he was off at work and finally had run off with the son-of-a-bitch who'd seduced her, as sure as gravity makes apples fall or gunpowder makes bullets fly.

For almost a year he'd lain in his king-size bed with that knowledge beside him, and all the while his feelings seethed and squirmed and grew. Hate, of course, enormously, but weirdly a kind of love too. Glandier had had as little intention of loving anyone, including his wife, as of becoming a murderer. Not from any active misanthropy but out of a developed skepticism toward the sort of behavior that went by the name of love in the world about him. Love was hokum, moonshine, b.s., manipulation. It was the weapon wives used on husbands and parents on children to get them to toe the line. He could still remember the day his mother had traded in the commodity once too often—"If you love me, you'll do it"—and he'd realized, gleefully, that he *didn't* love her and therefore didn't have to obey her. That dog-biscuit sort of love was a useful tool for training children, but less and less effective as one developed a reasoning adult awareness of one's own self-interest. Glandier believed, with his favorite economist, Milton Friedman, that self-interest was the best regulator of social relationships in a free economy. He believed in striking the best bargain possible and devil take the hindmost. He believed in paying as low a wage to employees as they could be made to accept and in treating wives in a similarly self-considerative manner. Therefore it had seemed very strange, and even neurotic, for him to have started loving Giselle at precisely the moment she left him in the lurch. But there it was, a love that could set him crying when he heard a song on the radio, a love that gave him nightmares of loss and abandonment, a love that wouldn't let him think of anything else for hours at a stretch but the textures of her body, the tones of her voice, the astonishing fact, unnoted heretofore, that his wife was an independently existing person with thoughts in her head that he could not begin to guess at. Indeed, until she'd disappeared, it had never occurred to him to imagine an inner life for her, nor, so far as he could recall, had she ever bothered to tell him much about herself. Some childhood memories, her preferences in food and furniture, an occasional announcement that she was "feeling depressed" (which he took to mean that she was on the rag), and a susceptibility to tears when she saw sad movies—that was about the extent of his data on her. As to sex, the presumptive cause of her disappearance, he had not known and seldom wondered whether, for all her well-nigh nightly willingness to let him get his rocks off, she had got any personal satisfaction out of it. Sex between them had had the character of a job designed by a time-and-motion-study specialist. Giselle had been called upon to show little in the way of initiatives. As to discussing these matters, Glandier had felt a reasonable, manly disinclination to inquire whether Giselle's occasional stifled exclamations or heavy breathing did or did not signify orgasm. In truth, sex had always seemed one of life's nastier necessities, something not to be thought of, a good reason for taking a bath.

Now, however, even though he'd killed her, he could

think of nothing else. He was becoming—there was no other word—a sex maniac. Not just in terms of the time he spent nowadays thinking about it, imagining it, craving it, but also in terms of the sort of sex that filled these musings, which was crazy, sick, sadistic, and irresistible as a dream. He remembered the moment of the murder with a confusing, beautiful sense of . . . there was no word at all, not satisfaction, not pleasure. More than anything he longed to experience that sensation again. He would look down at his hands as they rested on the polished wood of his desk and get horny as his mind would rehearse the motions of strangulation, the quick tightening of the right thumb on her windpipe, which yielded to the pressure not as a garden hose might, with even pliancy, but collapsing with a sudden snap like a tougher-than-usual Styrofoam cup. When he was fucking Libby or Sacajawea the same dear memories or even weirder fantasies fizzed through his head until, at that moment of orgasm, they suddenly reversed their valence and became nightmares.

For Glandier wasn't completely a monster. He could feel guilt and shame as well as the next man. He didn't *want* to be a sex maniac any more than he'd wanted to be a murderer. Sometimes he did try to avoid such thoughts, but it was impossible, living alone, always to keep looking in the opposite direction from sex. The TV would remind him, in an ad for a shampoo, of the way Giselle's hair had swayed, the most delicate of pendulums, above her bare shoulders, and his fingers would quiver with excitement and nothing would answer but jerking off. Or a story in *Analog*—when he read for pleasure, he read science fiction—would swerve unexpectedly in the direction of sex.

Admittedly there were times when he *sought* assistance and stimulus. His favorite masturbatory aid was the fiction of John Norman, author of *Raiders of Gor, Hunters of Gor, Marauders of Gor, Slave Girl of Gor*, and, as well, of a nonfiction guide to the same shadowed realms, entitled *Imaginative Sex.* In that book Norman not only provided the yummy "recipes for pleasure" beloved by fans of the Gor series but he argued, as well, for the essential normalcy of man's need to beat, rape, and abuse and, by these means, to dominate the woman he loves. Despite these reassurances, Glandier was not always able to free his spirit of a certain weight of guilt, especially at such times as his imagination exceeded Norman's, passing beyond the permitted bounds of the captured-by-pirates or raped-by-a-monster fantasies to reveries of murder and dismemberment. Could such desires be reconciled with Norman's attractive thesis that sadism and masochism were the natural and inevitable outcome of the evolutionary process? Glandier could well imagine an era when every man was a huntsman and every woman a potential prey, but the prey, once captured, had to be domesticated, surely, not killed. There could be no survival value, in an evolutionary sense, in the murder of one's sexual partner—and so it even seemed logical to feel some guilt on that score. Sometimes, guiltily, Glandier considered returning to the couch of Dr. Helbron and discussing the matter in a cool, grown-up, analytical way, but the danger of admitting too much always prevented him from acting on such self-improving impulses. So long as he was unwilling to confess to his wife's murder, he seemed doomed to relive it. Hell is a tape loop that keeps playing the same stupid tune over and over and over forever and ever and ever.

CHAPTER
11

Tuesday morning brought a major dislocation at Techno-Controls. The long, bitter, undeclared war between Glandier's friend and ally, Jerry Petersen, and the resident boy wonder of marketing, Michael Sheehy, had ended in a decisive victory for Sheehy. Petersen was out on his ass, and Sheehy was now a V.P. with five hundred square feet of office space on the fourth floor right down the hall from Roy Becker. Glandier felt sure that worse was still to come. Sheehy's opinion of the R & D program was well-known: fat to be trimmed.

Such was his stated opinion of Glandier as well. Sheehy with his long hair and lean figure, his open collars and gold necklaces, represented the greening of Techno-Controls

Corporation. He was a jogger, a liberal Democrat, a Knight of Columbus, the father of six children, and only four years after joining the company the most successful salesman it had ever had. He and Glandier had taken an immediate instinctive dislike to each other, which had escalated to abhorrence (on Glandier's side) when the Sheehys had moved into 1240, five houses up the street from Glandier, a broad red farm of a place with an acre of lawn and flower beds and, towering over the wood-shingle roof, seven magnificent willows that had been planted when the original pre-suburban marsh had been drained back in 1947. Glandier's own pair of willows were bonsais by comparison. Now Sheehy had stuck up a goddamned windmill in his back yard. Sometimes on summer nights, watching the tips of the whirling vanes from his bedroom window and straining to hear its little *squeak-ticky-ticky-squeak*, Glandier would have slow-burning fantasies of sneaking over to 1240 and dynamiting the fucker.

What rankled even more than the windmill, the wound to his ego that wouldn't heal, was an encounter that had taken place in the company parking lot a year ago, just before the murder. Sheehy's mileage-conscious Japanese import had slid into the space beside Glandier's imposing Chrysler, and there on Sheehy's bumper was a fluorescent-orange sticker bidding the world to *Save the Whales.* Whales, for Christ's sake! Whales, in Minnesota! Next thing, Sheehy would be going around with a surfboard.

"Hey there, Mike," Glandier had saluted his enemy as he was unfolding himself from behind the steering wheel. "If I see any whales in danger today, I'll do what I can to save 'em."

Sheehy emitted the dry, perfunctory chortle that was his standard response to Glandier's jokes, a non-laugh that as much as said, You turkey. "You do that, Bob."

They moved toward the side entrance of Techno-Controls, shackled together by the force of their mutual resentment.

"Not that I've seen all that many whales around here lately," Glandier went on, rubbing it in.

"Oh, I don't know about that, Bob. You get out to Lake Minnetonka sometimes, don't you? If that wasn't you I saw out there last August, then I swear to God it must have been a small sperm whale." With which, and a hearty all-in-good-fun slap on the back, they had parted.

A dumb joke and a grudge scarcely worth bearing (there had been no witnesses) except for Glandier's conviction that if Sheehy despised him as much as he despised Sheehy it would only be a matter of time before Sheehy used his leverage with Roy Becker to arrange his ruination the way he'd arranged Petersen's.

At eleven there was a valedictory gathering in the office of Petersen's assistant, R. R. Welles. While Petersen, sober and subdued, tried to look politely shell-shocked, Welles kept steering the conversation away from the one relevant concern that Petersen's friends shared that moment: their own necks, next on the line. Veer where he would, however, all detours led back to that highway, just as, nationally, all economic indicators were pointing to recession, cutbacks, layoffs, and further disaster and disgrace. No one lingered at the obsequies. Glandier shook his old buddy's hand, muttered an obligatory bland denunciation of the triumphant Sheehy, and assented to Petersen's politic lie that they would keep in touch. Welles loyally suggested a farewell lunch, but to everyone's relief Petersen vetoed the idea.

Back in his office on 2, where he'd gone to get his overcoat, Glandier found a message to call Joy-Ann Anker. "Urgent," Miss Spaeth had written on the pad. What of any urgency could happen in Joy-Ann's life—unless her cancer had branched out in some new direction? Or was that just wishful thinking? Whatever, he couldn't risk forfeiting her goodwill at this juncture. He'd have to return the call.

"Hi," he said brightly, when she finally picked up the phone after seven rings. Joy-Ann was definitely slowing down.

"Bob. I wouldn't have called you at work, but I couldn't get hold of you last night. Are you busy right now?"

"Sort of. What's up?"

"Oh, this is so . . . darned embarrassing. There's no one who can overhear us, is there? Your secretary?"

"She's at lunch. What is it?"

Joy-Ann drew an audible breath. "Would you know anyone, maybe some young person there at your office, who uses—um, drugs?"

"Drugs? What kind of drugs?"

"What this is about, Bob, is that I need some marijuana." Glandier guffawed.

"No, honestly," she insisted. She told him of Sister Rita's visit the day before and of what she'd said concerning the beneficial results marijuana could have in combating the side-effects of chemotherapy.

"Now I've heard everything. A nun who smokes pot. Jesus Christ."

Joy-Ann was silent long enough to imply a pro forma mortification, then plunged on. "That's my reaction too, of course, but Sister Rita insists that it works. The thing is, Bob, I don't know where to go to get . . . you called it 'pop' just now, didn't you? See, I don't even know what to call it. I wouldn't know how to begin to buy any."

"And you think I do?"

"You know more people."

"Not those people."

"Haven't you ever tried it yourself?"

"No, certainly not."

Which wasn't entirely true. He'd had the stuff three or four times in his college days in the early '60s and thought it

43

an inferior substitute for getting drunk. By the '70s, when grass had got to be almost as common as lawns, even in Willowville, Glandier was already committed to a life-style on the other side of the generation gap.

"Don't you know someone you could *ask?* It couldn't hurt to ask."

"Here at the office?"

There was a long silence. Glandier reminded himself of the mortgageless house and the fact that Joy-Ann was very nearly dead.

"I'll see what I can do."

He made the promise without any intention of keeping it, but then—this was Tuesday—as he was heading in to the Bicentennial it occurred to him that either Libby or Sacajawea would be able to supply him with whatever proscribed drug he might want. Hookers were all supposed to be addicts, so nothing could be more natural. Even so, when the moment came to pop the question he felt as shy about it as the first time he'd asked the price of a blow job.

Sacajawea didn't seem to notice his awkwardness. She just shook her head resignedly and said, "Things are tight right now, very tight."

Glandier, relaxed and good-humored, with his attention still focused on sex, considered making a pun but thought better of it. "I'd be willing to pay a little extra."

"So would I." She laughed. Then, just as he'd promised Joy-Ann and just as unhopefully, "I'll see what I can do."

CHAPTER
12

But no, it had not been Bob. It was only the clock in the bedroom, striking four.

Valves had dilated and she had felt the mix of her blood darken with a familiar fear. Only now, only here in the grave, secure against the influence of all the predatory forces in the world above that made fear rational and necessary, only now, only here, could she smile, though facelessly, at the memory of what she had seen when she had entered the bedroom, drawn by the summons, the warning, of that clock: His face floating disembodied on the glass oval of the dresser, framed in a metal frame, but *living*, the eyes alert, the lips released from the long enchantment of their smile—it was a wedding photograph—to curl up in the asymmetric sneer that prefaced his major pronouncements.

"Giselle!" the photograph said, seeming more surprised than she. And then, more lingeringly, "Giselle."

If she had made no reply it was not through doubting the reality of the apparition.

"Giselle, honey, come here and gimme a kiss. I'll tell you a secret if you do. I'll read your fortune."

She shook her head.

"Don't, then. I'll read your fortune anyhow."

"I wish you wouldn't."

"The next time we meet, sweetie, I am going to kill you. Sure as hell, I'm going to strangle you. With these two hands." The face in the photograph looked annoyed; it had no hands with which to threaten her. With sadness, with even a touch of resignation, it resumed the false smile of their wedding day and spoke no more. It was only a photograph again, inert, a piece of paper covered with glass.

She knew that what she'd just witnessed wasn't, in some sense, real, just as the flames about the boy's head and the black emanations from her purse must have been unreal. But she believed the photograph's prophecy no less because it was the product of her own imagination, and she began at once to act on that belief. Trusting in God, as the ribbon over the temple on the five-dollar bill had instructed her, she removed the fuzzy slippers she'd been wearing and got into a pair of sneakers, a relic of high school, that she dug out of the back of the closet. (Bob disapproved of sneakers.) Balanced on one knee and then on the other, she tied the laces with a sense of wonder at her own purposefulness. Then, rising to her feet, she almost lost her new-formed purpose in the glistening pool of the most potent illusion she'd yet encountered, as it floated, wraithlike, in the dresser mirror.

Often in that very mirror, and more often in others, she had debated with herself whether she was beautiful or only

46

pretty. After so much scrutiny those features ought to have seemed familiar. Yet now the face in evidence before her was a stranger's—and grotesque, a Halloween mask of old habits and artifices through which the eyes of her awakened soul glinted wonderingly. The Ankers had had a spaniel when Giselle was a girl, Ginger, named for the dancer Ginger Rogers. Ginger had been similarly credulous in front of mirrors, always persuaded that her image was an autonomous being, a friend, an enemy.

The lacquered hair, brittle as a bouquet of dried flowers; the waxed lips that were the color of a Ritz cracker box; the pink plastic buttons clipped to her ears; the black lines traced around her eyes. All so strange! And even stranger now, knowing that the rosy original of that mask had vanished as irrecoverably as the image from the mirror. Here in its grave it moldered and shriveled, like food dropped behind a stove, a pervasive, inescapable presence.

So sad, so fascinating: no wonder she had hovered over it then, trying to teach the waxy lips to smile, the clenched jaw to relax, the pinched nostrils to accept a deeper, livelier breath. But the poor raddled creature would not be instructed, would not be pitied. "Leave me," the red lips insisted. "Now."

So, with a kiss, they had severed.

There was something still to be done before she left the house, but what? She returned to the kitchen, where the seven talismanic Magnapads hung on the refrigerator door. Three of them, the Rainbow Assortment, she remembered were to be a gift. She took them, certain again of her purpose, and set off through the front door and down the flagstones to the gravel-glittering street. Her cotton-polyester housedress fluttered about her thighs. Lawns of comfort and luxury quivered with green life. A woman like the woman in the mirror looked up from the flower bed by which she was

47

kneeling and said her name, "Giselle," waving a claw of crimson metal. She waved the Magnapads in reply. Behind the next house the whirling vanes of a windmill quickened, squeaking, and veered southwestward, showing her the direction she must take.

CHAPTER
13

Alice Hoffman squinted disapprovingly at the little glass pipe with the floral decal. "I swear I can't feel a thing."

"It sneaks up on you," Joy-Ann said, "like a Manhattan."

"The power of suggestion, that's all."

"I can't explain it, but it seems to work. I'm not sick to my stomach all the time, the way I was. That's the main thing."

"Aren't you afraid the police will find out somehow and arrest you?"

"I was a little nervous at first, but if you think about it, why would the police come here. They've got better things to do." Joy-Ann lifted the glass pipe to her lips, held a forefinger delicately over the other end, and sucked. "Drat, it's out again."

"No more for me, anyhow," Alice declared, fending off temptation with palm upraised.

Joy-Ann tapped out the ashes into an ashtray and refilled the bowl from the half-depleted Baggie. "Life," she said, and shook her head.

As that might prove to be an awkward subject with Joy-Ann, Alice could come up with no rejoinder. She thought it inconsiderate of her friend to be dying at home instead of in a hospital, inconsiderate but also interesting. If someone had been hit by a car outside her house, Alice would have had to go out and take a closer look. By the same token she couldn't resist dropping in on Joy-Ann from time to time to marvel at her strange new glamour—the weight she'd lost, the wig she had to wear now, all the clothes. Except for the dark rings under her eyes, which the makeup didn't quite disguise, and a slight trembling at times in her fingers, she seemed to be in A-1 condition. The house was another story. The house was a mess, but then it usually had been, even before her cancer.

"I think I told you about that book Sister Rita brought me. You know me, I'm not much of a reader, but when the—" She paused uneasily before the forbidden word, like someone just learning to swear. "—the marijuana turned out to be such a godsend, I thought it would only be fair to read some of the book. So—" She put a match to the bowl of the pipe, drew in a breath, and let out the smoke in a whooshing sigh. "I started it, and it—was—a-*mazing*. The basic idea, you see—"

"You've told me all this already, Joy-Ann."

"But it's so *true:* the basic idea is that death is a blessing in disguise."

Alice nodded in pious, resentful concurrence. "Mm, yes, of course."

"Oh, not like *that*. What *she* said, the author, is that a

50

dying person might as well forget the things other people ordinarily worry about, 'cause there's nothing anyone can do about any of that, and instead concentrate on the things you really love. Flowers, for instance."

"Oh yes."

"Except in my case I've never cared all that much for flowers. But I do love music. So yesterday I did what she said in the book, I went down to the basement and I dug out the box with all my old seventy-eights that I hadn't listened to in years—"

"Joy-Ann, really! You shouldn't be going down in the *basement.*"

"No, the book says don't coddle yourself. Anyhow, what do you think I did then?"

What Alice thought Joy-Ann *should* have done was to straighten up the mess in her living room. Or, supposing that was too much effort, she could have started work on the needlepoint pillow kit Alice had given her for Christmas and that still hadn't had its cellophane wrappings taken off. However, she was too polite to say so. "I couldn't imagine."

"I danced."

"You *danced?*"

"First to 'Black Magic,' and then 'Blue Skies.' My two favorite songs. I hadn't heard either for years, I guess, and there they were, just gathering dust. I should lend you the book."

"Joy-Ann, I think you should think twice before you use any more of that marijuana. Dancing, in your condition!"

"Oh, but Alice, it was nice. I didn't *exert* myself. I just sort of floated around. Very gently. I felt better than I've felt in months. Anyhow, the point I was getting to. . . . Isn't it a lovely day?"

"Isn't it," Alice agreed with a crisp little smile, as though acknowledging a personal compliment.

"So do you think we could go for a drive? You did say, last week, that you'd take me out to the cemetery as soon as the weather got warm enough."

"Oh but Joy-Ann. The *cemetery*?"

"I never did see where they put her. The funeral was all I could handle. And there's no one else I can ask, certainly not Bob."

"But it's certain to be upsetting."

"On the other hand—" Joy-Ann set down the glass pipe beside the toaster in a manner expressive of obstinacy and inner peace. "—it *might* be a great comfort. Another thing the book says is put your house in order."

"Well, that's true enough," Alice said, with a significant glance toward the living room.

"Meaning, that a person should take care of all those things that keep getting put off till next week. The book says, 'Let next week be this minute.' I'd get out there by myself if I had a car and knew how to drive. I suppose I could take driving lessons. The book says it's never too late to learn a new skill. There was a woman in Toronto who learned French well enough to speak just four weeks before she died."

"Why would she do that?"

"I think she had relatives who were French. Anyhow— would you?"

"Oh, I suppose."

Alice tried to sound put-upon, but in fact she was grateful for the opportunity to pry a little deeper into the scandal surrounding Giselle Glandier's death. Alice was Joy-Ann's oldest neighbor. She'd babysat for Giselle, scolded her out of trees, gone to her high school graduation and her wedding, visited her when she moved out to Willowville, and sent her a Christmas card every year. But when she'd suddenly disappeared into the blue, Joy-Ann had been strangely reluctant to discuss what might have become of her daughter or where she could have gone to.

To Las Vegas it had turned out—but why? For the gambling, like her father? Joy-Ann swore that Giselle had next to no interest in gambling. To see her brother, Bing? Joy-Ann, who hadn't had anything to do with her son since he'd left home in 1966, said the police had told her that Bing hadn't even known his sister was living in Las Vegas.

Alice had her own explanation, which was Sex. Sex would account not only for the way she'd run off but for the way she'd been found as well, strangled to death and raped in the bathroom of her efficiency apartment in the Lady Luck Motor Lodge.

Alice could understand her friend's reluctance to dwell on so painful a subject, but it was aggravating to be living next door to a genuine murder mystery (Alice had read practically every word that Erle Stanley Gardner had ever written) and not to know any of the details, not to be able to talk about it.

But on the drive to the cemetery Joy-Ann fell into one of her moods, and even when Alice accidentally went through a red light she couldn't be roused from her dazed admiration of dead lawns and leafless trees silhouetted by the sky's bright, uniform blue.

The lawns of the cemetery, by contrast, were already feeling the influence of spring, and the matted browns and yellows of last year's grass were interleaved with green. No need to stop at the gatehouse to ask the way, since Giselle had been buried next to her father. Bob, without ever saying so outright, had made it clear that he didn't want his wife anywhere close by when it came time for him to be buried. An understandable feeling, Joy-Ann thought.

It was annoying to be able to understand Bob (whom she'd never really liked) and not to have a glimmering of what it was possessed her daughter to run off to Las Vegas. She'd simply appeared at the back door one summer afternoon, without so much as a handbag, nothing but three magnetic potholders (which still worked, after a dozen launderings, just as Giselle had said they would), to announce her intention of "taking a vacation," not saying where, and to ask for the money for her ticket. At first Joy-Ann supposed there'd been a quarrel that Giselle didn't want to talk about, but according to Bob, whose surprise (and anger) surely had been genuine, that was not the case.

Finally Joy-Ann had decided that the explanation must lie in Women's Liberation. Her daughter had never seemed the sort to be caught up by Women's Liberation, exactly the opposite, really, but you could scarcely turn on the TV these days or open a magazine without seeing something about how unfair and degrading it was to be a housewife. Bob, God knows, was just the sort of husband Women's Liberation was trying to stamp out. Compared to him, Dewey had been a saint. Reluctantly Joy-Ann had given Giselle the money she'd asked for, thereby saddling herself with a much heavier burden than the guilt of sharing her crime (if that's what it was): the burden of a secret she'd never been able to tell anyone. How could she have explained—to Alice, for instance—that she'd made no effort to stop Giselle's departure, or even to delay it? She didn't understand it herself. While they were together it had seemed the natural thing to do, regrettable but necessary, but the moment Giselle had waved goodbye from the taxi from outside the bank where they'd gone to make the withdrawal it seemed crazy.

Ah, but Giselle had looked so beautiful that day, like one of those new movie stars who manage not to look like movie stars, and Joy-Ann had always been a sucker for good looks. Dewey had been a regular Prince Charming, if a little on the short side, and Giselle had inherited all his best features—the nose, the eyes, the slightly dimpled chin. Whereas Bing . . .

But Joy-Ann preferred not to think about Bing and had the

wonderful ability—an aspect of the gift of grace—not to think of things that might make her feel guilty, angry, or depressed.

"She's not *here*," Alice Hoffman said, when she'd reached the side of Dewey's grave, several strides ahead of her friend, who could not, despite the weight she'd lost, keep up an ordinary walking pace.

"Nonsense, she has to be."

But in fact Giselle's grave wasn't there. The marker to the right of Dewey's was for Roberta Liebergott, and the one to the left was for Lester Anker, Joy-Ann's great-great-uncle, born all the way back in 1891, dead in 1964. Giselle was nowhere to be found.

"It isn't possible," Joy-Ann declared, with a feeling both of indignation and, incongruously, of hopefulness, as though it might be possible that her daughter were not, after all, dead.

"They've made a mistake," declared Alice, whose distrust of constituted authority was larger than Joy-Ann's. "They've put her in someone else's plot. Probably this Roberta What's-her-name. Look, she died just about the same time last summer."

"They couldn't make a mistake in a matter like this. They couldn't."

"We'll have to check. There must be a directory back at the gate, where the guard was."

"She must be right *around* here," Joy-Ann said, with a dismal look to where the car was parked, fifty yards away.

"You stay here. I won't be a minute. This is outrageous." And Alice, in a glory of indignation, went striding off to the car.

It was outrageous, certainly, but Joy-Ann couldn't help feeling relieved to be given a moment alone by Dewey's grave. She ought to have thought to bring flowers. Did the

55

dead keep track of such things? She'd find out soon enough. Unusually for Joy-Ann, this reflection on her own exceptionally mortal situation didn't trigger tears or even melancholy. The weather was too warm, the lawn too green, for gloom to take over. *Blue skies*, she crooned subvocally, *nothing but blue skies heading my way.*

Where could they have put Giselle? Imagine, making a mistake on such a scale! Would they have to dig her up again? What an awful idea.

She looked around to see if there were any graves that seemed new, and there was one plot three rows ahead and four markers to the right where the grass had a sparser character. She knew by the clenching of something inside of her that that was her daughter's grave.

Was it her heart? But there was nothing wrong with her heart.

And then she could smell, as distinctly as though she'd stepped into her own kitchen, a smell of burning chocolate. She remembered the day that Giselle, who must have been eleven at the time, had set out to make brownies and then, watching a program on TV, had forgotten all about them. Dewey had made the family eat the incinerated brownies that night, as a lesson in home economy, and now, as impossible as the smell of cooking amid these acres of graves, the taste of that dessert was on Joy-Ann's tongue.

The smell and the taste of the brownies made her even more certain that the grave in question was Giselle's. Why then this reluctance to approach it and be sure? I'm being silly, she thought, though that was not at all how she felt as she began, despite herself, to walk on a zigzag course between the low granite markers.

She noticed, as she drew nearer, the sharp blades of a daffodil (Or was it an iris? Until they bloomed, all flowers that sprang from bulbs were the same to Joy-Ann) thrusting up from the raw dirt at the foot of the grave.

And there, sure enough, on the low headstone was her daughter's name and the years of her birth and her death:

GISELLE ANKER GLANDIER
1952–1979

Someone called her and she looked around. It was not Alice; Alice's car was nowhere in sight. In any case, Alice would not have addressed her as Mummy.

It's my nerves, she thought. As who would say, It's the wind.

And then she saw that the plant at the foot of the grave, which had not borne any bloom a moment ago, was fully grown and in flower. Joy-Ann was prepared to believe that her other senses might play tricks on her but not her vision. Her eyes had never failed her.

She knelt down to take a closer look at the impossible flower on her daughter's grave, and only when she was on her knees did she see that it wasn't a flower at all that blossomed from the plant's thick stem but a small pink hand. It grasped Joy-Ann's finger and tugged at it, as a child might, struggling to keep its balance as it took its first faltering steps.

Just as Joy-Ann died, Giselle's voice shrilled delightedly in her ears: *Mummy, I'm free! I'm free! Oh, thank you so much.*

CHAPTER
14

In the first glory of her freedom she could think of nothing but the fact that she was (it seemed) herself again. For days all her attention had been focused on the growth of the flower above her, as it pierced the friable topsoil and thrust conscious leaves into the light. Her spirit had intertwined with bulb and blade until she had almost come to accept, in more peaceful moments, that she was to become a flower, simply and forever that. And why not? Could one have wished for a pleasanter afterlife than this, to sip at the air and the rain, be visited by bees, and relax in a calm appreciation of the sun? Hadn't those hours of sunbathing by the pool of the Lady Luck Motor Lodge been the happiest of the memories she'd had to rehearse during her entombment, the most illuminating?

But such moments of acceptance had been rare. She would grow impatient with mere radiance and begin to twist, like a key in a faulty lock, up through the living tunnel of the stem to the small node of potentiality at the slowly unsealing tip. Does every flower feel such an eagerness to unfurl itself, to spin earth's inert straw into the gold of life?

And then she had blossomed, all in an instant, out of the earth—and out of the flower. The last link between spirit and corpse was sundered. She was free, and she soared upward in her freedom like a jet of water rising from a fountain, upward until she reached, as all things will, a point of equipoise. Something still bound her to the world below, but only as birds must from time to time relinquish flight and settle to earth. No longer, however, would she be confined to a sphere of sentience narrow as the cemetery. She could feel her spirit literally expand, like an ever-widening bell of fireworks, almost (it seemed) to the horizon, and then fall back amazed and exhausted.

Near and far, large and small, all relative dimensions became unfixed and fluid. Her mind, immense in itself, seemed to enclose all consciousness of the cemetery below as in a waterdrop, a crystal ball hovering in the surrounding blaze of light; the moment of her blossoming to birth seemed to have taken place quite as long ago as the birth of her physical body. Of the circumstances of her second birth she could remember only the touch and tug of her mother's hand, her own responsive cry of delight. All that followed was lost in the rapture of release. She did not know, yet, that the release had produced an equal and opposite reaction. She did not notice, on the ground by the grave, Joy-Ann's sprawled body, daffodil in hand.

And God, Who is said to see all things, did He notice? Surely it had been a kindness in Him, and in keeping with His partiality to the Ankers as a family, that He had blessed Joy-Ann with one of His most precious gifts, a swift and unexpected death coming at a moment of inward grace. Of her He had shown Himself solicitous; the same could not be said of His regard for Giselle. Though she thought herself free, she was, in fact, no freer than the wind, or any more conscious of the forces that would now direct her actions.

She would haunt her husband. Even in the grave Giselle had foreseen that, had sensed that the bond that had united her to her own corpse and now anchored her still to the waterdrop world below was in a sense covalent with the bond of her marriage. For this, and for the danger it would put her in, God was not, however, to be blamed. Having set in motion the great clockworks of atom and universe, having introduced thereto the element of random action, He must follow the rules of His creation, as an artist must follow the incised lines of the sketch that will become, in its finished state, the gigantic fresco of His Last Judgment. He must allow to humans, as to electrons, some degree of indeterminacy. Not even His favorites can escape flu viruses or muggings or the greater mischance of a ruinous marriage. Giselle, in marrying Robert Glandier after a two-week courtship, had erred, through laziness and lust. Now even in death she had to live with the consequences of her original mistake. All those years as Glandier's wife had deformed the shape of her spirit so that even after receiving the gift of grace, and even in death, she remained wedded to him, attached, powerless to turn her attention anywhere but westward, to Willowville, to the house there, to the man in the house who had murdered her.

CHAPTER
15

"Mr. Glandier, there's a call for you. A woman who won't give her name but says it's extremely important." Miss Spaeth struck an attitude of aggrieved obstinacy, planting her hand on the doorjamb and jutting her hip sideways.

"Probably my mother-in-law." He took up the phone and said hello.

"Hello, is this Mr. Glandier?"

"It is, yes. Who is this?"

"This is Alice Hoffman. I'm a friend of your mother-in-law, Joy-Ann Anker. Actually we've met a few times, at Joy-Ann's."

"Yes, I remember. What can I do for you, Mrs. Hoffman?"

For an instant Glandier thought Alice Hoffman was being

strangled. Then he realized she was sobbing.

"What is the matter, Mrs. Hoffman? Are you all right?" (And if not, he thought to himself, I'd like you to tell me how that could be any concern of mine.)

"It's Joy-Ann, Mr. Glandier. She's dead. I took her to the cemetery, and then—" She broke off into more slobbering.

"You took her to the cemetery?" That was expeditious, he thought.

"To see Giselle's grave. She'd never been there, and she wanted me to drive. I never thought when I left to look for the gatekeeper. . . . It must have been the shock."

He was too confused and too pleased to think what to reply or what to ask. He had just got used to the idea that the chemotherapy was working and that Joy-Ann might linger on for a year or longer. What luck.

"Mr. Glandier?" Alice Hoffman inquired at last.

He tried to take a businesslike tone. "Yes, yes. As you say, the shock. Where are you now, and where is Mrs. Anker?"

"They took her to the hospital. But she is dead, there was no doubt about that. When I came back, it couldn't have been five minutes later, she was lying on the grass right by Giselle's grave. With a flower in her hand. I thought I'd have a heart attack myself, Mr. Glandier. I mean, there was no *warning*. This morning she seemed so cheerful. It was her idea to go out there, I didn't want any part of it. I think it must have been the—" Alice paused and shifted down to a whisper. "—the drugs you got for her. But don't worry about that. I looked in her purse before the police came. And afterward, back home, I remembered where she kept that stuff, so I went in through the back door—Joy-Ann never locked the back door—and I took it out of the jar in the drawer with the dishtowels. That's where she'd been hiding it."

"Mrs. Hoffman, I don't see what any of that has to do with me."

"No, of course not. Or with me either. Only I don't want to have it in my house."

"Flush it down the toilet. Put in the garbage. It's no concern of mine."

"But you did buy it for her. I don't know, it seems like destroying evidence."

"You haven't told anyone about it, have you?"

"Certainly not. But if they ever asked—of course there's no reason they would ask, I suppose, but still, if they did—what would I say?"

"Mrs. Hoffman, there is no reason to become any more upset. I'll do whatever will make you feel better. I suggest that you don't talk to anyone else before you feel calmer. Just stay home. I'll drop by in an hour or so. You live next door?"

"Across the street. Number Ninety-seven."

"I'll be there as soon as I can," he said, and hung up. Only then, his hand still clamped tight around the sweaty receiver, did it occur to him that he hadn't asked where Joy-Ann had been taken.

Dead! And the house his. An impulse to celebrate swept over him, to make noise, to dash about. If Joy-Ann's corpse had been available, he would have embraced it. If he'd had a glass he would have thrown it against the wall. But here in his office he couldn't so much as let out a whoop or throw a punch of symbolic pleasure into a pillow. He just stood there thinking of the money and quivering under the impact of his own good luck. If he'd killed the old woman himself he could scarcely have felt more pleased.

CHAPTER

16

Looking blithe and slightly unreal in an apricot-color safari suit and canary-yellow Qiana shirt, Bing Anker reached into the cage of retumbled numbers, took out one ball, and leaned into the microphone: "N-thirty-one. Ain't we got fun. N-thirty-one." He pressed 31 on the console, and the number lighted on the board above his head. "Still no winners?" he demanded of the half-filled hall. "Well, spin 'em again, Sam." His foot touched the pedal; the cage whirled; the numbered balls avalanched over each other like clothes in a drier. Bing reached in, took out a ball, called the number: "Again, an N: N-forty-two. I wouldn't do it, if I were you. N-forty-two. Still no bingo? This is getting to be *preposterous!*" He exaggerated the plosives in the manner of Sylvester Pussycat and was rewarded with a sprinkling of chuckles. He punched 42 onto the board, spun the cage and drew: "I-sixteen. Sweet sixteen, and never been—"

"Bingo!" shouted a woman at the back of the hall. The usher approached her and confirmed her win: a vertical line in the N column and a horizontal line across the center of the card.

"Well, that was a sweet sixteen indeed, and the jackpot is a juicy *two hundred dollars!*" He held up a fan of twenty-dollar bills and beckoned the winner from her seat. "Unless you'd *rather* have a kiss?"

The winner mounted the steps to the stage unsteadily, clutching both railings. She looked as though she'd die before she got back to her seat.

"Oh, I can see it already. It's just my money you're after. They're all the same, these out-of-town women. Gold diggers, every last one of them. The Gold Diggers of 1980."

There was loyal laughter from his regulars in the front rows, but facing the spectacle of the case history who'd now almost reached his seat of judgment center stage, there could be no larger-scale levity. The woman's eyes were fixed on the money with the undisguised, anxious hunger of an addict or a starved pet. He switched the money, teasingly, to his left hand and confronted Lady Death with the microphone.

"Congratulations, Mrs.—" He arched an interrogative eyebrow.

"Collins." Her eyes glinted suspiciously.

"Collins!" he repeated in a loud voice, and the regulars, knowing his tricks, giggled in anticipation. "I'm sorry, we're out of *collins* mix, but every winner gets—" He pressed a button that triggered the bugle call. "—a free glass of California champagne. Mindy, where is Mrs. Collins's champagne?"

Mindy, in slithery pink satin, came out from the curtain

with the two champagne glasses on a tray. He took his (a ginger ale), and Mrs. Collins, with evident reluctance, took hers. They toasted. The bingo players applauded. Making a face, Mrs. Collins bolted the champagne, put the glass back on the tray, and waited for her winnings.

He confronted her again with the microphone. "And where do you *live*, Mrs. Collins?"

Her lips moved soundlessly.

"How's that again, Mrs. Collins?" He held the mike closer and turned up the volume.

"*Kansas City*," boomed through the hall, and the ladies had a good laugh at the winner's expense.

"Kansas City, here we come, they've got some pretty little women there, and *one* of them has just won today's first Blue Cross Special of two hundred dollars. There you are, dear, and congratulations." Bing handed Mrs. Collins the money.

As the usher led Mrs. Collins off the stage, Bing pattered on, announcing the next game, and the prizes: for the first vertical row, $10; for the first horizontal row, $20; for the first double diagonal, $50; and for a full card, $250. A full-card game could take forever, but business was light, and the special attraction of bingo, from the customers' point of view, was that they could linger over it all through the afternoon and still lose less than they would have at the slots. In that respect Bing considered his job humanitarian, on a par with nursing or styling hair, but more importantly it was show biz, glamour, razzmatazz, a stage with Bing at the center and down front an audience, bless them, who listened, who laughed at his lame jokes, who pretended, along with him, that they were on a television game show instead of just marking time at a jerkwater bingo hall. For those who lacked the money or the moxie to lose at high speed in the grown-up casinos, here was bingo with dignity, here was a home.

"Bing," said the tiny voice in the earphone pinned behind his ear. He switched the microphone to the office and asked what was up.

"You just got a phone call from—um, an important phone call. It came in the middle of the last game, and the individual wouldn't stay on the line. But maybe you better let Mindy take over for now. She left the number you're supposed to call back."

"What in the world is so important it can't wait till my break? This must be a real disaster. Did my mother die?"

"Uh. . . . I—uh—"

"She did, didn't she? How's that for psychic powers? Actually she's been about to pop off any moment, so I can't say I'm shocked, and I can't say I'm very sorry, since we haven't been on speaking terms since 1966. Still, she *was* my mother, wasn't she? Do you think I should tell the ladies? They'll all think it's terribly sad and dramatic, which it is, I suppose. It just hasn't sunk in yet. I'm probably in a state of shock."

"I wouldn't say anything now if I were you, Bing. Some of the ladies might get upset."

"Oh, I wouldn't be flippant."

"It's not that. It's just the idea of *anybody's* death. It's not something they want to think about."

"Well, you're the boss, sweetheart. Tell you what. They're getting restless. Why don't *you* reserve me a seat on a plane to Minneapolis. Sometime after eight, so I'll have time to pack and grab a sandwich."

"Mindy'll take over the calling, Bing. You don't have to keep at it now."

"But this is my *life*," Bing insisted, then thumbed the microphone back to the PA system. The trumpet blew, the cage revolved, and Bing reached in to take the first number:

"In the G column, fifty-three. Fifty-three and fancy-free. G-fifty-three.

"Under B, B-thirteen. Lucky for *someone*. B-thirteen.

67

"In the O column, seventy-five. Seventy-five and still alive. O-seventy-five.

"O, again. O-sixty-nine. *No* comment on O-sixty-nine."

The ladies giggled.

Bing winked.

The cage revolved.

CHAPTER
17

Part of the beauty of the sunset—and the sunset is always beautiful—is the fear it inspires. Night and the view it opens into the void above cannot help but be unsettling to anyone lately attentive to the sun. The sun is warm and friendly; it informs us that the sky is blue, and if that is not the sky's entire truth, we seldom refuse to be taken in by the sun's report. We don't say, *That blue is just an illusion, a trick of the atmosphere. In fact, the sky is black and space a vacuum.* But at sunset we're reminded that even if we avoid saying this, it is so. The sky is black. The moon is lifeless, and the planets too, and the stars, though many, are far away and exert no influence across the light-years on our small lives.

She had expected all this to change in the afterlife. She

had thought the stars when they appeared would have some new message she'd been deaf to before, but they were the same stars she had looked at from the balcony of her motel room in Las Vegas. They reminded her now, as then, of her own smallness and fragility. Though she had entered on this new, not entirely material existence, she felt no certainty that she could not still be destroyed as quickly and utterly as a moth lured to a bug light. What did she know, more than a moth, of the forces that governed her existence now?

There was fear in that thought, surely, but not so great as to be insupportable. The fear was a kind of string leading her back (the wind of that first elation had dropped, and she could feel herself wobbling like a kite about to plunge) to the safety and stability of the ground; it was a line of moonlit pebbles pointing the way home.

But where was home? Below her the city spread out its seine of lights in feeble but effective contradiction to the prevailing dark. Headlights negotiated the grid of streets and clustered on the long double curves of the expressways. Their energy seemed as feeble, their progress as slow, as the similar configurations she had sensed in the grave—the worms tunneling through winter soil. Where amid all these interweaving lights and purposes was her light, her purpose? Could she choose, for instance, that van and follow it? that lighted porch behind its still-unbudded hedge of lilacs? that window of blue flickerings where someone watched TV?

The kite string snapped, and she felt herself tobogganing down the steep slope of the night. In the exhilaration of the long spiraling descent, she did not consider where she might be bound. To the bottom, wherever that might be. To ground.

Then, without transition, she found herself pinned, like a mathematical point, infinitely small, to a single winking photon of light. Not even light: another kind of energy. It

70

pulsed, faster than the fastest disco beat, while beyond this less-than-nutshell to which she'd shrunk there roiled a kind of smoke, a blackness unlike the inert blackness of night and space because it was capable of motion, desire, and purpose.

The blackness bulged and extruded a filament like the long tongue of a lizard. The black filament curled around her and began to squeeze. At its first actual touch she knew the blackness to be her husband. She had returned, unwilling and unconscious, to her own home and was trapped in it. Like a ghost weighed down with chains and groaning, she knew herself to be no longer autonomous: a function, instead, of the blackness that was Glandier, a mote in the dim corridors of his consciousness, too insignificant to bear noticing. Even more than when she had lain within the grave, a captive of her own corpse, she felt the horror and panic of imprisonment. She would have screamed, but lacked existence. There was nothing she could do but feel his presence surrounding her, thickening and growing blacker.

CHAPTER
18

It was still early as Glandier pulled into his blacktop driveway. The willows and windmill behind Michael Sheehy's house were black silhouettes against cloud stripes of gorgeous, gory red. "Someday, motherfucker," he promised, "someday!" But he was able, tonight, to consider the long postponement of these ill intentions with something like equanimity, if not downright benevolence. A sweetening of $80,000 could neutralize a lot of acid. Already, in his magnanimous mood, he had okayed funeral arrangements far in excess of Joy-Ann's strict requirements. At the same time he'd amused himself by insisting that the cemetery correct its mistake in having planted Giselle in the wrong plot. *Wake up, sweetheart* (he'd sent by psychic telegram), *it's Resurrection Day!*

The one sour note had been struck when Flynn, Joy-Ann's lawyer, had insisted that Bing Anker be notified of his mother's death. Glandier had pointed out that Bing and his mother hadn't been on speaking terms for years. Why raise false hopes (Glandier had urged benignly) and involve the poor sap in the expense of a wild goose chase? Flynn wouldn't argue. He'd just offered Glandier a choice between making the call himself as next of kin or letting Flynn make the call. "You do it," Glandier had told him, then waited at the side of his desk while the call was put through. When Bing answered, it turned out that he'd already been told of Joy-Ann's death (by that meddling bitch Alice Hoffman) and had started to pack. Bing had asked Flynn if he could stay at his mother's house, and Flynn passed on the inquiry to Glandier, who did a long double-take over the tip of his cigar and finally answered, "You've got to be kidding."

Glandier resented the growing likelihood of a wrangle over the inheritance. Bing Anker's coming to the funeral could only mean that he was expecting a slice of the pie, perhaps even all of it. Not that he stood a bat's chance in hell of getting so much as a nibble. When Bing Anker, at age seventeen, had left home to become a faggot in California, he had written himself out of his mother's will. Joy-Ann had never stopped feeling acutely sensitive to the shame of having her only son (who had always gone to Catholic schools) turn out to be a cocksucker. Glandier, naturally, had lent his own moral support to Joy-Ann's occasional expressions of outraged orthodoxy, and he could do so without feeling the least hypocritical or self-serving, since he quite genuinely hated faggots under any circumstances.

An annoyance, but (knowing that Joy-Ann's will was in order) only a minor annoyance, the merest flyspeck in a five-gallon pot of ointment. Rejoicing was therefore in order, and to that end he'd brought home two big bags of groceries and a carton of booze from Byerly's. In the kitchen he turned on the oven in readiness for a pizza and ordered the groceries into categories of freezer, Frigidaire, cupboard, and immediate consumption. Then, after he'd unboxed one of the pizzas, stuck it in the oven, and set the timer to ding in twenty minutes, he peeled the skin of foil from a plastic tub of dip and emptied a bag of rippled potato chips into a mixing bowl. This was the life.

He thumbed the cap off a bottle of Heineken's and carried bottle, dip, and bowl out to the living room, where he settled, bowl in lap and bottle and dip on the armrest, into the sighing recliner, sighing himself in complementary fashion. He lifted the bottle in mock salute to the deceased: "Here's to you, you old scumbag."

As the first icy swallow struck like a breaker against the rocks of his thirst, he remembered the pictures of Giselle and of her mother that he'd at last be able to retire from his den to the junk heaps in the basement. Now that his life was no longer being patrolled by a mother-in-law, there was no one in the whole fucking city who had any claim to be allowed inside the house. His privacy was absolute and inviolable, a castle. Luxuriously he scooped up dip with a potato chip, but at the moment he opened his mouth for the first creamy crunch his senses registered an acrid and altogether inappropriate smell of burning chocolate.

CHAPTER
19

She awoke bathed in brightness. The sheets, the walls, even the roses by her bed were all immaculately white. So white and so unshadowed that at first only by blinking could she make out these constituent shapes. Isn't it lovely, Joy-Ann thought, before it occurred to her to wonder where she was or how she'd got there. More oddly, when those questions did arise, they didn't seem very important. It sufficed that she was being taken care of. Her wristwatch had been taken from her, and that was a nuisance, since without it any long wait would stretch out to eternity.

But what was she waiting *for?* And could she really object to an eternity spent so pleasurably? For she *was* comfortable, wonderfully comfortable, as fit in all ways as the woman in the ad for Anacin who is able, again, to lift that heavy frying pan. The pain was gone from inside. She felt relaxed, cheerful, dapper.

Since no one had told her she shouldn't, she swung her legs over the side of the bed and wiggled her toes into fluffy pink slippers. Her nightgown—really more of a negligee—was the same pink with infinitely many ruches and ruffles, a fashion model's dream. She shuffled her feet in fox-trot patterns and then, without a moment's thought, whirled around, twice, on her right toe.

She froze then, worried that she might be seen and ordered back into bed. Where *were* the nurses and doctors? When would they bring her dinner, and would there be something for dessert besides that rubbery Jell-O you always get in hospitals?

Looking for answers, she opened a door, but it turned out to be the door of the closet, and the closet was full of more questions: Could this gown of golden feathers be for her? And what possible explanation could there be for the harp?

For that—she twanged the largest of its six strings—is what it was, a harp! Joy-Ann could not play a harp. She'd never known anyone who could. She'd never *seen* a harp before, not this hand-held variety, except in pictures of angels.

Only then did it dawn on her that she had died and gone to heaven.

"God?" she called out, though not loudly since this was, besides being heaven, a hospital too.

There was no reply. Either He wasn't paying attention or she wasn't qualified yet to deal with Him directly. Well, there would be plenty of time, if this was heaven. She wasn't really feeling impatient, only a little antsy.

Wasn't it funny, though, to think that heaven was just the way everyone had told her it *wouldn't* be. Full of harps and angelic robes. Funny, but nice, too, in an old-fashioned way.

•It was a bit like stepping off Hennepin Avenue (which had gotten to be so sleazy) and finding yourself in one of those old-fashioned soda fountains that looked ritzy and simple at the same time.

She tried to recall if she'd left anything important undone down on the terrestrial plane, but the immediate past was hazy. She'd been dancing to the Bing Crosby record, and then she'd written the letter to Sister Rita. But that was yesterday. Today she'd gone somewhere with Alice Hoffman, and then . . .

The closet door opened to admit a nurse in a charming little white cap just like the caps the nurses wore on *General Hospital*.

"Joy-Ann Anker?" the nurse read from her clipboard.

"That's me."

"Already out of bed. My, that was a quick recovery. How are we feeling?"

"Actually, I've never felt better."

"Good. Let me just—" She lifted Joy-Ann's hand and pressed a finger to her inside wrist, taking her pulse.

"I love your cap," said Joy-Ann. "It makes you look like Diane, on *General Hospital*."

The nurse smiled and touched the cap in an absentminded way.

"I hope we're allowed to watch TV here," Joy-Ann said.

"Of course," said the nurse, pointing to a beautiful white Zenith that Joy-Ann had somehow not noticed till now. "There's even Home Box Office."

Joy-Ann observed that although the nurse was taking her pulse she wasn't using a watch to time the pulse against. "Aren't there clocks in heaven?" she wanted to know.

"Oh, *this* isn't heaven, Joy-Ann. More what you might call a kind of halfway house. Time goes on here pretty much at the pace you're used to, though it's true we don't have any use for clocks. We all know the time instinctively here. And

77

it's time right now, my instincts tell me, for *you* to get back in bed and *rest*."

"Rest? But I feel I'm bursting with energy."

The nurse nodded knowingly. "Yes, but what you *should* be feeling, Joy-Ann, is deep, calm inner peace. Now—" She pulled back the coverlet of shimmery white silk and waited for Joy-Ann to return to bed. Reluctantly, Joy-Ann submitted to the nurse's divine authority.

"Rest!" the nurse insisted once again, and went out through the closet door.

To the right of that door, on the wall just across from the bed, was an embroidery sampler that Joy-Ann had not noticed before, though it represented the only note of bright color in the otherwise so white room. The sampler showed a rainbow in a bright blue sky with elm trees on either side of the rainbow, elms as tall as the elms you used to see shading Calumet Avenue in the days before the blight, and in the foreground below the elms a winding brook, and all along the edge of the brook were flowers—violets, bluebells, daffodils, irises; flowers of spring—and beneath the flowers, cross-stitched in colors as bright as a rainbow of petals, the first of the Beatitudes:

BLESSED ARE
THE POOR IN SPIRIT
FOR THEIRS IS THE
KINGDOM OF HEAVEN.

CHAPTER
20

To speak of any spirit as "disembodied" is to say no more of it than that it is a spirit. Spirits in their nature are bodiless. Yet we all understand, in an a priori way, that somehow our bodies of flesh and blood, these "selves" of ours, are governed by something immaterial. We may resist calling that something a spirit or a soul, but we are quite certain that our actions are not determined in some simplistically mechanical way, as by the gears of a clock. At the very least we must partake of the nature of automobiles (or they of ours), requiring a spark—that is, a process volatile as fire—to set us into motion. Where, in that case, is the human spark plug located? What is the source of the fire? Where do spirit and flesh connect? In the liver, as some Greek philosophers believed? In the pancreas, as Descartes guessed? In the brain, as a

Gallup poll has shown to be the current consensus? The correct answer is (d) none of the above. Soul connects to body not at the juncture of some particular organ but at a certain *depth*, at that level of the microscopic where microscopes no longer avail—smaller than the smallest components of the living cell, smaller even than the twining lattices of DNA, deep within the spinning orreries of the atom itself and then still deeper until cause-and-effect melts to mere statistical probability. There the soul lives and enjoys its autonomy, which seems, from our more macroscopic view, a bit illusory.

But just as light is sometimes better understood as particles than as waves, so with the soul; sometimes, in certain extraordinary circumstances, it will establish fixed residence not at a depth but in a place: a locus, or focus. In Giselle's case it was in the corpus callosum of her husband's brain. The corpus callosum is the bundle of fibers that links the brain's two hemispheres. Its function is to regulate, pattern, and cross-index the flow of all conscious and unconscious thought. Admittedly, this tells us little about the corpus callosum. Enough for now to note that it is there, the deepest point, as it were, in the stream of Robert Glandier's consciousness, and there, caught in it as in a net, was Giselle, full fathom five.

Having only moments before been conscious of such sublime vistas, having so lately won free from the confinement of the grave, it was all the more tormenting to be imprisoned again and to have no notion of how it had happened or how long it might go on. Resistance was not possible, for there was nothing she could exert her will against. She felt as though she had been suspended in a black, viscous fluid, which was subject to sluggish eddies, currents not so much of hot and cold as of degrees of ill health, malice, and fear— patterns of turbulence in the diseased mind of Robert Glandier as he groped his way toward a reciprocal awareness that his wife had returned from death to haunt him.

CHAPTER
21

In the oven the cheese nubbles on top of the pizza were just starting to get gloppy, and the kitchen was full of its smell. So what could explain the smell of burning chocolate, vanished now but still distinct to memory? Nothing explained it. This, however, was not an acceptable verdict, and Glandier, returning to his bowl of potato chips, applied himself to solving the mystery. A vagrant odor from a neighbor's kitchen? Hardly likely. An olfactory hallucination? Glandier did not like to think himself susceptible to such things, but it was a fact recognized by science that the mind could have short circuits just like computers. So he thought he'd smelled chocolate: was that any different, really, from the way the melody of some old song can pop into a person's head for no good reason? It was not, and the mystery was filed under "Solved."

Even so, when he raised the green beer bottle to his lips, he did so hesitantly, as though it might contain something other than beer. And there was, when he let it wash, fizzing, across his tongue, something about the aftertaste it left, a kind of staleness. A second taste was, if anything, odder— behind the coldness and the carbonation a flavor almost of pond water.

Fuck it, he thought, I'm coming down with a cold.

He picked up the remote control from the end table, switched on the TV, and flipped soundlessly from channel to channel. Nothing, nothing, and nothing again. Too late for the news and too early for serious titillation. Maybe he should treat himself to a Beta-Max with some of Joy-Ann's money. Just the idea was enough to start signals of arousal sparking. His cock stirred in its cocoon of Munsingwear; his jaw dropped, his mouth grew dry; the rhythm of his breathing altered. God damn it, there had to be *something* on television that could do the trick!

He flipped channels again and hit the end of a Buick ad, the eagle spreading its feathers as it alights on the car's trademark. Glandier must have looked at the same image a hundred times and never even noticed it. Why should it have suddenly become so unsettling? Why didn't it come to an end? How many times did the fucker have to flap its wings before it got where it was heading? Just as Glandier was beginning to suspect that the problem might be in his equipment, not the TV's, the Buick ad faded and the entertainment commenced. It was a pursuit adventure about a blue Chrysler being chased by a red Thunderbird. The Chrysler swerved around a bend; the Thunderbird followed, squealing. The Chrysler whizzed through an intersection against the light, just missing a large van. The Thunderbird braked and spun about a full 360 degrees. The Chrysler pulled off the highway, and for the first time the camera approached close enough to let Glandier see the driver's face.

She smiled at him. Her lips were a dark, rusty red, like blood that has begun to dry. Her hair swayed in motions slow as the eagle's spreading wings. Slowly she removed her sunglasses, slowly raised blue-tinged eyelids to look at him. There was nothing of love or forgiveness in her recognition—only contempt, accusation, derision. He wanted to kill again, and swift as that wish he found her in his arms, not an image on a screen but a physical body alive and writhing. Her fingers tugged at his belt, undid his fly. He made no attempt to repulse her or resist, in part from a fear that to do so would make the apparition more real, but also from an intuition that no harm was intended him, only pleasure.

The red lips parted. The blue-tinged eyes looked up into his face, as though asking permission or awaiting command. He nodded his head, and she started to give him a blow job. At first he just lay inert in the relaxed curve dictated by the recliner, but then, yielding to the momentum of his need, he slid lower.

Now her mouth was pressed to his mouth, and he could feel all particular awareness dissolve into one grand continuous slurp of need and greed forever gratified, renewed, fulfilled. He shot his load, and closed his eyes, and when he opened them she was gone. His bottle lay on the rug beside the recliner in a still-foaming puddle of beer. The potato chips were scattered everywhere, the bowl shattered in four pieces. The dip was spread over his pants and on his hands and in his pubic hair.

In the kitchen he could hear his wife stacking dishes in the cupboard and singing, rather loudly, the new commercial for Geritol.

> "Get yourself a bottle of Geritol,
>   Geritol, Geritol.
> Get yourself a bottle of Geritol,
>   And the walls come tumbling down."

83

Jesus Christ, he thought, either I've really gone off my rocker or I have just fucked a ghost. The idea that he could be going crazy made him uncomfortable, even a bit afraid, though only in a rational way, the way one would fear a bankruptcy impending in the distant future. Another part of him reacted with a weirdly straightforward satisfaction. Quite simply, he hadn't had such a good solid spine-tingler in ages, and if it was a ghost he'd been fucking, then good for him and good for the ghost. He was ready already for a second helping.

CHAPTER
22

"Father Windakiewiczowa?" Bing Anker dropped his shoulder bag into the aisle seat and leaned across the middle seat to offer his hand to be shaken. "It *is* Father Windakiewiczowa, isn't it?"

The old priest, out of his collar and wearing a rumpled gray suit, blinked owlishly through wire-framed lenses and submitted to Bing's recognition. "I'm afraid I don't quite—um, recall. . . ."

"Bing Anker: Joy-Ann Anker's son."

The priest nodded, though Bing was certain, from the vagueness still in his eyes, that no bells had been rung.

"Is this seat taken?" Bing lifted the straps of the seatbelt and slid into the middle seat. "Such a nice coincidence. Are you still at Our Lady of Mercy, Father Windakiewiczowa?"

The priest nodded. "Um, Mr. Anker, wouldn't you be more comfortable, if—"

Bing quickly switched to solemnity. "Oh, I never thought—you haven't heard the news, have you? My mother died. Just this morning. No warning."

"I'm sorry to hear that." Reluctantly the priest adjusted his manner from annoyance at Bing's having taken the seat beside him instead of the aisle seat (the plane, after all, was virtually empty) to condolence and availability. He had not expected his holiday to give way so quickly to pastoral duties.

"It was a blessing, really," said Bing, cinching the seatbelt with a grimace of satisfaction at his ever-unconquerable thinness. "She'd suffered so terribly. And there surely can't be any doubt as to her going to heaven. Though she may have to spend a *little* time in purgatory, since she died without receiving the Last Sacrament. But that doesn't really matter, does it, Father—if a person has lived a *holy* life?"

"Of course," said Father Windakiewiczowa uneasily.

"Maybe you'd like to say a rosary with me!" Bing suggested brightly. "In her memory? Or is that something I ought to provide an offering for? It's all so awful—I'm returning home practically broke, and I have no idea *where* I'm going to stay. But I can't really fail to show up for my own mother's funeral, can I? Maybe you'll be saying the mass. That would be a truly strange coincidence, wouldn't it?"

The flight attendant tapped Bing on the shoulder and asked him to put his shoulder bag under the seat. Then she took orders for drinks. Bing asked for rosé wine, and Father Windakiewiczowa ordered two Bloody Marys. Then, to forestall Bing's further nattering, Father Windakiewiczowa took out his breviary and excused himself: he had to read his office.

Father Windakiewiczowa was steadfast in this reverent

purpose all through takeoff and for the next fifteen minutes, but when the liquor cart at last reached row 21 he had to make a choice. He succumbed to his carnal appetite, whereupon, as he'd feared, Bing folded up the airline magazine he'd been reading and resumed his air of bland conviviality.

"Dare I ask, Father—were you lucky?"

"I beg your pardon?"

Bing winked knowingly. "Were you lucky? This *is* why people visit Vegas, generally—to get lucky. There's no *sin* in it, is there? Leastways not if you're a Catholic. That's one thing that has to be said for Catholicism: they leave you room to breathe. One can gamble. One can booze. And one can—Well, that's about it, really, but it's *something*. So, tell me, were you lucky?"

"No," said Father Windakiewiczowa, "I wasn't."

"Well, Rome wasn't built in a day." Bing unscrewed the cap from his bottle of Gallo rosé, poured it into the plastic tumbler, and offered a toast. "Here's to your better luck *next* time."

"And to the memory," said Father Windakiewiczowa, not without consciousness of malice, "of your mother. May she rest in peace."

"To Mom," Bing agreed warmly.

"And were *you* lucky?" the priest demanded.

"Me?" Bing tittered. "Oh, I'm just an employee. I call out the numbers at Old Pioneer Bingo Parlor on Searles Avenue, out near Woodlawn Cemetery, if you know where that is. So luck doesn't really enter into it for me. Except that I consider myself lucky to live in Las Vegas."

"You like Las Vegas, do you?" the priest asked in a tone he usually reserved for the confessional.

"Oh, I'm crazy for it. I think Las Vegas is the secret capital of the country. The one place democracy actually works. You think I'm kidding, don't you? Not at all. Stand by any crap table or roulette wheel and look at the *mix* of people around you. Where else in the world will you find millionaires on speaking terms with ordinary riffraff like me? Not in very many *churches*, for all their talk of brotherhood. No, the real melting pots these days are the casinos, and I think it's because people can express their deepest feelings there. The comparison Father Mabbley always draws—" Bing broke off and looked at the priest slyly across the top of his tumbler. "Did you happen to meet Father Mabbley while you were there by any chance? He's the pastor of St. Jude's. No? Next time you're there you must hear one of his sermons. Especially if you've been on a losing streak. Father Mabbley will cheer you up more than three watermelons.

"Anyhow, to return to his comparison." Bing took a sip of his rosé and resumed. "Father Mabbley says that for lots of people Las Vegas serves the same purpose as a pilgrimage to Lourdes. First, there's the hope for a miraculous cure, which in this case is financial rather than physical, but the idea in both cases is that God should *intervene* on a material level. Some miracles *are* performed, enough to keep the reputation of the place alive, but the real importance of a pilgrimage isn't whether your prayers are *answered*, it's the fact that they're expressed, the fact that something is *felt* at absolute gut level. Even if it's only despair—despair for one's material condition, that is. Because the next step after despair is freedom. Once you realize that all the *work* you've been doing, and the money you've been trying to save, and the mortgages, and the car payments—once you realize that that's all just crap, then you can begin to feel spiritual freedom."

"Well, it's an interesting theory," said Father Windakiewiczowa, "but somehow I can't quite believe that a priest . . . Father Mabbley, you say his name is?"

Bing, who had the happy facility of getting drunk on very little alcohol, spluttered into his wine, and then (the joke was all the funnier because it could not be shared: Father

Mabbley's nickname among a large circle of his parishioners was Queen Mab, but try and explain *that* to Father Windakiewiczowa!) spluttered again. "Excuse me, Father," he got out at last. "Something went down the wrong tube."

Father Windakiewiczowa glared at Bing, as though in prelude to a reprimand, but short of reminding him, again, of his mother's death he could think of nothing to bring to bear. Instead, he reached up and switched off the light above his seat. "Well, if you'll excuse me, Mr.—um—"

"Anker. Bing Anker."

"Yes. Well. I think I'll try and grab some sleep. I'm a little worn down and—"

"Oh, surely, Father. Let me turn out my light too. But there *is* one thing before you do go to sleep: I was hoping you'd hear my confession."

"Your confession," said Father Windakiewiczowa with undisguised dismay. "Does that mean that you are still— um, a practicing Catholic?"

"A *believing* Catholic, certainly," Bing qualified. "As Father Mabbley says, there are no atheists in casinos."

"This Father Mabbley, he's your usual confessor, I take it?"

Bing nodded and continued, contritely, "I would have gone to Father Mabbley, naturally, but he was out, and I wanted to be on the first plane I could get. And then when I saw *you* it seemed, what's the word? Providential."

"And you are—um, actually in need of confession?"

Bing heaved a sigh. "Yes, Father, I'm afraid so. There are rather a lot of sins that are definitely mortal and some others right on the edge. So if I want to take communion at Mom's funeral mass—and how would it look if I didn't?—I'll have to go to confession. Won't I?"

"How you look is not the issue. You must feel a sincere contrition and be resolved never to sin again."

"My goodness, I know *that*. I'm a graduate of Cretin, after all. Naturally, I'm dreadfully sorry for *all* my sins."

"Well. In that case." With a sigh of admitted defeat Father Windakiewiczowa reached under the seat before him for his valise and removed from it a two-inch-wide strip of purple silk faced with white. "My stole," he explained. He placed the stole around his neck, bowed his head, and made the sign of the cross.

"In the name of the Father," Bing recited, "and of the Son, and of the Holy Ghost. Bless me, Father, for I have sinned. It has been four years since my last confession and in that time I have done these sins."

"Please!" the priest hissed. "Whisper!"

Bing bowed his head contritely and leaned toward the old man's ear to whisper his sins. Father Windakiewiczowa interposed few questions, but even so the catalogue of Bing's sins took fully twenty minutes to be told. When he was done, he was given a penance of twenty-five rosaries, the last of which had not been rattled off till the plane had landed and the last piece of luggage, which was Bing's, had been retrieved from the carousel.

"Well, *that's* taken care of," said Bing with satisfaction. He dropped the glass beads in his pocket and took up his canvas suitcase. "I'm pure again."

CHAPTER
23

The darkness burst and she found herself—in human form and wearing a blue cotton dress—in the kitchen of the Willowville house. The refrigerator growled. The clock on the wall hummed. The light glared on the white enamel. It was as though she had been returned, unchanged, to the moment when, in this same kitchen, the world had suddenly been stood on its head and she had begun to see, clearly, the beauty and madness about her. Ah, but it was not the same. What had then seemed lovely and laughable now fairly radiated menace. The very light from the recessed fluorescent fixture seemed dirty somehow, as though particles of that earlier enveloping darkness were mixed in with the waves of white.

She could feel him pushing his body out of the recliner and walking heavily toward the kitchen, in the way one feels the sagging of bedsprings or the rolling of a boat. Part of her being was still embedded in his, a function of his deformed imagination. Another part was free and autonomous, but the nearer he approached the more tenuous that freedom seemed.

He reached the doorway, saw her, and stopped. Just as when he'd come upon her at the Lady Luck Motor Lodge, she experienced contradictory extremes of dismay and of lassitude, the same refusal to confront, even by a word, the source of so much—hatred, could it be called? No, for it was too unfocused. Call it simply evil and never try to understand.

"Fucking hell," said Glandier.

She would have fled or made herself invisible—anything to avoid further knowledge of him—but her freedom of movement was limited in ways not yet clear to her. As much as when she had writhed in the casket's confinement, she was subject to laws she did not understand but to which her actions accorded with instinctive aptness.

"I don't believe in ghosts," Glandier asserted in a tone of childish truculence, as though he might bully her into disappearing.

Ah, if only it could be that simple! If only there were no knot between them. But ghosts, evidently, have no say in whether they will haunt someone, or whom they will haunt. Would the manner of the haunting be equally outside her control? she wondered. Would she have to hoot at him, and bleed, and rattle chains?

"Aren't you going to *say* anything?" he demanded.

A good question. Did she *want* to say anything to him? To scold him for having murdered her? Absurd. What would be the point of talking to him? Wouldn't any speech between them serve to tighten the bonds that she would rather see dissolved?

"I've been under a strain," he insisted. "And this is some kind of hallucination. Isn't it?"

She smiled and, though she knew it to be a lie, nodded yes. She could feel his fear, like a string between her fingers waiting to be plucked. She did not wish to see what that fear, released, would make him do.

She wished herself *away*.

Swift as the wish she vanished into the turbid darkness of his corpus callosum. Then, with a thought, emerged in the bedroom.

The room seemed full of smoke. It billowed up under her footsteps like the ooze stirred from the bed of a stagnant pond. The mirror above the dresser had darkened almost to opacity and gave back no image of herself. She knew at once that these dark vapors were a residue of his presence, as was the smell that emanated from the trellised roses of the wallpaper—a blast of corruption like the stench that explodes from an icebox of rotted groceries.

She began then to feel panic, for there seemed to be no way to escape his pervading presence. She wished herself *outside* the house, but nothing happened, unless the glimmering of red within the coiling darkness of the mirror might be an echo of that wish. She went to the bedroom door and tried to turn the knob, but the physical world would not yield to her ghostly touch. She felt it, cool and smooth and curved, but could not make it move. It was as though all the world were carved from one monumental block of marble.

She heard him approaching the bedroom. Not heard, but registered the intenser pressure of his presence. Then he stood within the doorway, glaring, baleful—and she could not resist the impulse to make him feel some part of the horror he inspired. She took the taut wire of his fear between her fingers and plucked it, once. At once his face convulsed, eyes starting, mouth agape, the tongue distended, and a scream tore from his throat. He fell to his knees and then, hamstrings spasming, to his side. She looked on for a while with curiosity, then, overcome with disgust, walked around him and out of the bedroom through the door he'd left open.

The front and back doors were both closed. There were two windows open, but they were screened. She was trapped inside the house. She would have to resign herself to that fact. With a sigh she sat down on the edge of the recliner and watched the first few minutes of the ten o'clock news. Reagan had been elected president and already, it seemed, someone had tried to shoot him. Otherwise nothing had changed. Various countries were in turmoil. The black smoke that had filled Glandier's bedroom swirled about the news studio and blanketed the streets of faraway cities like an immovable layer of smog. It was all too depressing. She found a corner of the living room from which the screen of the TV was not visible. I'll try and sleep, she thought, and at once she was asleep.

At the same moment, in the bedroom, Glandier's convulsions ceased and he sank into a dreamless oblivion.

CHAPTER
24

Joy-Ann was watching another replay of her wedding day in April of 1949, when the nurse (whose name was Adah Menken and who had been, she claimed, a world-famous actress and poet back at the time of the Civil War) came in with a tray of carrot sticks and sour cream dip and a bottle of real French champagne.

"Goodness!" said Joy-Ann. "What's the occasion?"

Adah Menken laughed, popped the cork, and poured the champagne into two glasses. "The occasion is that you're moving up to the next level of blessedness." She handed Joy-Ann a brimming glass and lifted her own in homage. "Congratulations!"

After the clinking of the glasses, Joy-Ann sipped and nibbled and went on watching, out of the corner of her eye, dear old Dewey, with his hair parted low to disguise his bald spot, and herself beside him in a white veil, only seventeen years old. Life was so amazing, and now it was all over, and that was even more amazing.

But it wasn't very polite to go on viewing Home Box Office when it was clear that Adah wanted to have a serious discussion, and in any case Joy-Ann had watched her wedding a dozen times already, so she aimed the remote control at the TV screen and blipped it off.

"Shouldn't I change?" Joy-Ann asked, remembering wistfully the gown of golden feathers she'd found the first time she looked inside the closet.

"What a good idea," Adah agreed. "We'll *both* change. I hate dressing like a nurse, if truth be told." She placed her emptied glass on the Zenith and went into the closet, re-emerging a moment later in an immense dress of burgundy velvet with panels of pink satin, the kind of dress that only exists in old movies. "Like it?" Adah fluffed out the thick folds of the skirt with catlike complacence.

"Oh, it's *lovely.*"

And the dress with the golden feathers was, if anything, even lovelier. Joy-Ann could have spent the rest of the day luxuriating in its extravagance, and possibly she did. Time was entirely subjective here in the afterlife, and minutes could stretch out into hours or melt away to nothing.

When she returned to Adah, the hospital room had disappeared. They were standing now in what looked like the lobby of a downtown theater outside the ladies' lounge. Far across the marble floor was an escalator with silver steps and a handrail of gleaming gold.

"There it is," Adah proclaimed in the tone of a hometown booster, "the stairway to Paradise!"

The steps mounted up and up until they vanished in the haze. You couldn't see Paradise itself, but you could hear, far, far away, a trembling of music.

"Will Dewey be waiting at the top?" Joy-Ann asked in a whisper.

"Well, no, not exactly. Dewey's in heaven, of course, but he's advanced to a level where neither of us would be able to recognize him as . . . Dewey. You see, after a certain stage of transcendental growth, a person isn't exactly a person any longer. You're more like a vast—" Adah opened up her arms in a universe-encompassing gesture. "—ball of gas."

"Inflammable gas, I'll bet," said Joy-Ann, bursting into laughter at the idea of Dewey turning into a hot air balloon. He always had let off the most atrocious farts.

"In a sense, yes," said Adah seriously. "In the sense that combustion is a natural metaphor for love."

"Oh, dear," said Joy-Ann in a stricken tone.

"What's wrong?"

"I'm not sure I'm ready for this. I mean, I'm probably not *worthy*. I remember the day Bing came home from school, just after Dewey had passed on, and explained that all anyone ever did in heaven was look at God's face. Which struck me, at the time, as kind of a dull thing to do, especially for all eternity. I know it's probably wonderful once you start to do it, but . . . oh, I don't know: my idea of a good time has always been to go dancing."

"There's plenty of dancing in heaven. Just take the escalator to the mezzanine and you can dance to the Day of Judgment. In fact, if you like, I can go that far with you."

"Would you like to?"

"Oh, I never refuse a chance to enjoy some higher bliss. And time stops completely at the mezzanine, so I wouldn't be in any sense shirking my duties down here. All work and no play, as they say." She held out her hand to Joy-Ann. "Shall we dance (oom-pah-pah)?"

Arm in arm and hip to hip they whirled toward the foot of the escalator. Anywhere else Joy-Ann would have felt funny waltzing with another woman, but here in heaven with her

own personal spirit-guide leading—and with such verve!—
what could be the harm? Adah hummed Richard Rodgers's
unforgettable tune, and their bodies swooped and tilted and
dipped and spun around, and even as they danced Joy-Ann
became thoughtful and asked, "Why *do* you stay at this level, if what you said yesterday is so: that every soul is always
free to move on to the next level up?"

"It's my earthy nature, I suppose, or as the French might
say, *nostalgia de la boue.*"

"Oh well, if you're going to speak French!"

"But you see, Joy-Ann, it was there I learned to love the
material world for itself. Not, you may be sure, in Cincin-
nati! Oh my dear, you can't imagine the Paris of those years.
The houses, the furniture, the clothes, and there was I in the
midst of it all, the leading scandal of my day. I was photo-
graphed with Dumas—in his shirt sleeves! George Sand was
my son's godmother! And when I appeared, virtually naked,
in *Les Pirates* at the Gaîté, nothing can express the splash I
made. Perhaps if I'd lived long enough I might have grown
disillusioned, but God was kind to me, as He was to you, and
I died in 1868 at the height of my fame. If it hadn't been for
the war and the terrible things that happened during the
Commune, I doubt I'd ever have stopped haunting Paris.
But there were all these poor souls wandering about in total
confusion, and since I wasn't quite so lost as they were, I felt
I had to help out. If someone asks you directions on the
street, you can't just tell them to bugger off. I can't, anyhow."

"And now you're in charge of all this!" marveled Joy-Ann,
their waltz having come to an end by the foot of the escalator.

"In charge? Scarcely that. Let's say that I try to be useful
to souls who are having difficulties making the transition.
There aren't that many of us who are willing to linger, as it
were, on the threshold. Most souls are too eager, once they

reach their staircase, to ascend directly to a higher existence. It's natural, I suppose."

"I suppose," Joy-Ann agreed without conviction.

Adah stood upon the gleaming silver plate at the base of the moving escalator and held out her hand invitingly. Joy-Ann hesitated, then took the hand she'd been offered and stepped onto the escalator.

"I've got this funny feeling," she said, "that there's something I haven't done."

"Oh?" said Adah in a tone of neutral inquiry.

"What a slow escalator," Joy-Ann observed. "It seemed to go much faster when we were just looking at it."

"It moves as fast as the soul wants it to. Perhaps something, or someone, is holding you back. That can happen."

"Who?" Joy-Ann insisted.

Adah looked over the side of the escalator to the floor of the lobby forty feet below. "I'm not permitted to tell you her name. . . . " She put only the lightest emphasis on the telltale possessive pronoun.

"Is it—?" Joy-Ann shook her head. "But that's impossible. It couldn't be Giselle. Surely by now Giselle is up there, with Dewey. Isn't she?"

Adah wouldn't look Joy-Ann in the eye, and suddenly she knew it *was* Giselle who was holding her back, calling to her. Giselle was still on the material plane, trapped there in some way, and she needed her mother's help!

"Is there a down escalator?" Joy-Ann asked. "I'll have to return. Giselle needs me. I can feel it."

"I'm afraid," said Adah, "we'll have to run." She lifted her velvet skirts and began to clamber down the upward-moving steps. Joy-Ann ran after her, not without a sense that she was much too old for such games. Only children who've escaped from their parents in department stores get into such mischief as this. The faster they ran, the faster the escalator seemed to rise, and soon Joy-Ann's legs were trembly

99

from the exertion. She had to remind herself that in reality she didn't have legs, that everything she was going through existed entirely in her imagination—the theater lobby, the escalator, the golden feathers of her dress, the wind that ruffled them. All that pertained to the senses (as Adah had explained) was a kind of mirage that the soul had to put up with until it got used to an entirely spiritual existence. But meanwhile this was a very potent illusion, and Joy-Ann began to think it might be pleasanter just to give in to the escalator and let it take her to the ballroom on the mezzanine. Already she could hear the million-string orchestra playing "Begin the Beguine."

Joy-Ann ignored the lure of the music and paid no heed to the pain in her legs and kept running down against the current of the steps. She was nearer now, and Adah caught hold of her hand and squeezed it for encouragement, and she *knew* then she'd reach the lobby, and when she did, an instant later, she let herself collapse into a feathery heap on the marble floor and just lie there gasping for breath and wishing she'd worn a dress that wasn't quite so tight about the midriff. Then she started to laugh, and Adah laughed along with her, and for the longest time that's all they did— just lay there on the floor in their evening dresses laughing like a couple of lunatics. Joy-Ann hadn't had so much fun in ages.

CHAPTER
25

Something was definitely going wrong inside his head—
something beyond the nonsense he'd been imagining, something physical. It felt like a shred of pork that had got embedded between two molars at the back of his mouth. He
had this maddening urge to pry it out, though there was no
way to get at it. Could it be cancer? he wondered. Never in
all the time old Joy-Ann had been shriveling away with her
cancer and her chemotherapy had he been disturbed by the
idea that that sort of thing could happen to him. Fear had
kept at a reasonable distance, like an animal that never ven-
tures within the city limits. Now the animal was snuffling
around the garbage can, dropping its spoor on his lawn, and
all because he could feel an itch, a gnawing, an ache dead

center in the middle of his brain.

I've got to go to a dentist, he thought. Not a rational thought at all, and then just as his car was pulling into the parking lot beside the dentist's office, he woke to a clearer degree of consciousness and realized that the aching wasn't only in his head, that his whole body ached from sleeping on the floor. He pushed himself up to his knees, then used the yielding edge of the mattress to lever himself to his feet.

Before he could take in just what it was, he knew there was something wrong *outside* his head, something beyond the jumble of dreaming, something physical. Then he saw it, scrawled on the wallpaper in crude, thick lines, a drawing of Giselle, her eyes staring, her tongue distended, his fingers gripping her throat. He didn't ask himself how he knew those few jagged lines were meant to be fingers, his fingers: he just knew. He knew, as well, that he had made this drawing himself, though he had no memory of doing so. Whenever he doodled this was the way he drew. The way, rather, he refused to draw, since to have evidenced any skill at drawing would have been a concession to the idea of art.

He rubbed at one of the eyes staring out of the wallpaper. The circle of crumbly, pale-blue chalk blurred, but not out of recognition. The drawing was no hallucination, and he had drawn it. No one else could have; no one else *knew*.

Unless (he thought) someone were to get in the house and see this. Then, sure as hell, they would know! The thing was worse than a signed confession. There was something in its very craziness that made it believable.

He had to erase it. Immediately. But how? The wallpaper was ruined. He'd have to strip off the paper or paint over it. Though possibly plain soap and water would serve for the time being. He reached into his back pocket for his handkerchief, intending to test his theory with a gob of spit. A piece of blue chalk fell from the folds of the cloth onto the carpet. It was the carpenter's chalk from the tool kit he kept in the bathroom closet. He stooped, with a small gasp, to pick up the chalk, thinking he might blot out the graffito by scribbling over it.

But when he stood before the drawing with the chalk poised, it was as though another hand had closed over his own, and instead of effacing the drawing, he wrote, beside it, in letters six inches high:

YOU ARE A MURDERER

Not (he thought) I AM but YOU ARE.

His fingers dropped the chalk. His foot lifted and ground it into the carpet. And then he heard her, laughing, and turned toward the mirror and saw her framed in it, taunting and tempting him with her nakedness.

He acted without thought, but it was his own act, no puppet–string compulsion. He grabbed the heavy green-glass ashtray from the bedside table and hurled it, discuslike, into the mirror.

The mirror shattered.

She was gone. But not (somehow he knew this) destroyed. She had retreated into some darkness where he could not follow.

The strangest thing in all this strangeness was that he suddenly felt much better. Was it simply knowing he was not insane? Knowing that he was being haunted, literally haunted, by the ghost of his murdered wife? No, it went beyond that. It was his feeling, his hunch, that he still stood a chance against her. Even though she was a ghost, she could be destroyed. How it could be done he didn't know, but he'd find out, and he'd do it, and it would give him unimaginable pleasure.

CHAPTER

26

As a seventh-grader Giselle had filled four pages of a nar-
row-ruled spiral notebook with a single endlessly repeated
sentence: *I wish I were dead. I wish I were dead. I wish I were
dead. . . .* She had had no particular reason to wish herself
dead, just a conviction that life ought to offer something
more than the tedium of sitting in a classroom listening to
the semi-senile Sister Terence explain about adverbs. Some
weeks after Giselle had scribbled that testimony to her boredom, Sister Terence had discovered the notebook and made
Giselle, as a penance, fill as many pages with its opposite:
I'm glad I'm alive. I'm glad I'm alive. I'm glad I'm alive. . . .

Sister Terence's lesson now seemed more pertinent than
ever, for time and again Giselle found herself wishing that

old, foolish wish—wishing, that is, for oblivion, since what could be accomplished, now, by wishing to be dead? She *was* dead, and death had proved to be no improvement on Sister Terence's classroom or on the years of marital monotony. She would rather have been back inside the grave than here in the rambler on Willowville Drive, where at any moment she could be summoned to Bob's side by some quirk of his psyche. She hated the sight of his gross, disproportioned body, of his dull, demented eyes, of the round lips that seemed to be nothing but the exposed portion of the digestive tract that governed his existence. Even more, she hated being made to hate.

She had not meant to laugh at him. She had not consciously prompted him to scrawl his confession on the wallpaper. He seemed in some way she could not understand to be able to read her mind. Or it was as though their minds had been joined in an unwilling marriage, each at the mercy of the other, subject to the other's caprice.

Then he had thrown the ashtray into the mirror, and as suddenly as she had materialized in the bedroom she had dematerialized out of it into this new region that seemed neither here nor hereafter; the kitchen, it would seem, but a kitchen not quite substantial, a kitchen of twilight and mists through which she drifted like a ribbon of cigarette smoke, never impinging on any surface, unable to formulate any fixed intention, the merest atom in the dance of other atoms in the air.

She remembered. . . .

Or rather there was something she knew she must try to remember: a place, a pattern, a purpose. And there was something here in the kitchen—a key to that place, a sketch of the pattern, a hint of the purpose.

Then, as it drifted, the mote of her consciousness fixed on it: a red-checked potholder that hung on the side of the icebox, next to the stove. It was stained now, stained quite dreadfully, but if she could ignore that stain, if she could focus her thoughts, she could . . .

She could go there.

She could leave this world and enter the other she'd first glimpsed at rare moments when she had lain in the bondage of the grave.

Like an infant that has first seized hold of the concept of "inside" and tries, and fails, to *enter* the cup into which he has introduced his fist, Giselle tried, and failed, to *enter* the potholder that hung on the icebox. She was, indeed, less capable now of entering that further realm that this shining spoke of than when she had first sensed its glimmering in the grave. Then, at least, she had not made the simple confusion between thought and thing, pattern and potholder. Now she accepted appearance as fact. Her mind drifted from seeming to seeming like a bored and resentful teenager let loose in the dullest of museums, wandering among the shards of third-rate Roman statues. Nothing made sense. Nothing was of any use. She felt herself dwindling. It seemed possible that she might be utterly dispersed to the elements and randomized like the gas released from a balloon.

And all this was his fault. Her husband, Robert Glandier.

She did not want to hate him. But it was necessary. How else, unless she hated him, could she destroy him? For that, unless she were to be destroyed herself, is what seemed to be required.

CHAPTER

27

Three blocks from the theater along the gleaming main street of Paradise was the most beautiful department store Joy-Ann had ever been inside of. All you could see when you entered were endless acres of perfume, cosmetics, and jewelry. They sat on a velvet loveseat beneath a gold-plated palm tree surrounded by tiers of amber flasks and bottles on Lucite shelves. There were white marble statues and magnificent floral arrangements of all the flowers beginning with B and an open box of Fanny Farmer's Family Assortment. Far overhead the ceiling slowly revolved in time to the strains of "I Dreamt I Dwelt. . . . "

"*Luxe*," said Adah, with a lazy smile, "*calme, et volupté.*"

Joy-Ann, though she didn't understand French, nodded

agreement. This came closer to her idea of heaven than anything she'd seen yet. Inside of each relaxation there was another relaxation and a peacefulness deeper than the balmiest sleep.

"But," said Adah, just as though she'd been reading Joy-Ann's mind, "first things first. We have work to do!" She pressed a button and a television, cased in the same white marble as the floor, rose up before them; another button, and the TV screen glowed with an inverted image of Adah's face. The camera drew back, and you could see that Adah had been bound naked to the saddle of a horse that was galloping furiously around a circle of men in top hats, while a large orchestra played a suitably thunderous accompaniment.

"Ah, those were the days," said Adah.

"You really *did* that?" Joy-Ann demanded, having figured out that the TV must have been tuned to Adah's own Home Box Office channel. On Home Box Office you could watch all the events of your past life in any order and as many times as you liked. Joy-Ann had spent practically all her time in the convalescent ward reliving her own happiest hours.

"Oh, hundreds of times—but never so well as there at Astley's. For six nights a week and at Saturday matinees I was bound to that horse, as you see me there, and borne about the stage fully thirty laps to the delight of all London. Including, I might add, the delight of Mr. Charles Dickens, who became my very special and devoted patron."

"And you didn't *wear* anything?" Joy-Ann marveled. "I thought things were stricter then."

"I wore a body stocking, of course—and I'll wager you're the first person it ever fooled. Though maybe not. Theater is ninety percent imagination, isn't it? And life's a stage. Ah, well, I've all eternity to watch reruns. Time and tide, time and tide."

Adah switched channels, and now it was Giselle on the

108

screen. She was sitting in the back seat of Bob's Chrysler, looking fraught, and wearing (it seemed) nothing at all. It was not, in this case, a body stocking. Her breasts were completely bare; that much was unmistakable through the car's window.

"I suppose it's old-fashioned of me," said Joy-Ann, looking anywhere but at the screen, "but I can't get used to indecency. Especially here in heaven and on TV."

Adah smiled. "Now, Joy-Ann, you know better than that. Think of Adam and Eve. They were naked all the time in the Garden of Eden. We're made in God's image, after all, so how can nudity be wrong? From the eternal point of view, that is."

Though Adah tried to adopt a mollifying tone, she was obviously amused by Joy-Ann's prudery, which only made Joy-Ann more defensive. "But *we're* wearing clothes," she pointed out. Why can't she?" She cast a reluctantly accusing glance at her daughter. People (fully clothed) walked past the car, seemingly oblivious of the naked woman within.

"Our clothes are only an appearance," Adah explained patiently, "just as your daughter's nakedness is only an appearance. The difference is that we can choose how we wish to appear, whereas Giselle, as a ghost, must appear in the form imagined by the person she haunts."

Joy-Ann foresaw a lecture and sighed.

"You must know that, in the Bible, Christ says 'Judge not, lest ye be judged.' That's what you're doing right now, Joy-Ann. You're judging by appearances."

"Oh, I suppose you're right. I'm not *blaming* her. But it is so like Giselle to be in the back seat of someone's car without a bra. I remember when she was only fourteen—"

"And I remember what Samuel Goldwyn said to me, after he first came to heaven and we were talking about drive-in movies. He said, 'The common touch begins in the back seat.'"

109

Joy-Ann allowed this a grudging smile, and Adah pursued her advantage. "Now listen carefully, because I'll only say this once. If you want to help your daughter, the first thing you have to do is get her out of that car. She's stuck inside until someone opens the door and lets her out. Which you can do, if you're willing to take an earthly form. But I must warn you that if you do, it will slow up your progress in moving on to the higher levels of heaven. Temporarily you'll be stuck here on this intermediate plane."

"Well, that wouldn't be so bad. It's lovely here in Paradise, even if it's not heaven. Tell me what I have to do."

"First put this on." Adah took an emerald ring from her middle finger and handed it to Joy-Ann. "It's a magic ring that lets you take on an available earthly shape. Not literally, of course, but from your daughter's point of view it will look like you're opening the car door, and she'll be able to get out. There's no time to get into the theory of what's real and what isn't. Her husband may come back any moment and drive her off somewhere else."

Joy-Ann shook her head sympathetically. "That poor man. As though he hasn't suffered enough already, now he has to be haunted. It's not fair."

"Suffered? Him! Whatever are you talking about?"

"Well, the way she ran off. And then later, learning how she'd died, in that motel. That had to be a terrible shock."

"You mean you don't know he murdered her?"

"Bob? Murdered Giselle? I don't believe it."

"Don't take my word. You can watch the whole thing on HBO. In fact, I'd been assuming you already had."

"Oh, I didn't want to look at what Giselle was up to there in Las Vegas. I could imagine that well enough! And I *certainly* didn't want to see her being murdered. I never liked the violence on TV."

"Well, there's no time now to explain all that. Go to her. Offer what help you can, but don't stay more than an hour or so, Earth time. Longer than that and you'll get side-effects."

"But—"

Adah waved aside her objection and, with the same motion, made the Lucite shelves part at the center and revolve 90 degrees to reveal an escalator with a large red neon sign over it that said DOWN. Joy-Ann stood on the steel plate at the top of the moving steps and looked down at the earth far below, all blue and gleaming and mottled with clouds.

Years ago on the eight-foot diving board at Lake Calhoun, Joy-Ann had learned there was only one way she could get up the nerve to jump from such a height. She took a deep breath and closed her eyes and stepped onto the escalator. After she'd counted to ten she opened her eyes (it took an enormous effort, for her eyelids felt heavy as lead) and found that she had already arrived at her destination. There, parked alongside a yellow line on the curb, was Bob Glandier's Chrysler with Giselle in the back seat, naked as the day she was born.

CHAPTER
28

Giselle closed her eyes and placed her hands palm down on her stomach and tried to *will* the queasiness away. Instead, a rocking sensation came over her, like the rocking of the seat on a ferris wheel, followed by an intenser queasiness. Could ghosts throw up? It was so unfair. She felt like a child, a carsick child abandoned in the back seat of the car while her parents were getting drunk in a bar. She was certain she'd feel better the moment she could get out of the Chrysler. Being naked wouldn't matter, since she was invisible to everyone but her husband (and he was aware of her only from time to time). But the door handle was a physical object, and she could not move physical objects, so she was trapped inside the car.

To be physically ill when you weren't even physical yourself—that was what rankled, that was the worst unfairness.

But was it unfair? What if she were being punished? This wasn't the hell of tortures and torments that nuns had described in school, but it was quite awful and getting worse. *Please, God,* she prayed (the first time she'd thought to pray since she had died), *no more!*

Then, almost as though in answer to her prayer (though it had been there all along; she simply hadn't noticed it till now), she saw a statue of the Virgin Mary standing in a niche in the windowless brick wall of the building the car was parked in front of. The statue was half lifesize and made of white marble flecked with dazzle like sunlight on snow. The Virgin's arms were opened in a gesture of gentle invitation, as though she were encouraging a child to walk toward her.

All right then, Giselle told herself, more in a spirit of defiance than of devotion, I'll pray to *her.* And, quite loudly, so as to be heard through the closed window, she called out, "Mary, mother in heaven—*help!*"

The statue lifted its head, rather stiffly, to smile at Giselle and, with the awkwardness of great effort, raised its hand to signal that it could hear her prayer.

There was a narrow strip of grass below the statue's niche, separating the sidewalk from the building. The statue looked down, frowning, at the grass, then carefully lowered itself to a sitting position, closed its eyes, and jumped, landing without a sound on the little throw rug of lawn edging the building. More limber now, it crossed the sidewalk and came up to the car to peer inside with blank white marble eyes. "Giselle?" it said, and before Giselle could think what to reply, it opened the car door.

Despite her passionate desire to be out of the car, Giselle hesitated. Once, at Caesar's Palace, she had got into an elevator with Red Buttons and been overcome by exactly the same shyness. Not the shyness of being naked (she'd been fully clothed in the elevator) but of encountering a major celebrity.

"Where are your clothes?" the statue demanded (in an oddly familiar voice), as Giselle stepped out of the car.

"I wish I knew. I was wearing something when I went to sleep in the living room. Then I woke up like this in the bedroom, just as Bob was waking up. I don't seem able to control my own actions any more. I couldn't get out of the house then, and I couldn't get out of the car now. It's as though there were some kind of string tying me to him. Wherever he goes I'm pulled along. Like when Bob got into the car, suddenly, *poof*, I'm in the back seat. It's awful. It's not as though I wanted to haunt him. I don't."

"Even though he murdered you?" the statue demanded. "He did, didn't he?"

"Yes, yes, but now it's as though he were murdering me again every day. I just want to get away. Can't you take me back to heaven with you? That's where you've come from, isn't it?"

Worry lines creased the statue's brow. "I honestly don't know. I mean, yes, that is where I'm from, or I guess I should say Paradise. There's a difference, though I can't explain it very well. It's still all very strange. In any case, one thing is quite clear: you can't go to heaven like that. Here—" The statue tried to take off its veil, but all its clothes were part of the same solid block of marble and could not be removed. "Damn," said the statue, giving up in frustration.

Its voice seemed so familiar, but still Giselle couldn't place it.

"O my Lord," said the statue. "Do you believe it!" It pointed to the street corner where a taxi had stopped and a small man in a shiny blue-gray suit was maneuvering a bulky canvas suitcase out of the back seat. "Talk about coincidences, this has got to take the cake."

The man paid the taxi driver and turned to face them. It was her brother.

"Bing!" Giselle called out.

But he walked straight toward them, utterly oblivious. She had forgotten how short he was, how delicate.

"Bing," she called again, even as she stepped aside to avoid being walked over.

"He can't see us," the statue said sadly. "We're on another plane, you know. But isn't it strange to see him here in St. Paul? How long has it been? It was either '67 or '66 when he left home."

At last Giselle recognized the statue's voice. "Mother! Is that *you*?"

The statue laughed. "Who did you think?"

"Well, you look like—" She could not quite keep from sounding disappointed. "—like the Virgin Mary."

"Oh, Giselle, don't be ridiculous. Though actually I suppose I am a saint now, in the technical sense. Though maybe not. I haven't been in heaven yet, not even as far as the ballroom. I was just on my way, when Adah—that's Adah Menken, who was a famous actress way back when—told me about you. It's a long story, and yours must be another. But couldn't we, just for now, follow Bing inside that building and see what he's up to?"

"Really, Mother, I'd rather not. Bob's in there too."

"But you're with me, and I'll protect you. That's what I was sent to do, and I've got this to help me do it." The statue held out its beringed hand and tilted it from side to side so that the ring's emerald flared in the light. "According to Adah Menken, it's a magic ring, though I forget in exactly what way. Anyhow it will protect you from him, for sure. We're on the spirit plane now. Keep that in mind and you'll be all right. On the other hand, if you'd rather wait out here on the street, that's okay too. I'll just take a quick peek at what Bing's up to, and then—"

The statue had pushed open the door of the building, and Giselle was able to see down the length of the inner lobby. Suddenly she realized where she was. This was the side entrance to McCarron's Funeral Home. She must have walked past it and seen the statue standing in its niche a hundred times when she was a girl. McCarrion's, they'd called it at Our Lady of Mercy.

"No, wait," Giselle said. "I'll go with you."

She took the statue's hand and together they walked down the long salmon-colored carpet toward the central foyer, off which branched the four rooms where the corpses were laid out for viewing. Giselle felt a growing, dismal certainty as to why Bing and her husband had come to McCarron's, but her mother seemed not to have an inkling. Or might it be that Joy-Ann had become so spiritual already that the sight of her own dead body was a matter of indifference to her?

"Oh, my," said the statue, pausing at the threshold of the first of the four rooms.

There was Bing, standing by the casket, and there, kneeling at the prie-dieu before it and saying a rosary, was Sister Rita from Our Lady of Mercy, and behind Sister Rita, sitting on a red velvet chair, with her makeup smeared from crying, was Alice Hoffman, Joy-Ann's across-the-street neighbor. Even though she was naked, Giselle felt oddly at home and comfortable. The room's furnishings and its baskets of pastel flowers put her in mind of one of the more old-fashioned cocktail lounges in Las Vegas, the way you might find it at 6 or 7 A.M.—the same hush, the same soft light, the same sense, among the few people left, of a loss that nothing can change.

She walked to the casket and stood at her brother's side and looked down tenderly at Joy-Ann's dead, painted face in its frame of pink satin ruffles. How thin she'd gotten! And what a good job the undertaker had done with the makeup. Joy-Ann really did look as though she were asleep. The smile was so typical, all tight across the teeth with just the slightest tilt of good humor at the corners of the lips. The same smile that Bing was smiling as he looked down at her.

116

Half sarcastic, half indulgent—the family smile.

The statue, too short to see into the casket, asked Giselle to lift it up. Obediently she stooped down and got her arms around it in a bear hug, then lurched up, staggering only a little under its weight. The statue placed its delicate hands on the side of the casket and bent forward, intent and amazed. "It's *me!* But I've been dead for weeks. It can't have taken that long to arrange a funeral."

"Time isn't the same when you're dead," said Giselle.

"Of course, I know that, but—oh, I look terrible!" White tears fell from the statue's eyes and bounced off the face of the corpse like hailstones.

Giselle took an unsteady step backward and lowered the statue to the carpet. "Sorry, Mom. You're just too heavy."

The statue made no reply. It stood motionless in the pose it had assumed through all the years Giselle had known it.

"Mom? Are you still . . . in there?"

The statue blinked. "Yes. Sorry. But I need a moment to myself, dear. Seeing myself like that was a bit unsettling. Here, why don't you take the ring Adah gave me and see if you can't find something to wear in that suitcase Bing was lugging around." The statue gave her its emerald ring and went to sit at the side of the room beneath a large basket of gladiolas.

With the confidence of having a magic ring and the caution of not knowing exactly how to use it, Giselle looked for Bing's suitcase and found it in a little checkroom to the side of the main entrance. With the ring on she could actually lift the suitcase by its handle, but the ring's efficacy stopped there. The suitcase was locked, and she couldn't open it. However, it was a cheap lock, no more than a glorified zipper and, with the leverage of a broomstick, quite easy to snap.

Bing's shirts were bright and assertive, like ties that had grown large and sprouted buttons. She set aside two she

117

liked, then tried on a pair of pants. They were impossibly tight. As a teenager Giselle had always been able to wear her brother's old blue jeans. Had she actually gained that many inches around her middle since then? Or had he got that much thinner?

Finally she settled for a short orange Dacron-and-cotton bathrobe and repacked the suitcase the way it had been.

Leaving the checkroom, she saw her husband in the front lounge where people went to sneak cigarettes. He was arguing with two other men. The older of the two looked vaguely familiar. The other, an anxious young man in a dark suit, was probably in charge of the funeral home.

"Naturally, I understand how you feel, Bob," said the older man (as soon as he spoke she remembered who he was—Judson Flynn, the Ankers' family lawyer), "but as I'm sure Mr. McCarron here will agree—" The young man nodded vigorously at this cue. "—what you're suggesting is simply out of the question. Whatever else, he's her son, and that gives him every right to be here. Legally."

"And morally," added the young man. Glandier and Flynn ignored him.

"*She* wouldn't have wanted him here," Glandier insisted angrily. "She'd have thrown him out on his ass."

"Actually, Bob, that remains to be seen."

"And what's that supposed to mean?"

"It means that maybe you're making an unwarranted assumption about Mrs. Anker's wishes."

"Stop throwing out your goddamn hints, Flynn, and come out with it. Did Joy-Ann change her will? Is that what you've been getting at ever since you got here?"

"All right, Bob, this is strictly in confidence, but that's about the size of it. It seems Mrs. Anker sent a letter to one of the nuns at Our Lady of Mercy just before she died. So help me, I only heard about it this morning; Sister Rita only *got* the letter this morning. I've read it now, and while I wish that Mrs. Anker had come to me directly, my professional judgment would be that her letter would stand up in court."

"So I'm going to be screwed out of the house by that faggot, is that what you're telling me?"

"No." Flynn smiled. "Mrs. Anker wanted you to share it, fifty-fifty. Unless he decides to live there."

"Fucking hell," said Glandier, quite loudly.

"Please, sir," said the young man in the dark suit.

"Fucking hell," he repeated still more loudly.

"Sir, if you can't control yourself, I'll have to ask you to leave."

"You're asking *me* to leave? Who do you think is *paying* for all this shit—the flowers, the casket, the fucking announcement in the fucking newspaper?"

"Mr. Flynn," said the young man, "would you take Mr. Glandier outside, please, till he's calmed down?"

The lawyer put his hand on Glandier's shoulder. "Bob," he began.

Glandier pulled away before he could say more. There was a crazed look in his eye, a knife-edge balance between hatred and horror. "Don't you touch me," he hissed, presumably at Flynn, though it seemed to Giselle that the warning was really aimed at her, as if he had begun to sense her hovering presence.

Should I? she asked herself, a finger poised above the filament of his fear. Would it be wrong to make him, again, convulse with terror—to which today would be added the shame of being witnessed? How many times might he be shattered and still rebound to daily life?

But no, to have exercised such power would have been to draw still tighter the knot between them. Even to imagine such revenges made her feel twinges of her earlier carsickness. She resisted the temptation and returned to her mother, who no longer sat pensive beneath the gladiolas but stood behind Bing and Alice Hoffman, eavesdropping on their whispered conversation.

"Oh, Giselle, there you are. You should have been here

just now. Poor Alice! I never realized what a friend she was. She's been so upset. Whereas Bing—'' The statue shook its head mournfully.

"Mother, please. We have to leave now. Bob's about to go, and I'm feeling sick again. In fact, I feel awful.''

"Best just to stay here in that case. Here, come sit on this step—'' The statue led her to the platform on which the casket was displayed. "—and close your eyes and hold my hand.''

Giselle did as the statue suggested, though she did not keep her eyes closed for long. In the darkness she could feel Glandier's anger whirling about, like a giant disengaged gear. She opened her eyes just as he passed the doorway and paused to throw one brief, baleful glance toward the casket. The statue tightened its tiny white fingers about her hand. Giselle took a deep breath and looked down at her bare feet. Glandier walked on down the corridor.

When she heard the Chrysler starting up, there was a wrenching sensation deep inside her stomach.

"All I can think of,'' said the statue, when the car could no longer be heard, "are the times he would come over, on Sunday mornings, and I'd make waffles for him, never suspecting a thing.''

Giselle, who had neither eaten nor thought of eating since she'd entered the afterlife, was overcome by a sudden overwhelming craving for waffles. Waffles with pools of melted butter inside each crispy square. Waffles and maple syrup and strips of bacon and a steaming mug of fresh-perked coffee at hand.

At the thought of the coffee the craving altered to its opposite. There wasn't even time to say excuse me. She pulled her hand free and turned to the side and vomited gluey strings of bitter green spittle over the salmon-colored carpet. She vomited until there were tears in her eyes. Then, as quickly as it had come over her, the nausea was gone.

"Are you feeling better now?" the statue asked.

"Much, thank you."

"You know what it is, don't you?"

"Earlier I was sure it was carsickness. That's what it felt like. Now, I don't know. It must be just the effect he has on me."

"Well, you could put it that way." The statue pursed its lips in a knowing smile. "What it really is, though, is that you're pregnant."

"But . . . that's not possible."

The statue lifted its hands, disclaiming responsibility. "Who's to say what's possible and what isn't possible, dear? When the doctor told me the first time, that was my reaction too. Dewey and I had been extra-careful, but I guess not careful enough."

"But, Mother, be reasonable. I'm a ghost. Ghosts don't have babies."

"Stand up and turn sideways."

"What?"

"Just do it, dear. We don't have all day. I'm supposed to be back inside of an hour."

Giselle rose and let the statue scrutinize her.

"This is just an estimate," said the statue, "but I'd say you're in your fourth or fifth month. Let me just—" It laid a marble hand on Giselle's stomach.

There was a squirmy motion within.

"Did you feel that?" said the statue.

Giselle nodded.

"And I'll tell you what else: it's a boy. You can call it guessing, if you like, but I've never been wrong yet."

Bing and Alice Hoffman had stopped talking. In the quiet of the funeral home all you could hear was the murmur of Sister Rita's Hail Marys.

CHAPTER
29

As usual on a Saturday morning, Jack's mother was off at Byerly's parking lot with Maryann and Judy, crusading against abortion. His father was jogging. Jack was in favor of abortion and against jogging, but he knew better than to express such unorthodox opinions in the Sheehy household. Eleven-year-olds are jailbirds one and all. They don't have freedom of speech or freedom of religion. All they've got is the distant hope of parole. Meanwhile Jack had a choice of (a) studying algebra (he'd accelerated way ahead of his age level in math and science), (b) watching a sappy cartoon adventure on TV, (c) visiting his friend Larry Willard, or (d) pursuing a life of crime. Crime was definitely the most exciting possibility, but it would have involved bicycling to a shopping mall beyond Willowdale, where he could be sure no one would recognize him if he got caught shoplifting. Jack no longer believed in gratuitous crimes, such as vandalism. For a while, when he was nine, he'd gone around sabotaging the neighbors' cars, puncturing swimming pools, and other such petty and profitless nastinesses. He'd been lucky enough to have grown out of that stage before he'd ever been caught. Actually he owed his present more virtuous life-style to his father, who had explained one morning at the breakfast table the principles of cost–benefit analysis, which was one of those ideas, like the x in algebra, that made so much immediate sense that you had to wonder how you'd ever *not* known about it.

Given these alternatives, Jack chose (e) none of the above, so it was altogether without plan or purpose that he'd gone out the back door to wander through the little forest of willows formed by the unfenced back yards of the houses lining Willowville Drive and the parallel Pillsbury Road. He tried to imagine what all this would have been like back in the prehistoric days before the Second World War when all Willowville had been a swamp instead of a suburb. There would have been lots of vines and giant lizards ripping at each other's long green throats with razor-sharp teeth. Jack didn't actually suppose that the Cretaceous had ended some time in the nineteenth century. He knew quite well that the heyday of his beloved *Tyrannosaurus rex* had taken place from 140 to 65 million years ago. It was only that he so much *wished* there could be a forty-foot-long Tyrannosaurus leaping about like a kangaroo and ripping the roofs off the houses while the residents of Willowville ran screaming out of their front doors carrying their most expensive portable appliances. Why didn't they ever show scenes like that in horror movies? Scenes from a realistic, scientifically correct point of view.

Jack walked along the edge of the cement-bottomed pond

of lily pads at the middle of the commons (as their communal back yard was know by those who shared it) and day-dreamed about lobsters. Could you create a lobster-sustaining ecosystem in a pond this size? If you could, it would be fascinating, since lobsters had such weird behavior. As soon as a lobster molts and is vulnerable to attack, other lobsters try and eat it, unless it's a lady lobster, in which case they have sex. Lacking real lobsters to study, Jack would have enjoyed seeing a documentary about the secret lives of lobsters or, even better, a movie about were-lobsters. It would start off with this scuba diver being nipped by a lobster in this experimental breeding pond that happens to be near an atomic power plant. There's been an accident at the plant, which the authorities have covered up, and—

This scenario was interrupted when Jack, coming to Glandier's back yard, noticed that the back door to the garage had been left open. That was unusual. Old man Glandier ordinarily kept his house locked up like a missile launching pad when he wasn't home. Jack took a quick scan of back windows overlooking the commons, then walked quickly across Glandier's yard and in at the open door. Sure enough, Glandier's car was gone. Could his carelessness have gone so far that he'd left the door *into* the house unlocked as well? There was only one way to tell. Jack looked around the garage for a pair of cloth gloves (he knew better than to leave fingerprints on anything), but all he could come up with was a brittle scrap of chamois. He scrunched it up to soften it, then tried the screen door, which was unlocked, and the door inside, which was also unlocked.

Jack stood on a landing of a stairway that went down to the basement in one direction and up to the kitchen in the other. Upstairs was definitely more interesting. He tiptoed up the stairs and stood in the kitchen doorway holding his breath, listening to his heart, enjoying the first big rush of fear through his body. With Glandier's car gone and no one else living in the house there couldn't be much real danger, but breaking into a strange house was always a creepy experience, and it didn't take a lot of investigation to see that this house was way up on the Strangeness Quotient scale. The kitchen looked like there'd been a battle in it. The floor was covered with garbage and broken dishes. Both sections of the sink were heaped with dirty dishes and stank with a week's gray scuzz. These were definitely signs of psychotic disturbance, definitely. And if old man Glandier was actually going psycho, wouldn't his father be tickled! Not that Jack particularly cared one way or the other about Techno-Controls office politics; he just responded instinctively to the possibility of mischief.

Nothing very strange about the living room. It was obvious that this was a house without a housewife, but the mess here was an average sort of mess—dust on the furniture, the stink of old cigars, piles of newspapers and magazines, a few potato chips crunched into the rug.

But the bedroom, oh boy! The bedroom was straight out of a horror movie. The dresser mirror was smashed to hell, and the pieces of it spread over the carpet and the unmade bed. There was an open can of white housepaint on the dresser, which someone had been using to paint over the flower-patterned wallpaper on three walls. Based on his own past experience, Jack recognized the irregular rectangles of paint as the shapes that happen when you're trying to paint over graffiti.

Graffiti on bedroom wallpaper?

Sure enough. At the left-hand end of the largest such patch of paint there was a ghost of the letter Y visible under the paint. Jack climbed onto the dresser chair and rubbed at the paint, which was still tacky, with the chamois scrap. YOU ARE . . . But that was as far as he could get before the chamois became useless.

YOU ARE . . . What? Jack felt as though he'd stepped into

the middle of his own Hardy Boys adventure: The Mystery of the Haunted Bedroom.

And then, just as Jack was about to leave, and just the way it would have happened to one of the Hardy Boys, he heard a car pull into the garage. He pushed up the nearest window, but the screen behind it was part of a combination, so that line of retreat was cut off.

The back door slammed shut. Jack was trapped in a lunatic's bedroom! The idea put him into an ecstasy of terror so overpowering that he almost didn't have the wits to hide under the bed before Glandier came stumbling into the bedroom. With a groan of weariness the fat man flopped down on the mattress, and the bedsprings sagged under his great bulk, driving the breath out of Jack's lungs and pinning him to the dusty carpet.

CHAPTER
30

There are numbers—the best known is i, the square root of minus one—that would *seem* not to be able to exist, being inherently paradoxical, and yet these numbers are needed to describe and measure actual events in the physical universe. Numbers, of course, are not in themselves real, yet it has always been the conviction of people at all acquainted with mathematics that the realm of numbers is in some ways realer than our own. "Realer" begs the question of how numbers can claim to be real at all, but if that question is not begged, the trapdoor of philosophy will spring open under our feet and we will find ourselves having to question whether *anything* is real—the sunrise that graphs itself upon the bedroom's venetian blinds; the leaves that rustle above a pool where a frog patiently waits to catch a fly; the taste of that fly; or a needle's pricking of a fingertip. But allow that there may be some "level of reality" where i is not irrational, and we stand on firm ground again, secure in our common sense, with no need for philosophy.

So it is with evil. Evil (as liberals insist) is a quality and not a substance; an adjective and not a noun. Hell and its legions of devils are a myth, a myth expressive of the capacity of every individual to perform or imagine actions his conscience or his conscious mind would utterly condemn. In most moral transactions, this theory serves reasonably well as a basis for interpreting our lives. However, in some circumstances evil does exist, not as an adjective but as a noun. This can happen when there has been some real interaction between the two realms—between, in this case, Glandier and Giselle. Then it may be that what had existed at the level of the number i is potentiated and released into our own world; the irrational becomes real. Not, of course, in such a form as even to cast a shadow across the grass, but rather (like i) as an electrical potential, a cloud, so to speak, with a charge of lightning—with this difference only, that the lightning is conscious, malign, and in communication with the entire realm of unpotentiated evil.

Such an evil grew now in Giselle's womb. Already the epidermis of the fetus had established its unique and changeless pattern of folds, ridges, creases, and flexor lines. Already a kind of consciousness glimmered behind the thin membranes of its eyelids, and spasms of infantine desire convulsed its mouth and fingertips from time to time. Already it felt an antipathy for the being in which its own being was enclosed and longed to tear loose from its confinement.

And each desire, each stirring of the evil in her womb, was like a knife stabbing and scraping from within, making her catch her breath and wait for the pain to stop.

Glandier had made her pregnant once before, early in

their marriage, and then, just at this stage of the pregnancy, had persuaded her to have an abortion. In the light of her Catholic upbringing no sin she'd ever committed had been half so grievous as that, the murder of her own wholly defenseless child, and so it seemed just, if not reasonable, that here in the afterlife she should pay for that guilt by bringing (as she believed) her aborted fetus to term. For if there are ghosts of people, why not of fetuses? Have they not, each of them, their murders to avenge?

Never during that first pregnancy or after the abortion had she spoken to her mother of what she had done, nor did she share her suppositions with Joy-Ann now, if only because Joy-Ann was suffering the threatened side-effects of too long a visit to the terrestrial plane and had no thought for any distress but her own. As they had left the funeral parlor, Joy-Ann had become of a sudden as heavy as the statue whose form she'd taken—and nearly as immobile. Speech cost her great effort, and her arms and legs would bend only at the hip and shoulder joints, like the limbs of some crude doll.

Now Giselle was trundling her—in a shopping cart she'd found in the parking lot of the Red Owl supermarket—to Sears Department Store on Lake Street. That was where the statue, in its strange, slurred speech, had asked to be taken, and Giselle, grateful for a task and a purpose, had not asked why.

It was not easy. Even with the statue helping, getting it in the shopping cart had taxed Giselle's strength to the limit. Then, a block from the supermarket, the shopping cart's left front wheel developed a proclivity to veer to the right, which either brought the cart to an abrupt halt or, if the right wheel didn't offer resistance, sent it careening off the sidewalk as though it had power steering. The statue would clutch at the wire rim of the cart and give a wordless yell of alarm, and then, when its erratic progress forward had recommenced, would moan unnervingly, incapable as any infant of dissembling its misery.

And all the while, every fifth or sixth block along the way, Giselle would feel the twist of the knife inside her womb and have to stop, close her eyes, and wait for the pain to pass. In the darkness of that waiting she remembered the dread she had felt during her first pregnancy—dread not only of her labor pains but of the child that would be born to her. She had been sure it would be born deformed. Dr. Jenner told her she was being foolish; she was young and healthy and all signs indicated a healthy birth, a normal child. But she could not be persuaded. She had been certain, irrationally but unshakably, that the child she carried was a monster, and it had been that certainty, and not her husband's arguments, that had given her the guilty strength to have the abortion.

And now that dread was born again, and lived in her womb, and there was nothing she could do, this time, but let it live and grow and come to term.

CHAPTER
31

As they approached the middle of the Lake Street bridge, Joy-Ann suddenly recuperated. The awful heaviness, the stiffness, the sensation of mentally grinding to a stop—all gone with just the popping of her ears. She turned around in the shopping cart and asked Giselle to take a rest. Giselle didn't have to be asked twice; she was worn to a frazzle.

"I feel so much *better*," Joy-Ann announced cheerily. "Do you know what I think did it? I think it's the bridge, having a lot of air and then the river underneath us."

But Giselle wasn't even listening. Joy-Ann put her hands over Giselle's, which still numbly gripped the handle of the shopping cart. "Poor darling."

"I feel terrible."

Joy-Ann sighed sympathetically. Having been through the wringer twice herself, she knew there were times when good advice was nothing but an annoyance. She couldn't understand why the Church had to be against the idea of test-tube babies. If the Pope were a woman and knew what pregnancy was like from experience . . .

"Isn't that strange," said Giselle.

"Isn't what strange?"

"The cars here on the bridge. Look at them, they're just creeping along."

"Well, I wouldn't complain. Most people drive too fast."

But it wasn't only the cars that were going slower, Joy-Ann noticed. Everything had gone into slow motion. The blue Mississippi below them seemed to be flowing like honey that had gone into the icebox by mistake, and on either shore the wind stirred the newly budded branches of the trees with the same weird sluggishness, as though the trees were seaweed and the wind the weariest of currents.

"Maybe," Joy-Ann speculated, "it's not the cars slowing down. Maybe it's us speeding up. Though come to think of it, it doesn't make much practical difference what you *call* it."

"I do wish," Giselle said, with a grimace of aggravation, "that I were in control of things instead of their always just happening to me. I mean, it could be useful to make everything go slower, if you could do it when you wanted to."

"Useful? It's pretty, certainly, but I don't see how—Giselle? Would you look down there—" She pointed with her little marble finger at a man standing in the middle of the river, standing, in fact, *on* the river. "—and tell me what you see?"

Giselle went to the railing of the bridge and looked down. "There's a man. With a big beard. And his head's bleeding. And I think he's *waving* at us."

"Do you suppose he's another ghost?"

132

"He's shouting something, but I can't make it out. Can you?"

"He must be a ghost," Joy-Ann decided, "or otherwise he couldn't see us."

"Bob can see us. Or me anyhow. Sometimes."

"But can he walk on top of water?"

Giselle cupped her hands to her mouth, leaned forward, and shouted as loudly as she could, *"What are you saying?"*

In reply the man on the water lifted his arms above his head and signaled "Come here" with his hands.

When Giselle pantomimed back to him, lifting her shoulders and spreading her hands, that this was impossible, he called up (Joy-Ann could just make it out), "Jump!"

"Jump?" Joy-Ann repeated indignantly. "Does he think we're crazy?"

"I don't know. It might be possible. I mean, for a while there I *was* able to fly."

"Have you tried it lately? It would sure beat hell out of walking the rest of the way to Sears. We've got a good thirty blocks ahead of us."

"No, once I was back inside my body, I stopped being able to fly. But maybe it's like in *Dumbo.* Maybe if I just believed hard enough, I could do it."

"As I recall, Dumbo had a magic feather. I wouldn't try it, if I were you. And I'm certainly not going to jump down there. Look at me: I'm made of stone. I'd sink right to the bottom."

"I wonder who he is, though."

"Listen, Giselle, if you want to make his acquaintance, that's fine with me. But let's get to Sears first. Please? The longer I stay here, the more likely it is that something even weirder will happen to me."

Giselle allowed this to be a reasonable demand, and they continued on their way. This time they continued without the grocery cart, since there was a bus stop at the other end of the bridge. While they waited for a bus, Joy-Ann could feel her body getting heavier again and her thoughts fuzzier, but even so, when the bus did finally arrive—traveling in slow motion, like the cars on the bridge—there was plenty of time to sneak onto it before the door hissed closed behind the last passenger. Then, at just about the pace that Giselle had pushed the grocery cart but so much more comfortably, the bus lumbered along Lake Street toward Sears.

As usual when she rode the bus, Joy-Ann couldn't keep from staring at the other passengers. They were old people and teenagers mostly, the old people in their winter coats, the teenagers already dressed for summer in T-shirts and light sweaters. A group of four girls were confabulating at the back of the bus in what would have been, at ordinary speed, a lively manner but seemed in slow motion thoroughly ridiculous, their voices retarded to something between the bleating of sheep and the croaking of frogs, their faces undergoing equally grotesque distortions, especially the face of the little blond girl who was chewing gum.

If they could see *me*, Joy-Ann thought, what would they think? What would anyone think, seeing a living half-life-size statue? She felt as though she'd turned into one of those punk people they showed sometimes on TV, someone weird and silly and threatening all at once, the only difference being, blessedly, that she was invisible.

Bleating and croaking, the girls at the back of the bus got off at Cedar. Giselle was curled up on the seat in front of the rear exit, asleep, her bare feet on the molded orange plastic of the seat. The bus was inching along at a slower and slower pace, and Joy-Ann was feeling logier and logier. But it would not do to fall asleep, so she set herself the task, which had kept her awake so often at Sunday mass, of thinking of a celebrity whose name began with the initials A.A., then of one with initials A.B., and so on, but for the life of her the only first name she could think of was Ann and the only last name, after a great deal of thought, was Anker.

And then, at last, just a few blocks ahead, you could see the square gray tower of the Sears Building soaring up from the drive-ins and car lots of Lake Street like a downtown skyscraper that had got lost. Now the only problem was whether the bus would stop and the doors open, but before she could even begin to worry about that, a black man, two seats behind the driver, reached for the signal cord and yanked it.

"Giselle," she said, tapping her daughter's right knee. "Giselle, wake up, we're almost there."

But Giselle, whatever Joy-Ann did, however loudly she shouted into her ear, refused to wake up. There was no help for it—Joy-Ann would have to get off by herself. Before the black man could block her way out the back exit, Joy-Ann hurried there and eased herself down to the lower step. The bus jiggled to a stop, its doors hissed open, and Joy-Ann hopped down to the curb. Sears didn't seem to have any customers that afternoon, and Joy-Ann paced back and forth in front of its entrance—a revolving door flanked by doors of brass-bound green glass—feeling herself get stiffer and creakier with every slow-motion minute. Apparently only if she were wearing the magic ring Adah had given her was it possible to accomplish something so physical as opening a door for herself. Not that she begrudged the ring to Giselle. But it was frustrating not to be able to do such a simple thing. This was what life must be like for pets. She remembered Alice Hoffman's little Sugar, whining and clawing at Alice's back door, wanting to get out.

At long last a shopper inside the store squeezed herself and her two shopping bags into one of the four compartments of the revolving door and set it in motion. Joy-Ann, who had finally, out of the blue, thought of a celebrity with

135

the initials A.A. (Alan Alda, who else?), was caught by surprise and didn't get into the section of the door opposite to the one the woman was at but had to wait for the next one. Which meant that, when the woman stopped pushing the door, Joy-Ann was caught inside. She stood there, trapped, while only some dozen yards ahead was the escalator that would have taken her back to Paradise. Ever so slowly the steps of the escalator rose to the next floor. Once or twice another customer would enter or leave the store, but never by the revolving door, always by the ordinary glass doors to either side—despite the signs that *asked* them to use the revolving door. If people only realized the harm they could do by not following the rules!

CHAPTER

32

—Father? Can you hear me? She's asleep now, the bitch, the ditch in which you planted me. We can talk.

—Dreaming.

—Oh, you're not dreaming. It's more as though we were using C.B. radios. Only you can't spin the dial. I'm what's happening, baby, as the deejays say.

—No.

—Yes. But if you're that anxious to deny my existence, why not plead insanity. On the other hand, why be in a hurry to deny me? I might be some use to you—once I've been born and grown a bit and you've thought of a name for me.

—Leave me *alone,* you little shit!

—Little Shit, is it? Not Beelzebub or Asmodeus? Of course, you lack a background in the so-called humanities. Not that *I* mind about that. In terms of your better damnation, your ignorance is likely to work to my advantage. Little Shit? Well, considering the source, I'm not surprised.

—Christ, what did I do to deserve this?

—Surely, that's not a serious question.

—

—The silent treatment now, is it? No problem there. I'll show you slides. A picture's worth a thousand words. This, for instance: bet you never thought Lizzy Spaeth had tits like that, huh. And this is you, fat as a *pig*, you are, and what'll we put in the thought balloon over your head? "Miss Spaeth, you are *late* again! I cannot let this continue!" And how about this one: you've got your hands around her neck, you are squeezing, she is choking, and she is not going to come back late from lunch ever again, is she? Now, look at the next one: you've taken out your Swiss Army knife and—

—Stop it. I'm not listening to any of this. You don't exist. I'm dreaming.

—Sure, right. Maybe you're more interested in disembowelings. This one is—

—Leave me alone!

—Careful, careful. That's twice you've asked that. I might take you at your word, if you ask a third time. Think of all the ways I could take that literally. I might "leave you alone" in the solitude of catatonia. Or up Shit Creek without a paddle. Because for all that I am your *son*, with whatever filial obligation that entails (and rest assured that it is not unlimited)—for all that I may feel an independent zeal to act on your behalf, I am not your friend. Oh, anything but. I'd like to see you rot in hell, and I've every confidence that someday I shall and you will. But in the meantime, Daddy-O, I'm at your service. Once *she* sets me loose.

138

—I know I'm sleeping. The pillow's wet where I've been drooling on it. I can smell the fresh paint.

—You were asleep, yes. But not dreaming. *You* haven't the imagination to dream my voice. Imagination has never been your strong suit. It's Mother who supplies the wit, as befits a spiritual nature. You're a *businessman*, right? From you I inherit pimples, pus, corruption. Shit.

He awoke, at last, by an act of will. Not from dreams but from the drowsing between dreams and waking. The mattress he lay on seemed to stir with its own life. He rolled over and opened his eyes in time to see the child's plaid shirt, frayed jeans, and red sneakers as he crawled out the bedroom door.

He pushed himself up on his elbows and rumbled an ineffectual "*Hey! Stop!*" Too late. By the time he was on his feet the back door had slammed closed. Some kid had been *under* his bed while he was asleep. That much was no dream, no ghost, no hallucination. He went to the bedroom window and saw the kid—it was Sheehy's brat—hightailing across the brown grass.

The kid had been inside this room, had seen the paint on the wallpaper (though not, thank God, what the paint was covering), and he was out free to blab about it to the whole neighborhood.

He tried to feel some anger. There was only fear.

CHAPTER
33

On the bus, before she fell asleep, Giselle had wondered what would happen if one of the boarding passengers were to sit on her. Though she was invisible to the living, she was probably not impermeable. She could not, for instance, walk through walls; without the ring her mother had left her she couldn't so much as open a door. This was not a major worry, little more than a fly-tickle of a question, and it hadn't kept her from sleeping through the bus's entire circuit down Lake Street to Hennepin and back again to the bridge, where the question was answered in the directest way. Someone getting on the bus sat down in the seat Giselle occupied, whereupon—*ping!*—she was displaced to the skirt of grass between sidewalk and curb. She awoke to see the bus bouncing ponderously up Marshall Avenue (which is what Lake Street became on the St. Paul side of the bridge). The world was still creaking along in slow motion, and she was still swollen with this preposterous, preternatural pregnancy. Nothing had changed except that her mother (so she supposed) had got off at Sears and returned to Paradise.

Natural and thoughtless as a ball rolling downhill, Giselle gravitated toward the bridge and its vistas of river and shore. Standing on the worn timbers of the pedestrian walkway, she regarded the trees clinging to the steep banks almost with envy. More peaceful even than sleep to be a tree. She could remember, though not very clearly (vegetation having an imprecise sense of time), the days or hours she had spent piercing with root and stem the crumbling cemetery soil, winning release into the light. No thoughts at all, only the rustling of leaves. Nameless, aimless, blameless.

"Excuse me?"

A hand touched her shoulder lightly and was withdrawn. She turned around to face a man who seemed to have recently been beaten about the face with a sledgehammer. Blood streamed freely from his left eye socket and from his mouth, dying the salt-and-pepper tangle of his long beard to a crimson that deepened to maroon and brown where it spattered his tweed coat.

"Please take no notice of my appearance," he said, dabbing nervously at his forehead with a handkerchief. Then, in a tone of elucidation: "I'm a poet."

Giselle, though momentarily alarmed, understood from the man's behavior that he intended no threat. "You're bleeding very badly," she said. "Don't you think you should be lying down?"

"Oh, never mind the bleeding. It's gone on like this for years now. It doesn't hurt. Except when I laugh." At which, as though in self-mockery, he laughed, exposing bloody and all-but-toothless gums; reflexively he grimaced with pain.

141

Giselle wondered if he might be in a state of shock. Accident victims were known to behave with apparent unawareness of their own injuries. Ghosts, however, probably weren't like living people in that respect, and if she were sure about very little else, Giselle felt sure this man was a ghost, the same she'd seen earlier that day standing on the river and urging her to jump.

"Do you read much poetry?" he asked.

She shook her head. "I don't read much of anything at all."

"It was you I saw up here an hour or so since, wasn't it? With the Virgin Mary beside you?"

"Actually, that was my mother."

"Ah," he said, with the offhand dejection of one accustomed to frequent disappointment. "And I don't suppose either of you *drink*? That, doubtless, would be beyond the bounds of hope."

"Are you thirsty?"

"I've fully eight years of thirst in me. It's been that long, you know, since my suicide."

"Eight years," Giselle repeated, stricken.

He nodded mournfully. "Eight years, and how much longer, while Adah Menken stands at heaven's gate, I dare not imagine. How did *you* kill yourself? I jumped. Not from this bridge, though. From the pedestrian bridge by the U. One hundred feet! I'd considered pills, but that seemed unmanly. In any case, I had my own prophecies to fulfill:

> "The assault on immortality begins.
> Put your rimes in order, marshal your thoughts,
> give it all a jump. . . .

"That's from the one where I complained that I'd never get the Nobel Prize. And I wouldn't have, you know, not if I'd hung on till my brain was pickled. But I'm in good company there. Ibsen, Frost, Nabokov, Borges. They can sense, you see, who's thirstiest—and it doesn't help to pretend not to be."

At last there was a break in the steady patter of his nonsense and Giselle was able to put in: "But I didn't kill myself. I was murdered."

"Murdered?" He seemed affronted, either at the idea of murder or at being contradicted. "By whom?"

Giselle looked down at the river. Why should she feel this reluctance to name his name? Could she still feel protective toward him? Or was it with her, as it was with rape victims and battered wives, a matter of shame? "It was my husband," she said at length, with a sense much more of going to confession than of pointing the finger of accusation. "He strangled me."

"And so now you're haunting him?"

"I suppose so. Though it's not by choice. I'd rather just stay out of his way, if I knew how."

"Live and let live, eh?" The poet tried to keep a straight face but after a moment burst into sputtering laughter.

Giselle looked down reproachfully at the gouts of his blood speckling her brother's orange bathrobe.

"Sorry, I could never resist a joke. But seriously—" A humorous look came over him but he was able, despite his professed incapacity, to resist laughing. "Seriously, um— what didn't you say your name is?"

"Giselle."

"Apt, very apt. Seriously, Giselle, it won't do you any good to avoid him. If you're stuck here, it's probably just so you will haunt him—and bring him to confess his crime. Heaven has a very traditional sense of justice in the matter of murder. Of course, it isn't fair to victims, but murder never is. Suicide's something else again. We have only ourselves to blame, and only ourselves to haunt. It can get very dull."

"How long will it go on?" Giselle asked.

143

The poet lifted his hands in a gesture of helpless perplexity. "How long? Who knows? Until Adah Menken is ready to release me, and that could be forever, since I will never—repeat, never—allow that *her* poetry is equal in merit to my own. For that, and nothing less, is what she demands. A lesson in humility, she insists. Let her claim she's a better cook, a better lay, I won't contest it. But Adah Isaacs Menken's poetry the equal of John Berryman's! I ask you! Have you ever *read* her poetry?"

Giselle shook her head.

"Of course not. No one has. No one should ever have to. Her name is deservedly erased from the scroll of memory. An actress whose greatest fame was for riding a horse while pretending to be naked. The wife of a prizefighter, a French novelist's whore, and the first *woman* to offer Whitman the flattery of imitation—all which I say in her favor. But her poetry is not to be believed, or forgiven. Take not my word, read it yourself. Here." He reached into the pocket of his tweed jacket and drew forth a small brown hardcover book and thrust it at Giselle. "Here is the infamy! Read it. Read just the first poem."

Giselle opened the book and started to read the first poem, which was entitled (meaninglessly) "Resurgam":

> Yes, yes, dear love! I am dead!
> > Dead to you!
> > Dead to the world!
> > Dead for ever!
> It was one young night in May.
> The stars were strangled, and the moon was blind with the
> > flying clouds of a black despair.
> > Years and years the songless soul waited to drift on
> beyond the sea of pain where the shapeless life was
> wrecked.
> > The red mouth closed down the breath that was hard
> and fierce.

The mad pulse beat back the baffled life with a low sob.

And so the stark and naked soul unfolded its wings to the dimness of Death.

A lonely, unknown Death.

A Death that left this dumb living body as his endless mark.

On the next page the poem went on to a section II and a section III. She peeked farther ahead and saw IV, V, and VI. Giselle was a slow reader and doubted whether the bleeding poet meant her to read at such length while he stood there, arms folded across his chest, scowling. She handed the book back.

"Well?" he demanded, arching his surviving eyebrow.

"Oh, it's not for me to judge. I don't know anything about poetry."

"I never supposed you did. But surely you know what you *like*? Everyone claims to know that."

"Well, actually, I did sort of like it."

He groaned.

"I can't say I always knew what it meant. But the feelings in it were feelings I've had often enough. Haven't you?"

"*She* sent you here. Admit it. She sent you here to tempt me, to torment me."

"Adah Menken? Oh no. I've never met her. My mother has, though. In fact, this ring—" She held up her hand so he could better see the ring. "—belonged to her. She gave it to my mother, and my mother gave it to me. It lets me open doors, and pick things up, and maybe do other things. I'm not sure what all."

"You have—" His manner shifted, quick as the turning of a page, from rudeness to reverence. He took her ring hand in his and raised it nearer his good eye. "Oh my. Oh my dear. My dear, dear Giselle. Eight years! Eight years I've suffered the tortures of Tantalus. Eight years of being summoned by the Ouija boards of suburban housewives and teenage girls wanting to talk with Freddie Prinze. Eight years with nothing to read but The Menken's moronic book, whose *one* well-chosen word is its title, *Infelicia*. When I look at any other writing, the letters turn to a gibberish of fishhooks before my eyes, for that has been her shrewdest stroke—dyslexia! Eight years cursed to wander the mortal boredom of these streets, haunting drive-in movies, reduced, even, to the *Tonight Show*! I! Unable, because I am a suicide, to travel five miles from the spot where I took my own life. With never a soul to talk to but suicides like myself, and even they remain at most a week or two, while me, me she makes languish like another damned Dutchman. Why even Nixon would rule heaven more fairly. And not *eight* years, Giselle, but eighty times eight years, for you have seen what time becomes for us unless we are summoned to be with one of them. You can see how the waters beneath us scarcely stir, how airplanes seem to hang suspended in the sky. Each afternoon becomes a month of Sundays. A fortnight is a year. And I have spent *eight years* so; maybe I'll spend a century more, for she is merciless, merciless, Giselle! But don't *you* be so."

"Oh, sure, if there's any way I can be a help. . . . "

"Oh my dear!" He got down on one knee and pressed her ring to his bleeding mouth. "*Such* help, *such* succor, such inestimable benefit. And it's only some six, seven blocks away, five minutes' walk. Less."

What's only five minutes' walk?" she wanted to know, though she had already decided to go with him, wherever. He was such a pitiful wreck, and (almost certainly) harmless.

"To the nearest liquor store. Oh, please, Giselle. One bottle, that's all I ask. One little pint of brandy, or possibly a fifth, no more. It's been eight years, Giselle. For Art's sake. Please."

There was a tear in his good eye.

She nodded her consent.

CHAPTER
34

"Sugar, you be quiet!" Alice Hoffman scolded, shaking a minatory finger at the yapping white-haired Scots terrier.

Sugar backed away from the front door but continued to protest the scent of the musk oil moisturizing lotion that emanated so powerfully from the visitor entering with Alice.

"Isn't he a darling," said Bing with grim affection. He squatted down beside his suitcase, held out his hands to be licked, and made kissing noises. To no avail; Sugar continued to bark hysterically.

"Sugar!" Alice insisted. "You stop that right now. Do you hear? Stop it! I'll put you *outside* if you don't stop right now."

"Usually dogs adore me," Bing said in a tone of martyred love.

"I don't have many gentlemen visiting me," Alice explained. "He'll quiet down in a minute or two. Meanwhile let me show you the room upstairs. No one's used it since my sister visited from Seattle last Christmas, but the sheets are fresh. Sugar, stop it!"

Sugar had advanced to within kicking distance and was daring Bing to try something. He interspersed his yapping with feints of snapping at Bing's trouser cuffs. Bing had never encountered a more ill-tempered dog.

"Scots terriers are my *favorite* breed," he said with the smile that had melted so many hearts at the Old Pioneer Bingo Parlor but which had no effect on Sugar, who rushed forward in an ecstasy of berserk daring and bit Bing's shoelaces.

"Now *that* does it!" Alice scooped up Sugar into her arms and carried him out to the kitchen and thence to the back yard, where she fastened his collar to the leash tethered to the clothesline. "Bad dog!"

Sugar went on barking.

Alice returned to the living room, feeling annoyed with her guest for being the cause of Sugar's display of temper. Ill-behaved pets, like ill-behaved children, can't be hidden away, skeleton-wise, in closets. They're always out there at center stage, clamoring to betray us.

"This is so kind of you," Bing told her once again. "Somehow I'd assumed I'd be able to stay at Mom's. It's so strange seeing the house there across the street and not being able to go inside. It's just the way I remember it. Except the elm is gone."

Alice nodded mournfully. "All the elms are gone now. The Dutch elm disease got them."

"And *she's* not there," Bing said, lowering his voice. "That's the difference I just can't believe yet."

Alice's face quivered, and tears welled up to wet the latest application of powder.

"Now, Alice, you promised me: no more tears. Remember

148

what Sister Rita said—my mother hasn't really left us. She may not be over there, across the street, but that's because in another way she's here with us, looking down and listening in."

"You really think so?" Alice snuffled. "Sometimes I wonder."

"I know so, Alice, and what's more I'll prove it. Do you have a Scrabble set around? Preferably the deluxe edition where the letters are on wooden squares."

"You want to play Scrabble? Now?"

Bing shook his head vigorously. "No, no, I want to get in touch with Mom. But not now. Later tonight, after it gets dark and we've both had a chance to *unwind*. Then I'll show you how to use your Scrabble set in place of a Ouija board. You do *have* a Scrabble set?"

"I think there's one around somewhere. Probably in the closet of Ben's old room, where I was going to put you. A Ouija board—isn't that illegal, though? I mean, for Catholics."

"The Church frowns on Ouija *boards*, but this isn't a Ouija *board*. It's much better." He smiled at his own deft casuistry. "As for the Church frowning, it was actually a Catholic priest who taught me Scrabble Ouija. Father Mabbley at St. Jude's Church in Las Vegas."

"Oh. Then you haven't—um, left the Church?"

"Good heavens, no! Why *ever* would you think that? I'm more devout now than when I went to Cretin, and when I was there, you know, I came this close—" He held up thumb and forefinger in a not-quite-closed O. "—to having a Vocation. I hope *Mom* never supposed that I'd lost my faith! That would have broken her *heart*."

"No, of course not. I was just assuming . . . I mean, Joy-Ann never heard from you all that time. And your being in Las Vegas and all. . . . " Alice trailed off into a flustered silence.

Bing assumed a look of mournful reproach. "Alice, I can

149

tell *you* have never been to Las Vegas. Las Vegas is an intensely religious city. As I was explaining last night on the plane to Father Windakiewiczowa, there are no atheists in casinos."

"On the plane?" Alice wrinkled her nose, either in puzzlement or as though literally sniffing out scandal.

"Oh, dear, now I have stepped in it, haven't I?"

"I thought Father Windy was on a retreat. That's what it said in the bulletin Sunday."

"Just forget I said anything. And anyhow, why can't people go to Vegas for a retreat?" Bing underlined his mischief with a little giggle of complicity; then, before it could be held against him, quickly changed gears. "This is so kind of you. Really! I don't know if I could have faced a hotel room tonight. Or afforded one, for that matter. Now why don't we sit down in this lovely living room—I swear it looks like a *photograph* from a home decorating book—and you tell me all about the trip you and Mom took out to see Giselle's grave. I want to know every detail."

Flattered and flustered in equal parts, Alice nodded compliance and sat down on the left-hand corner section of the aquamarine vinyl sectional. "It's hard to believe," she began, "that it was only the day before yesterday that Joy-Ann and I went out to the cemetery. . . . "

CHAPTER
35

"I hope you're not the sort to bear grudges," said the bleeding poet, holding out his plastic tumbler for a refill. "Ordinarily I'm not a rapist."

"I wouldn't have called that rape," Giselle assured him. "More just an ordinary grope."

"In my heart it was rape." Berryman furrowed his brow and shook his head in self-accusation. "As though any woman would want to be pawed at by a bloody cadaver. Has that damned bottle disappeared again?"

Giselle looked around for the bottle of Chivas Regal, which had indeed vanished from where she'd put it down beside the box on which she was sitting. It was the the oddest thing. The ring let her take any bottle off the shelves, open it, drink from it, possibly even smash it to bits, but the moment she looked away from it and stopped thinking of it, it returned to where it had been, resealed and untasted. It was as though as a ghost one could eat and drink only the ghosts of food and liquids. "Just a minute," she told Berryman, "I'll get us another."

Berryman continued to bask in self-reproach. "And you so pregnant you look like you modeled for the Venus of Willendorf. My God, I've behaved like a beast."

Who was the Venus of Willendorf? Giselle wondered, pushing herself up to her feet. She *was* hugely pregnant, that was so, and if this John Berryman had been any sort of gentleman, he'd have offered to get his whiskey for himself. Ah, but of course, he couldn't; *she* had the ring, and wasn't about to lend it to him. She was not such a fool as that; nor he, to do him credit, such a fool as to suggest it.

She crossed the store to the Scotch section, where she had to wait for a girl with an empty knapsack on her back to make her slow-motion choice among the various prices and labels. It wasn't possible to reach the shelf the Chivas was on till the girl had moved aside.

"Once," said Berryman, raising his voice, "in one of my Pussycat poems, I wondered if Hell would be any worse than what we've got, here and now, on Earth. What do you think?"

Her only answer was a laugh. She'd had that much to drink that she no longer felt shy in front of the poet, who turned out, for all his talk about how famous he'd been, to be a pretty average person. A bit of a lech perhaps, but a clumsy lech, a lot like the Cretin senior, Ron Plotkin, she'd dated in her sophomore year. At last the girl with the knapsack decided to take a gamble on the second-cheapest Scotch and moved out of the way. Giselle took the Chivas from the shelf and returned to the little conversation pit they'd made by stacking Gallo boxes in the untrafficked corner of the store devoted to liqueurs and sherries.

"Put it another way," he went on, undaunted by her laugh. "Is this Hell, and am I in it?"

"This?" She laughed again. There was something so silly about him—the self-importance combined with the self-pity and both so much at odds with his intelligence. "No, this is Minneapolis. Or I should say St. Paul, this side of the bridge. Here, hold out your glass." She broke the seal on the bottle.

Berryman held out his plastic tumbler, and she splashed Chivas into it, then into her own. They toasted, pliant brim to brim. Then he took a long grateful guzzle, while Giselle swirled her Scotch around and around the unmelting ice cubes she'd taken from the store's freezer. At last she took a sip.

"Do you think," she asked, "that it's really worth paying so much more money for Chivas Regal? I mean, can you actually taste the difference?"

"I used to think I could. But whether *this* stuff tastes different is a problem in epistemology."

Giselle looked at him as though she'd caught him cheating at cards.

"That is to say, since what we're drinking isn't entirely *real*, its taste must be based on what we each can remember of Chivas Regal back when we were alive. Assuming you had some then?"

"Oh, lots of times. When people were losing heavily at the tables they'd order this stuff probably more than anything else. Heavy losers like to look like big spenders."

"Can I ask a personal question?"

He meant, she knew, a question about sex. On the walk to the liquor store, they'd exchanged quick but candid accounts of their lives and deaths. He knew about her murder; she knew about his suicide. They'd also talked about sex. It was then he'd made his pass at her, after which the conversation became a lot more abstract and impersonal.

153

"Ask."

"Why did you go to Las Vegas?"

"I told you. I had this vision, I guess you would call it. My husband's photograph started talking to me. He said he was going to kill me. I suppose I should have wondered if I was going crazy, but I'm glad I didn't. I didn't even pack a suitcase. I just walked out of that house and kept walking."

"But why Las Vegas?"

She shrugged. "I felt lucky. And I was right about that. I never had to do a lick of work the whole time I was there. When I needed money I would just go somewhere there were slots, and I would have this kind of tingling feeling for which one was going to give me a jackpot. I almost never had to put in more than four quarters before the bells started ringing."

He shook his head and attempted, so far as his disfigurement permitted, a knowing smile. "I find that just a little hard to believe."

"So? What can I say? Some people *are* lucky. Oh, I know what you're thinking. You're thinking, There she was, a little suburban housewife who gets bored with Willowville and decides life is going to be more exciting as a hooker."

He lifted his hands in denial. "I never said that."

"No, scarcely anyone would ever come right out and *say* it, but a lot of them thought it. Or they left money, which is the same thing. But do you know who were the absolutely nicest people? The losers. Someone who had just lost everything he owned—or at least everything he could lay his hands on. They would make love to me like they were Adam and I was Eve and the garden of Eden had just been invented. It didn't last long, usually, but while it did it was terrific."

Berryman nodded. "That seems reasonable."

"I wonder if that's why my husband killed me. I never really considered it till now, talking to you. But it's likely, isn't it? He must have found out where I was somehow and come there and seen me with someone else and gone crazy; it's a theory. I really have no idea how his mind works. I probably never did."

"Didn't he say anything?"

"No. There was a note at the desk at the motel where I was staying, saying that a Mr. Glandier was looking for me, and I thought, 'That's it, time to check out.' I went up to my room, but he'd managed to get inside ahead of me. The door was unlocked. And he didn't say a thing, just strangled me. But do you think that's why? Do you think it was jealousy, as simple as that?"

"I . . . couldn't begin to guess. I've never met the man." His wounds began to bleed more copiously. It seemed a way of blushing. He took a long desperate swallow of whiskey.

Giselle smiled and touched his knee. There was something about him, his shifts back and forth between bubbling excitement and a silky sort of gloominess, that brought back to life a whole slice of her year in Las Vegas. The way she'd floated along the Strip or through the casinos, amazed by the lights and the swarms of people, disconnected from everyone else, colliding with other people's eyes, nothing making the least bit of sense or needing to, and then one night, bingo, out of the blue, just like it happened in every song, she would meet the one stranger who understood everything that was happening just the way she understood it, and for a night or a weekend they would tell each other their stories and make love and eat dinner and say goodbye. Such a weird and wasteful way to have lived, it seemed now. Though better, far, than the way she'd lived before.

Berryman had set his glass down and taken a handkerchief from his coat pocket to try and stanch his bleeding. The handkerchief was brown and crusty from earlier use and accomplished nothing. He put it back in his pocket and reached for his glass, which had disappeared. "Damn! Again!"

155

"Here," said Giselle, "have mine."

He accepted her glass, and said, "You still haven't answered my question, you know. Not about Las Vegas. The question before, about hell. Don't *you* ever feel condemned?"

"Not really. Confused, often enough. But condemned would be like condemned to death, wouldn't it? And we're dead already."

"Not necessarily. You can be condemned to pay a fine. That's the root of the word—from the Latin *damnum*, a legal fine. I thought by killing myself I'd just slip away unnoticed, as I might have left a party without saying goodbye to my hosts—without paying the fine. I truly didn't expect an afterlife. Oh, I wrote my share of religious poems, and very orthodox they were in their way. I couldn't, after all, let Eliot and that lot have *all* the glory. The Metaphysical tradition was mine as much as his. But an actual, literal afterlife, like this, with rewards and punishments and gatekeepers? Believe me, if I'd foreseen such a possibility, I'd have taken Hamlet's advice more seriously."

"Which is?"

"Hamlet said he'd have wanted to kill himself if he could be sure it would be like going to sleep and never dreaming. He equated hell with a nightmare. That's a rough paraphrase; Shakespeare says it much better." Berryman struck a declamatory pose, switched on an English accent, and recited:

> "To die, to sleep;
> To sleep: perchance to dream: ay, there's the rub;
> For in that sleep of death what dreams may come
> When we have shuffled off this mortal coil,
> Must give us pause."

He paused, and repeated the last phrase, as though to his prompter: "'Must give us pause.'"

A maudlin throb had entered his voice, and from maudlin, Giselle knew, a drunk could quickly progress either to raucous or to stupified. How was he to be kept sober enough to be helpful (as he'd promised he would be; he had been present at many deliveries performed by an obstetrician friend of his in Rutherford, New Jersey) at the crucial moment? She did not want to sneak off into a dark corner like a cat dropping a litter of kittens.

"Damn," he said.

"What's wrong now?" she asked, setting the bottle to the side of the box she sat on.

"The rest is silence. I can't remember another word of that soliloquy. I used to know virtually the whole play by heart. My mind's becoming a sponge—a *dry* sponge. And now the *bottle*'s missing!"

She looked down beside the box: like the white elephants you can't stop thinking about for fifteen seconds if someone tells you *not* to think of them, the bottle was still there. But really, he had to be slowed down. "Don't you think you've had enough for the moment?"

Berryman cracked the plastic cup between his fingers and threw it on the floor, where the ice cubes went skating about the linoleum. "I don't think it's fucking fair," he shouted, "that I should end it all and then end up in the same situation I was in before, with you acting like a goddamned ward mother!" Then, suddenly as his anger had flared, it faded. "Though, of course, that's exactly how Dante designed his Inferno and kept its torments keen. The sinner must repeat the sins of his earthly life, but in their platonic form, so to speak."

She wished he could talk about something besides all the old books he'd read, though so long as he talked about anything at all she supposed she ought to be grateful. Talk (his own talk, about his own problems) seemed to be, much more than booze, what he stood in greatest need of.

157

And so for the longest time they talked. They talked about Hamlet and various poet friends of Berryman's who'd killed themselves (and whom Adah Menken was punishing, like him, with a kind of house arrest), and whether any of them had intended, in their hearts of hearts, to succeed at suicide, and whether it was ever really the best or the only way out of a drastic problem. The afternoon went on and on, and customers went in and out of the store like zombies seen in instant replay, and the shadows of the houses crawled across lawns and sidewalks and began to cross the street, until, the sky growing overcast, these varied shadows were swallowed up into a single shadow and that shadow thickened to twilight, and all the while the poet went on, not always about suicide or his own books or the suicides or even the books of other famous poets, but sometimes about matters of more general interest, such as the essential differences between men and women and between rich people and poor people, and their similarities too, and about the way things worked in the afterlife, especially for spirits like Adah and Joy-Ann who had got loose from earth and could move around in what Berryman called the Aether.

"The Aether?" asked Giselle.

"The Aether, the Other Side, Heaven—whatever you call it, it sounds like you know what's there. And I don't, and who knows if I ever will? But sometimes . . ." He sighed poetically. "Sometimes I feel so close to breaking through to—well, wherever. Have you ever looked closely at the shadows of the ripples that the drops of water make, falling from a shower head into a full bathtub? The ripples bounce back from the sides of the tub and make interference patterns with new ripples expanding from the impact point of later droplets. Sometimes I'll close my eyes and there'll be patterns like that, only incredibly vast. And I know that if I could *enter* that pattern—"

"For me," said Giselle, "it's a crisscross pattern. Like a

pie-crust or a potholder. But I get the same feeling. I want to get inside it, as though it were a sleeping bag, and zip it up behind me and just *be* there."

"Yet from what you said about your mother's experiences there, and from things that Adah Menken has let drop, *their* heaven doesn't sound at all abstract. It's about as different from this world as St. Paul is from Minneapolis. Just the Other Side of another kind of river."

"Yes, but Mom did say she hasn't gone the whole way to heaven yet, and where she is now she doesn't see other spirits about, except for Adah Menken. So maybe it's different for each person, the way your ripples are basically round and my crisscrosses are square."

The telephone began to ring, as it had twice before since they'd come into the liquor store, but this time the owner of the store continued clearing the register and getting ready to close, seemingly oblivious.

"That's odd," said Berryman. "When it rang the last time it was deep and drawn-out, like a bell tolling. Now the sound isn't being slowed down. Do you suppose—"

"—that it's for us? I'll see."

Giselle went to the phone and picked up the receiver. Beside her the store's owner was making bundles of one-dollar bills.

"Hello?" she said.

"Hello, Giselle. This is Adah Menken. Could I speak with Mr. Berryman?"

Giselle held out the phone to Berryman. "It's for you."

He groaned. "I knew it. I knew this was too good to last." He answered with a "Hi" of resignation and thereafter said nothing but "Right," "Got it," and "Mm-hm," like an employee in a very subordinate position. Before Giselle could ask after her mother, he had hung up.

"I warned you this would happen," he said. "Someone right in this neighborhood is setting up a séance, and I've

159

got to be there. Such a damned waste of time. They'll want to know things I haven't got a clue to, and even when they ask a question I can answer, my dyslexia makes it almost impossible for me to give a coherent reply on the damned Ouija boards."

"But what about—" She did not say "me" because, in truth, she did not mean "me." Instead she placed her hands over her protruding abdomen.

"You're welcome to come along. It's not that far off. The corner of Calumet and Carver."

"That's where I grew up! Is someone having a séance in *our* house?"

"Are you on the northeast corner, yellow stucco with brown trim, cyclone fencing around the back yard?"

"That's Alice Hoffman's house. I saw her at the funeral parlor today. I'll bet she's trying to get in touch with my mother. Which is a little peculiar. I mean, she's a Catholic."

"You'd be surprised the people I've seen using Ouija boards," said Berryman. "Priests and nuns." He winked with his good eye.

"No. You're just saying that to shock me. Aren't you?"

"Maybe. See for yourself. Are you coming?"

"Yes, please. I promise I won't interfere."

"Interfere all you like. If you can spell, we'll give Alice Hoffman a séance that'll knock her socks off. But before we set off, would you—um, be so kind? I promise I won't become incapacitated. I'll just have enough to stop the fear and trembling."

Giselle nodded her acquiescence and, as they left the store, took another bottle of Chivas Regal off the shelf. She gave it to Berryman, and he carried it clutched to his chest beneath crossed arms, like a child on his way to bed cradling his teddy bear.

CHAPTER

36

"Would you believe," said Bing, mincing the carrot to atoms, "that I once weighed a hundred and *eighty* pounds? At my height; can you imagine?" He slid the pulverized carrot off the chopping block and into the pot.

Alice Hoffman regarded the pile of raw produce on her kitchen table with dismay. She seldom had to confront vegetables that weren't frozen. "Do you really need that much?"

"Oh, this soup isn't for just one meal. It should see you through an entire week. Every day just add a little something different, a pinch of this, a nuance of that. When I started the Prettykin program I didn't eat anything but this soup for a *month.* Soup for lunch, soup for dinner, and for breakfast a grapefruit, a tablespoon of bran to keep the bowels moving, and sometimes in the evening, when I lost all self-control, some thin turnip slices."

Alice, who hated turnips, looked at the vegetables with even more alarm. "This is all very nice of you, Bing, but it really isn't necessary."

"Nothing is *necessary*," said Bing primly, as he turned his attention to a large rutabaga. "Fitness isn't *necessary, a* youthful figure isn't necessary. But you will feel so much better, Alice, if you take off just twenty pounds. Thirty would be still better, but *at least* twenty. And I can help you do that. I have seen three other women through the Prettykin program, and every one of them was in worse shape than you. You see, this isn't a diet—it's a new *life-*style. You will change your eating habits, and you won't want to eat a lot of refined sugar and high-cholesterol fats. Beans! There are wonderful things you can do with beans."

"But—"

He lifted the paring knife and wagged it in silent reprimand. "It's little buts like that," he recited, "that lead to big butts."

She sighed resignedly and returned to the dining room, where the table had been prepared for Scrabble Ouija. Bing claimed to have read about Scrabble Ouija in the *National Enquirer.* A medium in Texas had by this means received some astonishingly detailed spirit messages and predictions from a number of dead celebrities, including Alfred Hitchcock. The lettered titles were spread, blank side up, across the dark polished wood. A pen lay crosswise over a tablet of Basildon Bond stationery. Expensive beeswax candles from the same shop in Highland Park that had supplied the stationery had been fitted into the two crystal candleholders, a gift, forty years ago, from her cousin Bea in Seattle. Bea, who had died barely a year ago. . . .

Alice felt terrible. She knew that what she and Bing were intending to do was a mortal sin, on a par with going to an astrologer or joining a Satanic cult. The only reason she was willing to go ahead with the séance in defiance of the teaching of Holy Mother Church was the certainty that nothing would come of it.

In fact, that was not the only reason, or even the major one; in fact, Alice simply didn't know how to say no to Bing Anker. She'd tried to stop him from making his giant pot of soup, but he'd refused to listen to her. He'd gone out and bought all those vegetables, and when she insisted that he shouldn't go to any bother in the kitchen, he'd somehow turned everything around so that it seemed he was under some kind of obligation, as her houseguest, not only to make the miserable soup but also to put her on his own private diet program. It hadn't even occurred to Alice, who'd held to exactly the same weight for the last thirty years, that she needed to diet. It was all very flustering. What Alice didn't understand was that she liked being flustered.

As he left the kitchen, Bing switched off the overhead light and then, after lighting the two beeswax candles, went about the rest of the downstairs turning off the other lights. He positioned his reluctant hostess in a chair on one side of the table, then went around the table and sat in the facing chair.

"Now, before we do anything else, we must clear our minds of all low, materialistic thoughts. Think of somewhere completely peaceful, maybe it's a lake, maybe it's a garden, and try to feel its influence over your spirit. *Relax* completely. No tension, no anxiety. You see, the spirits can't use us as their mediums unless we're clear of all the ugly static that attaches us to the material plane. Have you done that?"

Alice nodded.

"Good. Now we'll *summon* them." Bing closed his eyes and rolled his head back and called out, in the voice he usually reserved for announcing the final, most suspenseful numbers of a bingo game, "O Spirits who have passed beyond this mortal sphere, whom the ignorant call 'dead'—"

Alice winced and sat a little stiffer in her chair.

"—but who in truth are more alive than we, come to us! Share your immortal wisdom with two humble seekers. Speak to this grief-stricken woman and show her that life does continue beyond the grave. All right now, Alice, hold your right hand out over the letters, and when I take hold of the wrist let it go completely limp so the spirits can guide both our hands. Don't use your own willpower. If you feel your hand being guided to the right, don't resist, go with the flow. And whenever the spirits definitely stop your hand from moving any farther in any direction, then lower just the tip of one finger until you feel it touch one of the tiles, and I'll pick that tile up. Understood?"

She nodded.

"All right. Now close your eyes, and I'll do the same, and wait for the spirits to have their influence. It may take a while."

While they waited, Sugar, in the kitchen, whined, apprehensive of this strange conjunction of candlelight in the dining room and the dim blue light from the gas ring in the kitchen and the smell of vegetable soup everywhere through the house. Then, his whines unheeded, he could be heard going down the basement steps to his particular haven and hiding place behind the electric water heater.

Alice could feel a pressure at the side of her hand tugging it to the left. Not exactly a pressure nor did it precisely tug, but it wasn't her own doing and it didn't *seem* to be Bing's, whose hand rested lightly on her wrist, exerting no pressure either to left or to right.

"The spirit is here!" Bing exulted. "That was *very* prompt. Now, first thing, we must ask his name. Or hers, as the case may be."

Something urged Alice's finger to dip to the table and touch one of the tiles.

164

"This one?" Bing scooped it up. "Keep going."

Alice—or, rather, Alice's fingers—continued to move in slow swoops above the table, hesitating, dipping, touching, and moving on, while Bing picked up the tiles she touched and placed them on the plastic rack, and then, as the spirit continued in spate, beside the rack on the dark wood of the table.

"It's stopped," Alice announced matter-of-factly. "Whatever it was isn't doing anything now."

Bing marveled at the old lady's showmanship. He considered himself a connoisseur of fakery, and Alice Hoffman had all the right instincts: she was born to be a medium. A pity there was no way he could tell her. What he *could* do was play the game with the same conviction that she brought to it. After all, it was his game, and it wouldn't do to be beaten at it by a complete novice.

One by one, with due solemnity, he commenced to turn over the tiles. The first four were hash—D J O N—and the fifth was a blank.

"D, J, O, N," said Alice with a hint of sarcasm. "What's that supposed to mean?"

"Not a lot," Bing had to admit. "It's close to 'djin,' which is some kind of supernatural creature. And I suppose you'd pronounce it the same as John. Maybe when *all* the letters are turned over . . ."

With somewhat less solemnity and proportionally greater astonishment, Bing reversed the remaining six tiles:

BURYME

"Jesus," he whispered. "What are the odds against *that* happening?"

"I think we should quit now," Alice said in a tone that exactly captured Sugar's abjectest whine.

"Quit? This is *fascinating.* Look, the next step after studying the message in the original order of the letters is you

165

rearrange the letters the way you would if you were looking for the best possible score in a game. This is what makes this technique so much more three-dimensional than a session with an ordinary Ouija board. For instance, look—if you just switch the fourth letter with the ninth, you get Joy and Burn. Then use the blank as an E: Joy Burned Me. Which is a perfect description for what it might feel like when you get your first look at heaven. Right?"

"But that's her *name*," Alice insisted, having no wish to ferret still deeper meanings out of "Joy Burned Me." "And she *hasn't* been buried yet. Do you really think . . . ?"

"Or consider this," Bing went on, rearranging the letters. "If the blank were a T, you'd get *Don't* Bury Me, and a J left over, as a kind of signature."

"Why would she say *that?*" Alice demanded, offended at the most fundamental level of good housekeeping.

"Maybe she'd rather be cremated?" he suggested. "Don't ask me. Ask *her*."

He held his hand out over the Scrabble tiles like a dancer offering invitation to the dance.

With a shiver of sweet submission Alice yielded to the temptation. Bing's fingers closed around her wrist. She closed her eyes and whispered, "Joy-Ann, are you really here with us?"

CHAPTER
37

"See what I mean about my dyslexia?" said Berryman. He stood behind Alice Hoffman, leaning forward so that drops of his blood fell, and vanished, into the crisp tinted cylinders of her perm. "It doesn't really help that I can *see* the letters. Their shapes keep shifting around. If you hadn't taken over and started pointing out the letters to get her to touch, it would have been alphabet soup as usual. Oh, and by the way, the name is Berry-man, as in straw-berry. Not Bury-man."

"Sorry. I didn't know."

Berryman shrugged. "So much for immortal fame." He solaced his hurt feelings with a swallow of whiskey. "Shall we return to work?"

"Do you feel anything yet?" Bing insisted of Alice.

She shook her head.

"Spirits, are you still there?" Bing demanded in a tone of jocular bullying suitable for summoning a waitress who'd been systematically ignoring his table. "If we were mistaken in thinking you might be my mother, then tell us who you are."

"Listen," said Berryman. "He's your brother, so why don't you take over?"

"Could I? I mean, can I tell him anything I want to?"

"Such as spilling the beans about your husband the murderer? Be my guest. So far as I know, there are no censorship rules, and if it does turn out that I'm violating some heavenly ordinance, so much the better. Maybe they'll stop sending me out to these damned séances."

Giselle went around the table to stand behind Alice Hoffman, while Berryman slumped gratefully into one of the slat-back dining-room chairs doing sentry duty on either side of the kitchen door. All the Scrabble tiles, which Giselle had earlier turned letter-side-up when she'd helped Berryman spell his first message, had reverted to their face-down position, just as the bottles at the liquor store had returned to the shelves the moment they'd stopped being thought about. Nimbly Giselle reversed the tiles again until she'd found a G—toward which, with little tugs and nudges, she guided Alice Hoffman's so wonderfully suggestible fingers. The I, the S, and the E had already been turned up, and both L's were discovered with little difficulty. Only the final E eluded easy detection. Then she turned it up, and led Alice's finger to it, and stood back to enjoy the effect of her revelation.

Bing reversed the tiles one by one with mounting dismay. Giselle suspected that he'd begun the séance in a spirit of mischief, meaning only to have a little fun at Alice Hoffman's expense. As a boy he'd constantly tried to spook his younger and ever-credulous sister with stories of ghosts and werewolves, and he didn't seem to have changed much in the however many years since she'd last seen him. Now it was her turn to spook him, and though it might be wrong of her, she was enjoying the idea.

"Giselle," Alice Hoffman said, bending her head sideways to read the letters that Bing had arranged for his own reading convenience. "That's your sister's name. So it isn't your mother who's with us, it's your sister."

"Yes, I can see that."

Alice was visibly less shaken by the message than Bing, for there was still, at the back of her mind, a comfortable cushion of doubt. It might be that they were in contact with the Other Side, but it might equally well be that Bing Anker was pulling her leg. She didn't know exactly *how* he might have gone about it, but she was content to remain ignorant of most of the forces that ordered her life. Whenever, therefore, events insisted upon being witnessed and disillusionment became unavoidable (as, for instance, during Watergate), Alice would feel doubly betrayed—first, for having been fooled, and secondarily for not having been fooled well enough.

"Well, do you think, there's some *other* explanation?" she asked, after a search through her own mind yielded no results.

"I couldn't tell you, off the top of my head, the odds of just those seven letters turning up accidentally in that order, but they must be somewhere in the trillions. So *something* sure as hell is here. Unless—" His eyes twinkled with the glimmer of a rational explanation. "Unless *you've* got a marked Scrabble set."

"What do you mean?"

Bing regarded Alice and realized there was no way she could be diddling him. Her stupidity was altogether too genuine.

169

"Do you mean you think *I* could be cheating?"

"No, no, no. No one's cheating." His lips twitched with a grimace of a smile, and he squirmed against the seat of the chair as though screwing down his ass for safety. "This is real. So—let's ask her the obvious question."

"The obvious question?"

"Giselle?" Bing looked up at the ceiling, where dim shadows of the stucco nubbles jittered in the candlelight. "If you're there, can you tell us—how were you killed? Who did it?" He looked at Alice. "Put your hand out over the letters."

Alice complied reluctantly. Bing's sudden lack of playfulness was making her nervous.

Giselle looked at Berryman questioningly.

"What can you lose?" he answered.

Once more Giselle guided Alice's fingers among the Scrabble tiles, quickly almost as a hunt-and-peck typist now, since from Giselle's viewpoint nearly all the tiles were faced letter-side-up. It was strange to see the turned-up tiles popping out of existence at the moment Bing picked up each reversed original and set it in order along the edge of the table.

Some while after Giselle had completed her message, Alice announced, "That seems to be it."

Bing turned over the letters:

R O B E R T M U R D E R E D W E

He puzzled over the w, then turned it upside-down to make it an м.

"Robert's her husband's name."

"I know," said Bing.

"But Joy-Ann told me, back when the tragedy took place, that he was fishing out at Rush Lake. And he must have been able to prove it, there must have been witnesses, or the police would have given him more aggravation. So I don't

170

think it's possible, what those letters say, and I think we'd better stop."

"No, please," said Bing with an urgency that only alarmed Alice more. "Not now. There might be some other explanation. Maybe the unconscious actually keeps track of all the letters even once they're turned over and mixed around. I mean, that's the usual explanation for Ouija messages, isn't it: the unconscious. But maybe not; maybe this is the real thing."

"That's what I'm *thinking!* That's why we should stop."

"Well, damn it, let *me* try." He held his right hand out over the letters and demanded in a tone of normal conversational anger: "So—is there some way you can *prove* what you're saying? Is there evidence?"

Giselle sighed. "Now how would I know that?" she complained to Berryman. "I'm a victim, not a detective."

The poet furrowed his brow. "You did say something earlier about a *note* you got at your motel. What became of that? Do you remember?"

"I put it in my pocket."

"Then surely the police would have found it. Unless your husband got to it first and destroyed it, which is probably the case. What were you wearing when he killed you?"

Giselle laughed at the absurdity of the question, which reminded her of the questions on *The Newlywed Game.* Then, realizing its actual relevance, she broke off. "I wasn't wearing anything. As soon as I got to my room I took off what I had on, because I wanted a quick shower before I checked out. And when I went into the bathroom there he was, waiting."

"So the note might still be in the pocket?"

"Conceivably. It was an orange pants suit that always made me feel like a light bulb inside it, it was so bright. But who knows what may have become of it."

"Maybe your brother could find out. It's worth a shot."

Bing, meanwhile, through all this discussion, had sat bolt upright, his hand extended over the Scrabble tiles as over the embers of a fire. His lips were pressed into a tight humorless smile. His right toe tapped out a slow semaphore of impatience on the braided rug.

Giselle tried to guide his hand, as she'd guided Alice's, but he seemed as rigid and unresponsive as a statue.

"I don't think he can feel me," she said.

"Some can't," said Berryman. "It takes a particular empty-headed kind of person usually. They have a different way of relaxing. The idea of trance state is more related to their usual approach to things."

"So what should I do?"

"Try the old lady again. She's still sitting there."

At Giselle's first touch Alice Hoffman let out a little shriek and then a shudder, but she didn't resist Giselle's directions. Her limp hand let itself be lifted above the table. Letter by letter Giselle answered her brother's question. Bing waited until Alice's oracular finger no longer moved above the hidden letters, then turned over the three rows of tiles that had accumulated before him:

FINDTHENOTE

INORANGEPAN

TSUITPOCKET

"Oh," said Alice Hoffman, as soon as she'd figured out that to be understood the second line had to be run on into the third. "Oh!" she repeated, pushing back her chair without warning, so that Giselle was instantaneously dematerialized out of the dining room. "I know what suit she means. I've seen Joy-Ann wearing it. And it's hanging in her closet just across the street."

CHAPTER
38

As the back of the wooden chair struck its head, the fetus in Giselle's distended abdomen writhed in protest and tore with its small fingers at the tissues confining it. For a timeless instant fetus and woman were whirled through the vortex of all possible spaces until, like the unique wooden ball that drops from the revolving wire cage into the bingo caller's hand, they found themselves in the single space determined by etheric necessity.

It was a corner bedroom of the Anker house on Calumet Avenue, across the street from Alice's. The very bedroom and, indeed, the very bed Giselle had slept in all through her childhood and adolescence. The same little dresser of chipped pink paint stood in the same corner between the window overlooking Calumet and the window overlooking Carver. The same curtains, their flowers faded to a paler pink, their flounces dusty, covered the windows and filtered the glare of the corner streetlight.

The fetus clawed and kicked, searching for egress. As its consciousness had grown, its will had grown in proportion, and it would no longer tolerate confinement. It had purposes and capabilities that could only be realized in the world outside the womb. Indeed, it was, at this stage, little more essentially than a purpose to accomplish some yet unimagined evil. This half-existent purpose pressed its mouth against the yielding tissues of the womb, trying instinctively to chew its way through. But the placenta, even when its infant gums could obtain purchase, was too elastic. It must have teeth if it would puncture the placenta. Like seedlings, its first teeth began to bud.

Giselle had never experienced the legendary pains of childbirth. She assumed the pains she experienced now were simply the pains all laboring mothers have had to bear through the ages—and she tried to bear them. The ring she wore allowed her to clutch the chenille bedspread when the pains were most intense, and when for a moment they diminished she was able to go to the window and raise it and call across the street to the poet, where she'd left him in Alice Hoffman's house. "Help!" she screamed into the spring night, as the Calumet bus rolled to a stop at the traffic light and opened its doors for a single passenger to alight. "John! I'm here—across the street, in our old house. Help me, please!"

The bus rumbled on along Calumet. Its passenger crossed the street and walked on past Alice Hoffman's house in the direction of Grand.

Giselle screamed again—a wordless throat-ripping roar of pain—and fell to her knees, clutching the sill of the opened window. The curtains fluttered about her in the night

174

breeze. Cars drove by on the street, and night walkers passed on the sidewalk, all oblivious of her cries. Only Berryman, in the house across the street, could be of any help, and he, without the magic of her ring, could not so much as open a door himself in order to reach her.

A light came on in Alice Hoffman's porch, and, blurred by the sounds of distant traffic, she could hear her brother's voice in alternation with Alice's.

She called again, "John! John, can you hear me?" But the only answering sound was a far-off squeal of brakes.

Now the porch door opened, and she could see, framed and silhouetted by the bright porch light, her brother, still in conversation with Alice. She could not make out Bing's words, but she knew their melody was meant to soothe. Alice, in her replies, did not evidence any response to that melody. Her voice had the timbre and rhythm of Sugar's barking.

Or did she, in fact, hear Sugar himself barking in the basement?

The question—the possibility of questions in whatever form—was rendered wholly meaningless by a new attack of what she assumed to be her contractions: sharp fast raps of pain, as though the beaks of large birds were pecking at her inmost tenderest organs from some point within. Her mouth opened and her body arched convulsively backward, as in the yoga position known as the Cobra. She stared at the juncture of the ceiling and the wallpapered wall as though these dimly amber, streetlit surfaces were a veil about to be parted, revealing a nightmare's most terrible meaning.

How long the pain continued at this pitch she had no way to know. While it lasted it was without end; when it ended she collapsed upon the floor, all thought wrung from her mind but a horror of what had been, a fear it might return. Then, as a sense of sequence and rationality became possible again, she supposed she had passed through the gates of her

175

ordeal, that the child she had carried—for how little time? an interval of twenty-four hours?—would be found beside her on the bedroom's worn carpet, newly born. But then she placed her hand on her distended stomach and knew the fetus was inside her still.

As though the pressure of her hand had released a trigger, there was another spasm of mind-annihilating pain. This time when she recovered, Berryman was with her, anxiously trying to soothe away her pain and his dread with talk.

"I heard you, but I couldn't come here. There was no way out of that house, and no way in here, not till your brother could persuade Alice Hoffman to let him have the key. It seems your mother always left one with her in case she went out and forgot her own. Can you understand any of this? Are you conscious?"

She nodded and smiled, or tried to.

"He's here now, looking through your mother's closet for that orange pants suit. That's how I was able to get in, sneaking behind. When I found you, you were all twisted around incredibly. And the baby was—" Berryman's hand knotted in his blood-moist beard. "—I can't describe it. As though it were trying to push its way out by main force. Your stomach would . . . distort—"

"Don't talk, please don't talk. Just help me get it *out*. It's going to start again."

"But how can I—"

"I don't kno-ow" The last vowel twisted away from speech into a tortured moan, and her back arched as though making a bridge for the expected pain to travel along. But it was a false alarm. The worst was still in abeyance.

"A knife," she insisted. "Get a knife."

"Oh, Jesus, Giselle, no, I couldn't do . . . a cesarean?" He shook his head emphatically. Then with an inappropriateness so gross as to border on aplomb, he whinnied with laughter. Instantly he rolled his good eye in self-reproach—then whinnied again.

176

He bit down on his lip to stop the laughter. "I was remembering," he explained in a contrite murmur, "the scene from *Gone With the Wind*. You know, when Melanie's about to give birth, and Butterfly McQueen has her great line?" He switched into falsetto. "'Miss Scahlet, Ah doan know nuthin' 'bout birthin'.' Which is to say that all my talk before about having helped William Carlos Williams deliver babies was just bullshit. Once, just once, I saw a *movie* about natural childbirth, and that's it."

"Please. Don't argue. Take my ring and go down to the kitchen and get a knife from the drawer. Just under the counter to the right of the sink." She took the ring from her finger and he accepted it.

For too long he could only stare at the ring. He felt as though he'd been married. He knew this was an inappropriate response. He felt that all his responses, all through his life, had been inappropriate. At the same time, and at a completely different level of awareness, he was also shit-scared.

"Now," she pleaded, literally on her knees. "Before it starts again."

"Right. Right, I'm going. Now."

He backed out of the room into the small landing and past the door of Joy-Ann's bedroom, where Bing was still rummaging in the closet. As he went down the stairs, he considered walking out of the house and away. With the ring in his possession he might spend the rest of eternity drunk. Earlier that day he'd schemed how to trick the ring away from Giselle for just that purpose. Now it was too late. The spirit of do-gooding had laid hold of him, a spirit he despised and distrusted, since in the past that spirit had led him from one moral pratfall to another.

The knives were in the drawer where Giselle had said they would be. He took the largest and most lethal-looking, a carving knife, then thought better of it and took a paring knife instead. The object was to make an incision, not to saw her in half.

Returning up the stairs, he reasoned that the flesh of ghosts must, logically, be unlike the flesh of the living. His own unstanchable wounds were proof of that. On the other hand, his endless bleeding was also proof that though ghosts might not sustain *mortal* injuries, they could (like the damned in Dante's hell) suffer harm; they did know pain.

Re-entering Giselle's bedroom, he found the light had been switched on and Bing was at the door of the closet, sorting through the tightly packed hangers. Giselle, invisible to her brother, lay on the floor, her stricken features chiseled into a tragic mask by the glare of the overhead bulb.

He knelt beside her, closed his eyes in quick betokening of prayer, and placed the point of the blade against the upper curve of her distended abdomen. A little pressure raised a pinpoint gout of blood, but the tissue beneath the outer epidermis still resisted the edge of the blade.

He pressed harder; the tissue tore; blood flowed from the fissure. Then, as she screamed, a small red hand appeared at the lip of the wound, clenching and tearing to make a wider opening. Berryman stared at the hand, at the two hands, unable to act.

With the motions of a person squirming into a tight sweater, the fetus pushed and elbowed its way from the womb's darkness. Its bulbous, misshapen head emerged from the ruptured flesh. It blinked into the light, and then with the reflexive action even infant fingers can perform it grasped the knife from Berryman's slack fingers and plunged it hungrily into his heart, into his throat, into his one as-yet-unblinded eye, and as the knife plunged and hacked, its little lungs sucked in their first breath of air and released it in a scream of shrill, clarion triumph.

CHAPTER
39

Now her, it thought, and twisted about, tangling its stunted legs in the coils of the umbilicus, to stare at Giselle where she lay, dazed but conscious, on the blood-drenched carpet. Their eyes met, but for a moment only, and then she turned her face away.

It felt cheated. It hungered to see horror, hate, aversion; something, in any case, on a larger scale than mere weariness and release from pain. It wanted to be the cause of, and feed upon, more, and more excruciating, pain.

It drew the paring knife from where it had been sheathed in the blinded poet's eye and used it to sever the umbilicus. Then, as, in its indecision, it sat licking blood from the knife blade, the little man who had been looking through the closet spoke. "By God," he said, "this is it." He turned around in the door of the closet with a yellow slip of paper in his hand.

The fetus—but it was a fetus no longer; neither could it be called a child, nor yet a demon. Let it be spoken of, rather, as a halfling, with regard to its divided nature, belonging as it did to both the physical world of patrilineal descent and to the immaterial matrilinear world—to both, but equally to neither.

This halfling, then, pulled itself across the carpet toward its newly formed, intenser purpose. Through the consciousness it had shared with its mother when she had stood behind this man at the table in the other house, it knew that this man, and the slip of paper in his hand, posed some threat to Robert Glandier. The halfling recognized Glandier as its father and felt some limited bond of loyalty. It meant to serve its father now by murdering his enemy. It lifted the paring knife in its little hands and plunged it into the part of the man's ankle just before the Achilles tendon. But instead of drawing blood, the knife dematerialized; it was a ghostly knife, taken from the drawer by the ghostly power of Giselle's ring; it had power to harm only another ghost.

Oblivious of the harm intended him, Bing Anker crossed the bedroom to stand beneath the overhead light, where he might better study the paper he'd discovered in the jacket pocket of the orange pants suit. At his third step, his foot passed through—and claimed possession of—the space occupied by the ghostly knee of John Berryman, who, at the first instant of this interpenetration, was translated out of the bedroom and into the space he'd worn for himself by his own habitual actions within the narrow sphere he was allowed to inhabit. There, beneath the bridge from which he'd jumped to his death, on the dark surface of the river's slow-rolling waves, he lay, blinded and mute, with blood streaming from his face, and throat, and heart.

"This is it," said the little man, holding the yellow slip of paper with the delicate fervor one might accord a winning lottery ticket. (Which in a sense it was—for the thought had crossed his mind that were Glandier to be convicted as his wife's murderer, he would lose any claim to the Anker house. Indeed, might not Bing, as Giselle's sole surviving heir, have a claim against Glandier's property? The mere speculation brought with it a rush of avaricious and vindictive pleasure quite as though he'd inhaled a popper.)

The halfling felt a corresponding welling up of rage. A bile of powerless anger bubbled up in its throat to blot from its mouth the lingering aftertaste of blood. It sputtered with fury. But this was no idle fury; it focused the halfling's purpose, made it alert to the cue that at that very moment the night breeze brought through the window Giselle had left open.

Grasping the flounces of the curtain, it pulled itself up to the windowsill. From there it was a short drop to the roof of the porch, a longer drop from the roof to the wooden steps below. The pain of the fall did not deter it; the halfling was indifferent to pain and injury.

Its legs were too misshapen—the merest unjointed stumps—ever to have allowed it to walk upright, so it crawled across the parched lawn and out upon the lightly trafficked street. Though agile, it was not cautious, and once it came near to being struck by a delivery van. As the van whizzed by, heedless, the halfling lifted its head to shriek a wordless curse.

It crawled across Alice's lawn to a half window opening to the basement. It hesitated a moment, listening, and Sugar, sensing its presence, gave over the querulous yapping that had first drawn the halfling's attention and began to howl in earnest.

The halfling dropped to the floor of the basement and found its way quickly in the darkness to Sugar's nest behind the electric water heater.

Upstairs, Alice turned from her fretful vigil by the front window, went out to the kitchen, and stood at the head of the basement stairs. "Sugar!" she shouted into the darkness. "You stop that right now!"

Wonderfully, she did not have to shout a second time. Usually on these occasions of mutual anxiety, Sugar and Alice would improvise a kind of duet, yapping and scolding in happy unison. But tonight there was not a peep, not a whimper. Alice, with an obscure sense of disappointment, returned to the dining room, where the Scrabble tiles still spelled out the messages of the séance across the dining-room table. She felt the keenest urge to sweep them all back into their box and retire the box to the back of the closet and and to relegate all that had happened at the séance to a correspondingly dusty corner of her mind.

There was a rattling at the door to the front porch. Had she locked it after Bing had gone across the street? How thoughtless of her. But when she went to the front window to look out there was no one at the door.

Then she heard the back door into the kitchen opening. "Bing?" she called out in alarm—and felt a blessedness of relief when it *was* his voice that answered from the kitchen: "Alice, you will not *believe* this but it was *there!* A piece of notepaper from the Lady Luck Motor Lodge, with—"

He was cut short by a snarl from Sugar and his own piercing scream. Alice reached the door to the kitchen in time to see him stumble back against the stove. His right hand was at his throat to fend off the scrabbling paws of the Scottish terrier, which, having failed to gain a purchase in his flesh, had fastened its teeth into the collar of his Qiana shirt. With his left hand he reached out to keep from falling. With fatal precision his hand went into the boiling pot of vegetable soup. He fell, screaming, to the linoleum, pulling the pot over as he went down. His head struck the corner of the icebox. Sugar, heedless of his own scalding, continued to

182

attack his unconscious, unprotected body, biting and tearing at his throat and the blistered flesh of his face.

"Sugar!" Alice screamed. "Stop that! Sugar!"

Sugar paid no attention to his mistress; he owed his allegiance elsewhere now—to the halfling that had gained possession of his small animal soul and controlled his actions as a puppeteer controls his puppets' twitching limbs.

Alice lacked the sense, or the courage, to attack the raging dog while its rage was directed at Bing. Instead she did what she would have done in any other emergency. She went to the telephone and dialed 911.

Before the number had rung twice, Sugar had run, yapping, out of the kitchen in pursuit. He jumped to the seat of the sectional and from there to Alice's shoulder. His teeth closed around her ear. She screamed and clubbed at the dog with the receiver of the phone. He was knocked to the floor but immediately sprang at her again. His claws ripped through her dress. She kicked at him. He bit at her foot.

She ran into the dining room, looking for something she might use to strike the dog with. Sugar pursued. She thought then—it was even an intelligent thought—that she must put a door between herself and the mad dog. She ran into the kitchen, clutched for the door handle, and slipped, screaming, on the soup that had slicked the linoleum floor. She was dead before her body had tumbled to the bottom of the basement stairs.

Suddenly the house was quiet except for a little voice emitted by the receiver of the telephone. Sugar, ignoring that voice, trotted to the foot of the stairs and sniffed at the blood welling from Alice Hoffman's fractured skull. Where a small puddle of the blood had formed beside her still neatly permed hair he lapped some up, then gave his body a vigorous shake to try and rid himself of the soup that matted his white hair.

He returned, after another taste of blood, to the dining

room and leaped up to the seat of one of the chairs by the table. Awkwardly, for his paws were not really meant for such a task, he disarranged the message spelled out by the Scrabble tiles. Then—his last task before he left the house through the little hinged door cut out for him at the base of the door to the back yard—he pried open Bing's clenched fingers one by one and took the piece of yellow notepaper printed with the letterhead of the Lady Luck Motor Lodge.

Just wait till Daddy sees this, the halfling thought. He'll shit.

CHAPTER
40

He woke unable to remember his nightmare, though it must have been a wet dream of sorts. (This he inferred as he unglued the glans of his cock from his flannel pajamas.) Then, as he stood blear-eyed before the bathroom mirror, untangling the umbilical cord of his shaver, a single image of the dream surfaced to remembrance—a glimpse of Bing Anker's throat as he, Glandier, prepared to sink his teeth into the pink flesh. He put the shaver down on the shelf above the sink and closed his eyes, trying to remember more and fearing what more he might remember.

It was a dream, and all dreams were crazy. Freud had explained that. The thing he must not do was lose the distinction between his dreams and the real world. Ordinarily that would not have been a problem; ordinarily he'd have driven to the office and settled down to work. Work and reality were geometrically congruent concepts. But today was Sunday and the office was closed, and tomorrow would be Joy-Ann's funeral, which meant that he'd have to kill time for two days till he could get back on the main highway of established routine. So, he must *do* something. Such as get the bedroom back in shape. Strip off the wallpaper, lay down a coat of primer, spackle where it needed it, and then paint the whole sucker some bright solid color that would blot out the memory of those insane graffiti. Such as?

Blood red: the image came unbidden. It seemed a joke at first, red droplets trickling down the side of a gallon can—who would paint a bedroom such a color?—but the trickles conjoined to form a puddle beside the fractured skull of Alice Hoffman, and he was on his knees, lapping up the blood with his tongue.

The nightmare again, nothing but that, but why did it seem so real? Why did he feel so certain that Alice Hoffman was dead? He could not have crossed the length of Minneapolis and murdered her—and Bing Anker too—in a somnambulistic trance. Then why this itch to phone the old biddy?

Did the why of it matter? It was an easy enough itch to scratch. He found her number in the St. Paul directory and dialed it.

At the third ring a man's voice answered. "Yes?"

Glandier's immediate reaction was to hang up, but he thought better of it. "Is this six-nine-oh, three-six-three-one?"

"It is, yes. Are you calling Mrs. Hoffman?"

"Yes, is she there? I thought I'd pick her up on my way to McCarron's Funeral Home later this morning. She was a friend of my mother-in-law, Mrs. Anker."

"I'm afraid Mrs. Hoffman has had an accident. Could I

have your name, please? I'll see that someone at headquarters gets back to you with more information, as soon as we know more ourselves."

"Is she . . . all right?"

There was a pause while the man at the other end of the line considered whether to part with this information. Then he said, "Mrs. Hoffman suffered a fatal injury last night when she fell downstairs. There was also a houseguest, Bing Anker, who was badly injured in what seems to have been a related accident. The details aren't entirely clear, and Mr. Anker is still unconscious. Would you know him?"

"Not really." Glandier again wanted to hang up but again thought better of it. He'd already mentioned his mother-in-law: they'd know who'd called. So, after suitable protestations of dismay, he told the policeman what little he knew regarding Bing Anker, then referred him to Flynn, Joy-Ann's lawyer. He tried to worm out more details about the accident, but none were forthcoming. Glandier was told he'd be contacted later in the day. End of conversation.

If it had not been simply a dream, what was it? Some kind of private news broadcast, apparently, but from whom?

He walked to the picture window and looked out across the featureless expanse of his front lawn, as though the answer might be there. And so it was, although he didn't at once recognize it as such. A white Scottish terrier sat in the middle of the lawn, looking alertly at the house. When it saw Glandier at the window, it rose, wagging its tail, and trotted over to the front door. There was no sign up or down the street of the dog's owner.

Glandier went to the door and opened it. He peered at the dog through the aluminum screen of the outer door.

Awkwardly, because of its short legs, the dog bounded up the three brick steps and deposited a small yellow wad of paper before the door. Then it backed away from the door, sat down, and looked up expectantly at Glandier.

187

Glandier opened the screen door and stooped to pick up the saliva-sodden paper. When he'd managed to smooth it out, the letterhead of the Lady Luck Motor Lodge was still legible, and enough of the message that he could appreciate its import.

Glandier stood back from the door while holding it wide open, and the white terrier bounded up the steps with an appreciative yap and entered the house. Its hair was matted and discolored. The flesh, where it showed through the matted hair, seemed inflamed. It trotted into the kitchen and plunked down in front of the gas stove, quite as though it had read Glandier's mind and knew just what he intended to do with the note from the Lady Luck Motor Lodge.

Glandier turned on the burner and held the note over the blue flame. It did not burn easily or all at once, but when it had finally been consumed to the last yellow scrap, the dog let loose a celebratory chorus of yaps.

Glandier smiled and got down on his haunches and patted the dog on its head. "Hey, little fella," he said, "what's your name?" The dog shook its head, and he saw the brass tag attached to his collar. The tag read:

> Hi! My name is SUGAR!
> If I get lost, please call
> my home: 690-3631.

The number was the one Glandier had looked up and dialed only a few moments ago, the number of Alice Hoffman.

CHAPTER
41

For a moment, waking in her old bedroom, Giselle forgot she was dead. She wondered why she had been sleeping on the floor. Her back hurt, and she was naked. Then, as she rolled to her side, the pain of the unhealed incision acted as synopsis, recalling the events of the night, renewing fear. But she was alone, the house was quiet, and the wound in her side seemed almost healed. There was an ache within, like a distant echo of the convulsive cramping pains she'd suffered in the night, and a soreness about the dark lips of the wound. But she was not disabled. When she stood, and when she walked, there was no bleeding and no sharper pain.

She saw the pants suit spread across the bedspread and,

thinking of her nakedness, stooped to gather the silken folds of orange cotton-polyester in her hand. Without the ring she might as well have tried to charm the paper from the walls, the paint from the frame of the bed. She had entrusted the ring to Berryman, and, as she had feared, he had made off with it. Where to, there was no imagining.

She could see, out the window, a police car parked along the Carver side of Alice Hoffman's house. Guilt wrenched at her spirit, for she knew whatever events had brought a police car there, the root of the blame was hers. She had been wrong, as a spirit, to intrude on the lives of the living, to be vengeful, to haunt. Revenge would only compound the original evil and give it larger scope. Poor Mr. Berryman—as though his own miseries had not been large enough! Now. . . But imagination balked before the possibility of his further, deeper pain. She must find him and—

Repossess the ring? Wasn't that, and not charity, at the root of her impulse? Nothing she could do, no choice she could make, seemed free of the flaw of selfishness and the hunger to see her husband suffer. Each day she spent outside the grave that hunger grew, as the child had grown within her womb. Starved of his suffering, the hunger fed on hers, on anyone's. It was a cancer eating at her soul, and she was helpless against it. Indeed, she held it to her breast and bade it feast.

Was there nothing she could do that would not lead her deeper into misery, brooding over, breeding horror? Then she would do nothing. She would lie in the bed of her childhood and sleep away the time. She would will her wound to heal. She would fix her thoughts on absence and enter the void behind her closed eyes and die, if she could, a second and completer death, beyond awakening.

CHAPTER
42

This must be, Berryman thought, waking, a lesson in poetry. I have entered the company of the illustrious blind. Homer and Milton stand at my side.

> O dark, dark, dark, amid the blaze of noon,
> Irrecoverably dark, total eclipse
> Without all hope of day!

As though the shifting volutes of the waves on which he lay were living Braille, the lines appeared before him whole, his memory miraculously restored:

> To live a life half dead, a living death,
> And buried; but, O yet more miserable!
> Myself my sepulchre, a moving grave,

> Buried, yet not exempt
> By privilege of death and burial
> From worst of other evils, pains, and wrongs,
> But made hereby obnoxious more
> To all the miseries of life,
> Life in captivity
> Among inhuman foes.

Milton, we *both* should be living at this hour! If I had tears . . .

But possibly he did. He lifted his fingers to his cheeks and felt the blood that still, in a ghostly, sourceless profusion, streamed down his face. What an example, what an inspiration, what a warning if his dear readers could have seen him now. He would hang a pathetically ill-lettered sign from his neck:

> Here stands One
> Who refused the Gift of Light.
> Now for his Sin of Suicide
> He's plunged into Eternal Night!

What heart would not break to see him here supine, rattling a tin cup? What passions of mourning might he not provoke, were he but visible? What pity, what waste, that none could know how abject, how fallen, how more wretched than other men or poets was John Berryman!

"John," said a familiar and somewhat peremptory voice from the all-enveloping void, "whatever do you think you're doing, lying there on your back?"

He sat up, at once gratified to have an audience and dismayed to recognize the voice of Adah Menken. He tried to speak, to ask her the needless (but, because he was blind, so pathetic) question, "Who's there?" But he was mute. Only blood issued from the wound at his throat. He was blind, he was mute, and he couldn't even write messages in his own

blood in the manner of Shakespeare's Titus, for he was dys-
lexic as well.

"What a mess you are," Adah said in a tone of reprobation
and disgust.

He bowed his head in solemn acceptance of his shame.
Who more shameful? None!

"Well, you're not wholly to blame," she conceded.
"Things got rather out of hand last night."

He shook his head vigorously and beat at his bleeding
heart with his fist, a *mea maxima culpa* to end them all.

"What a thespian the world lost in you, John. Not James
E. Murdoch himself, one of our nation's greatest tragedians,
with whom I had the honor to play Lady Macbeth—an
honor, alas, I was too unseasoned to merit—not even he
could improve upon you for general tragic carriage."

He turned his head aside, as though ashamed, offering his
profile.

"But all that's by the by. I've come to say I'm sorry. Joy-
Ann Anker has made me understand how unfair I've been to
you and Miss Plath (impossible, even now, to think of her as
Mrs. Hughes) and that other one. So this morning I promised
Joy-Ann I'd release all of you from your terrestrial bonds
and let you go to heaven. But *first* I'll have to ask you for
that ring."

Instant as her asking, he smelled a scam. If she were prepared to offer salvation as the price for the ring, then it must
be worth a good deal more. He made a fist of his ring hand
and with his right hand touched his throat, as who would
say, Give me my voice and we will bargain.

For a long while he received no answer but silence. He
thought Adah might have gone away, but even then he was
confident she would return. He thought of the Nibelung's
ring and all the wonderful singers who had died for its pos-
sessing, or from longing to possess it: Alberich and Mime,

Fasolt and Fafner, Siegfried and Brunhilde and even Brunhilde's horse. Truly, rings could inspire considerable desire.

This was another ring, of course, with other and still untested capabilities. But the fact that Adah was willing to pay such a price for it meant that he might ask for virtually whatever he wanted. And today, for a wonder, he knew exactly what he wanted. Love and revenge, in that order.

He felt Adah Menken's fingers on the lips of his wound. It was like stepping under a sun lamp. The wound in his throat healed.

She touched his heart, and that wound healed as well.

She placed her hands over his eyes. But when she removed her hands, he remained blind.

"Sorry," she said.

"That's all right," he said, sincerely cheerful (for surely in heaven his sight would be restored, and in the meantime he didn't half mind belonging to such a noble tradition). "Two out of three isn't so bad. Now sit down here beside me—" He patted the rippling surface of the Mississippi. "—and tell me what you want this ring *for*."

CHAPTER
43

Sleep was not in the cards. As well hope for rain from a blue sky, blood from a turnip. How little time ago she'd strained for release from her grave; now she would almost have returned willingly. Oh, for a bottle of Nembutals, her standby on wide-awake nights in Willowville in a dark room filled with the sound of her husband's snores.

She rose from her bed and roamed through the house—or through as many of its rooms as she could enter without the help of the ring. Outside it had begun to rain, completing the likeness to the endless hours of early childhood when she'd been imprisoned by bad weather in this same tiresome circuit of empty rooms. Her problem now as then—nothing to do, nowhere to go, a world outside too fearful to be thought of.

As in the grave, she used her memory to pass the time, mining the house for cues and clues. Grandma Anker's needlepoint pillow evoked a wearisome chronicle of nights spent sitting beside her on the couch resisting knitting lessons. She remembered the spring the vacuum broke and she'd been delegated to pick the carpet clean of Ginger's sheddings. And Bing with his nose buried in *Valley of the Dolls*—it was still there in the bookcase—for the second or maybe the third time through.

And here in the kitchen, hanging by the magic of their magnets from the side of the icebox, were the three potholders she'd bought from the disturbed redheaded boy on the day she'd taken flight from Willowville and brought here to her mother as a goodbye present. Red, blue, and yellow, the Rainbow Assortment.

Far off, over the hush of the rain, she could hear . . . was it the crying of a baby? The sound distressed and attracted in equal measure. Sometimes it seemed less the wailing of an infant than the whining of a dog. But just as she grew certain that what she heard was a dog—probably Alice Hoffman's Scottie, across the street—the sound would go out of (or come into) focus and she knew it to be an infant's cry, her own child's, calling to her, demanding her. Hungry.

The strangest thing about this sound was not the way it would shift its meaning but the fact that it seemed to be coming not from outside the house, which would have been logical, or even from another room, but from *inside* one of the potholders hanging on the icebox.

The red potholder.

When she touched it, the barking or crying grew louder. The tip of her finger tingled. The sensation spread through her body in waves, and then her body altogether disappeared, and she had entered the space she had so many

196

times before sought to enter and failed: a pattern of crossed lines, an immense red-checked veil that parted now to reveal another veil, identical to itself, toward which she fell as toward a net. But the net parted, or she passed through its interstices, and the pattern was repeated, mindlessly, meaninglessly, again and again, until the white spaces within the red lines gradually darkened, like a twilight that slowly deepens to night. From time to time she would hear the barking of the dog, and then there was a larger darkness and a deeper silence and sleep closed around her like a blanket being tucked into place by a gigantic hand.

CHAPTER
44

Glandier was on the phone with the police when Sugar, who had been lying down drying off after his shower, suddenly leaped up in a frenzy of barking and scooted into the kitchen. Glandier knew very little more than the police about what had happened at Alice Hoffman's, but he'd been told that they were looking for her dog, and so he clamped his hand down over the phone's mouthpiece and made only the quickest and most noncommittal responses until it was safe to excuse himself and hang up. All the while the damned dog had gone on yapping.

When he went into the kitchen he found Sugar, his front feet up against the icebox, snarling and barking and making lunges at the potholder that clung, by its magnet, to the top of the icebox door.

Glandier looked at the dog with disgust. "You want the fucking potholder?" He took it off the door and threw it to the floor. "So *take* the fucking potholder! But for Christ's sake don't start in with that kind of noise when I'm on the phone with the police."

It seemed insane to be talking to an animal as though it were some damned employee, but this clearly was no ordinary animal. Apparently Sugar had managed to murder Alice Hoffman and done almost as much for Bing Anker. The police said both of them had been severely bitten, in addition to their other injuries. Glandier could fill in the details from his dream.

What's more, Sugar seemed to understand him. When he talked, Sugar would listen. When Sugar wanted something, he knew how to get it. Like the way he'd made a beeline for the bathroom and jumped into the tub, demanding a shampoo.

What the dog wanted with a potholder Glandier couldn't imagine, but he seemed content now that he had it. He'd taken the potholder back to his mat of newspapers and lain down on top of it with a look, which Glandier didn't think he was imagining, of considering just what to do next.

Which (Glandier told himself) was something he too would do well to consider. Whatever had happened at Alice Hoffman's, it would not look right if her dog were found here: "Well, Officer, *I* can't figure it out either." The police would not consider that an adequate response.

Sugar seemed to have reached a decision, for he bolted up from the newspapers and, snapping up the potholder, made his way to the far end of the kitchen, where he took up a position of readiness at the side of the door going out to the garage. He whined to be let out.

Glandier was of two minds whether to let Sugar have his way. He didn't want the neighbors to see Sugar, but neither did he want Sugar to become upset, given his known capacity for self-assertion. Also, he didn't want Sugar to piss on the floor, and that in the end was the deciding factor.

It was already dark. No one would see the dog, and if they did no one would suppose he was Glandier's. Maybe the little fucker would disappear into the nowhere he'd come from. He could hope.

The phone rang. The police again? But no, what reason would they have to be calling back? It was his office, probably. Without him there to make decisions, entropy would soon be making major advances at Techno-Controls. In his more confident moments, Glandier actually believed that; at other times, such as now, it was what he longed to be assured of. The problem was that the office wasn't likely to be calling on a Sunday evening. He picked up the phone on the sixth ring and said, "Yes?"

"Hullo, who's this?" said a voice that caused Glandier an instant inward cringe.

"That's what I'd like to know," he answered in his most official, prickly tone of voice.

"Hey, Bob, ole buddy, how ya doin', fella?" Then, when this elicited no reply: "This is Nils here, Nils Gulbradsen."

"I recognized your voice."

"Where you been keepin' yourself, man? Thought we'd see you up here for the ice fishin'. Now that you got yourself your own cabin an' everything."

"Always meant to. Never had the time."

"Hey, Bob, you gotta *take* the time, man. All work and no play, you know the saying. How 'bout coming up this weekend?"

"The weekend's over, Nils."

"Hey, man, I thought you was an executive. Executives'

weekends is over when they say they are. Right? Anyhow, how long a drive is it? Not much more than an hour when the traffic's light. So pile in your car and come up here and grab yourself a couple northerns before the season starts and they're all snapped up by ya-hoos from the Twin Cities." Nils made a hooting sound meant for laughter, and added, "Nothin' personal intended. I know you're basically a country boy at heart."

Glandier said nothing. He was livid.

"Thing is, Bob, I thought you and me could maybe have a little business talk while you was up here."

"It'll have to wait a couple months or so, Nils. I'm completely tied up here. Executives don't always have the kind of freedom you seem to think."

"Yeah, well. The thing is, the fishing season starts on May twelfth, and that doesn't give me a whole lot of time, does it? I mean, there's not a whole lot I can do without some *investment* capital. The fucking cooler's on the blink. Half the fucking boats are rotted through. But I say, Look on the bright side. Think of the situation I got here as an investment *opportunity.* That's what I told old Knudsen at Farmer's National. Know what old Knudsen told me? Go fuck yourself. Not in so many words, but that was the basic message. I'd've liked to take his fuckin' leather desk set and shove it up his fuckin' ass."

Glandier smiled. He had a personal weakness for imbecilic obscenity and often tried to mimic those, like Nils, who had obtained true mastery. But tonight, with the smell of blackmail so strong in the air, he didn't feel like playing the game by Nils's rules.

"I thought," he said, "you were going to get the resort in shape with the money I gave you for the cabin."

"Yeah, well. Ten thousand just doesn't go that far these days. Now what I was thinkin', Bob, is you and me being

201

partners. It wouldn't have to involve any work for you. I'd run the place, keep it all in good shape, handle the bait and the boat rentals and all that."

"And I'd just supply the investment capital?" Glandier asked.

"Wouldn't hurt to discuss it, would it? Over a couple beers."

Glandier couldn't trust himself to reply. He knew his wisest move would be to stall for time, but that required a friendlier tone than he could command at just this moment, when all he could think of was murder.

"Unless you'd rather have me drive into the city. I could do that."

"No. No, you're right—I could use a vacation. Tell you what, Nils, you see that my cabin's in shape, icebox plugged in, some wood for the stove. I'll drive up there tomorrow, or Tuesday at the latest."

"Hey, that sounds more like it, ole buddy. We'll tie one on, like—" He paused, and in his imagination Glandier could see his gap-toothed smirk, the tobacco juices staining his stringy beard, the bleary eyes, the prosthetic hand. "Like we did last summer!" This time the hoot of Nils's laughter was repeated in arrhythmic bursts.

The point of the joke was that Nils and Glandier had not, in fact, tied one on together last summer, or at any other time. Nils had, however, provided Glandier with that alibi for the time he'd flown (out of Madison, in neighboring Wisconsin) to Las Vegas and murdered his wife. Glandier in return had bought a lakeside shack from Nils for over six times its original asking price. A perfectly straightforward business arrangement that had been concluded to their mutual satisfaction. Only now, Nils was telling him, it had not been concluded.

"See you," said Glandier coldly, and hung up.

202

Sugar was waiting outside the kitchen door. The pot-holder was nowhere in sight.

"Couldn't stay away, huh? Well, come on in but don't get comfortable." He held the door open, and when the dog had come in he stooped down to unbuckle his collar. "How's that, a little better?"

The dog tilted his head sideways, eyes fixed on Glandier, alert with suspicion.

Glandier slipped the collar into his pocket, intending to throw it into a different part of the lake from where he would dump the dog's body. He would also need one of the large three-ply garbage bags and some rope. Though fishing line should serve as well as rope, and there was plenty of line in his tackle box.

He scratched Sugar behind his ear. "How'd you like to go fishing, Sugar? How'd you like that?"

Sugar barked and did a quick claw-clattering dance on the linoleum.

Glandier eased himself back to a standing position with the help of a kitchen chair. In the glow of satisfaction that came from having found a new short-term goal and plan of action, Glandier unwrapped the cellophane from a fresh cigar and lit it off the gas burner on the stove.

CHAPTER
45

How nice it would be, Joy-Ann had thought at first, to be a nurse. Even the idea of bedpans hadn't daunted her, though probably bedpans weren't necessary in the afterlife. What she hadn't imagined was this situation: Alice lying there comatose through all the long slow hours of eternity, never stirring, seeming not even to breathe, a bump on a log. If what Adah said was true and everyone's first reaction to the afterlife was an expression of their most fundamental nature, then Alice Hoffman's fundamental nature was certainly the opposite of peppy.

Still, Joy-Ann enjoyed wearing the uniform. Anything was better than going around as a three-foot-tall Virgin Mary, which had been for all too long the aftereffect of having overstayed her visit in the world below. Now, except for a certain marblish quality to her complexion, Joy-Ann was herself again, and very grateful to Adah Menken for having gone down the heavenly escalator to Sears and rescued her from the revolving door.

She *did* wish that Adah would return from her present errand of mercy to Mr. Berryman, since the comatose Alice did not provide much social stimulation. Indeed, to be brutally honest, Alice Hoffman had never been the life of anyone's party. Still, neighbors are neighbors, and Alice certainly hadn't deserved to be killed by that Scottish terrier of hers. Alice would not have been able to grasp the fact that Sugar hadn't been acting of his own volition, and the dog's attack must have seemed a terrible betrayal to poor Alice, who'd doted on him.

Like many another nurse in the same situation, Joy-Ann turned to the TV for relief. Home Box Office no longer exerted quite the same irresistible fascination as when she had first started watching it. Too often her curiosity had made her witness things she would rather not have to remember: Giselle's murder, Bing's actual sexual practices, and even poor dear Dewey's pecadilloes with a waitress who'd worked at a Rexall's in downtown Minneapolis. There are some things you're better off not knowing about your loved ones, and Joy-Ann had promised herself that she wouldn't tune to Home Box Office in the future to spy on her family's private lives.

However, keeping in touch with their present situation was another matter, and Joy-Ann had no compunctions about flipping from channel to channel to see how matters stood with Bing and Giselle. Poor Bing was lying unconscious in a hospital bed, his head turbaned with bandages, his arm connected to an IV bottle with clear plastic tubing. The sight of him lying there made Joy-Ann feel like an imposter in her nurse's uniform. Doubly an imposter, for there was as little she could do to help Alice in her hospital bed as she could to help Bing in his.

She thought of Giselle and switched channels, but the only image that resulted was a perfectly static view, like a test pattern, of a shallow concrete pond in someone's garden. The surface of the pond was stippled with raindrops. Beyond its farther rock-rimmed edge was a bed of tulips not yet in bloom, and beyond the tulips an expanse of lawn bounded by willows and suburban homes. It would seem to be the back yard of Glandier's house in Willowville, though Joy-Ann had no recollection of such a pond.

Again she thought of her daughter and switched channels. The image wavered and held steady. So much, thought Joy-Ann, for Home Box Office.

Before she switched off the TV it occurred to Joy-Ann that since Robert Glandier was her son-in-law she might be able to use Home Box Office to find out what he was up to. Maybe she could even track down Giselle through him, if (as Adah had gloomily foretold) she'd gone back to haunting her husband.

With a grimace of disclaimer (for it was not Joy-Ann's fault that the man was her son-in-law; she'd warned Giselle that she was much too young and good-looking to be marrying someone that old and that fat), she thought of Glandier, turned the channel selector, and—*blip!*—there he was in more than living color: his face luminously green, his graying hair now neon blond. He was in a small, shabby room unpacking groceries from a cardboard box. HBO's unearthly cameraman did a slow pan about the room, a technical feat that entirely escaped the notice of the program's sole viewer; Joy-Ann took technology quite as much for granted now as when she'd been alive in St. Paul.

The camera's pan revealed: a linoleum countertop piled high with two six-packs of Grain Belt; bags of Cheetos, of garlic-flavor potato chips, of Doritos; a can, already popped open and sampled, of Frito Enchilada Dip; Ritz crackers; port-wine cheddar cheese spread; two frozen pizzas; a tube of liver sausage; Planter's Beer Nuts; Land O' Lakes butter, ketchup, mustard, mayonnaise; two pounds of Oscar Mayer bacon; a loaf of rye bread, another loaf of pumpernickel; four fat hothouse tomatoes, a head of iceberg lettuce, and a large bottle of Baco-Bits.

Her son-in-law had never seemed so alien to Joy-Ann as at this moment. To have made such a pig of himself at some grocery store and not to have yielded to a single sweet. No cookies, no ice cream, no Sara Lee cake—it seemed perverse and unnatural.

But the camera did not let her ponder this judgment, for it moved on to show, through a doorless doorway, the foot of an unmade bed, then crept along a warping wall of painted planks that successive vacationers had transformed into a kind of commemorative bulletin board: *Midge & Norm— Smoochin' Heaven—June '63; Fargo Steamers 1965; Disco Sucks; Bobbi G; The Johnsons, Rapid City; Good Pussy 183-8351;* and, once again, *Midge & Norm—Can't Get Enuf of Your Love!*

It dawned on Joy-Ann that this must be the lakeside cabin Bob had talked of buying just after Giselle's death. "To help him get over the tragedy," as he'd explained at the time. She couldn't believe a fusspot like Bob would have bought such a dump as this. The camera glided by the last graffito and passed through a doorway into a cramped sunporch. The cardboard-and-lath ceiling was buckled and stained with rain, the screens were ruptured, and you could almost smell the mold in the old davenport. Just outside the windows was a rickety dock with one aluminum rowboat tied to it, and there at the foot of the dock, gnawing a large meaty bone, was Alice Hoffman's Sugar. As the camera zoomed in on the dog, he looked up from his bone and growled, not just Sugar's usual display of bad temper but a growl that Joy-Ann felt to be personally directed at herself. Behind her, on the hospital bed, Alice Hoffman stirred and murmured.

Glandier passed in front of the window, carrying a rod and tackle box, which he stowed in the back of the aluminum boat. He left the dock and passed by the window and out of sight around the side of the house. The dog barely bothered to glance up at him as he went by. Glandier returned with the oars of the boat. After he'd passed by Sugar and just before stepping onto the dock, he dropped one of the oars and turned around, raising the other above his head and bringing the blade of the oar down, axlike, across the dog's back.

It was not a killing blow. Sugar began to yelp. As Glandier raised the oar again, Joy-Ann saw a bleeding child struggle to disengage its body from the body of the dog. The child's legs were stunted, its face grotesque, the sort of face you'd only ever see in a medical book and then have to look away from.

The oar came down across the dog's head. Sugar collapsed, quiet and quite dead, across the bone he'd been gnawing, but the child, if it was a child, had pulled itself free from the dog's corpse and was crawling over the mud and pebbles of the shore and into the reeds at the edge of the lake.

Glandier, oblivious of the child, proceeded to stuff Sugar's body into a black plastic bag.

As though uninterested in detailing the dog's interment, the camera looked up and out across the overcast waters of the lake. The child had vanished, but out beyond the reeds, wading on its spindly, stiltlike legs, was a heron. Joy-Ann remembered Glandier's telling her that Rush Lake was famous for its herons, which nested on an island at the center of the lake and could be seen every day flying back and forth across the water or fishing along the shore, like this one, disdaining to notice their human competitors.

The heron spotted a prey, dipped its long beak into the

water, and raised its head so that you could follow, inch by inch, the progress of the swallowed morsel down its throat. The heron gave a single shudder of its body, then spread its wings and bore itself aloft into the air.

As the heron flew away, Alice Hoffman began to choke convulsively. Joy-Ann went to her side and helped her sit up. The choking became more violent. Each spasm covered the starched sheets of the bed with a spray of wet black crumbles, like the soil sold for potting houseplants. After a final wrenching convulsion, Alice went limp in Joy-Ann's arms. Joy-Ann eased her back against the pillow. What seemed a large tulip bulb was lodged in Alice's wide-open mouth. Small maggots wiggled in the dirt spattering the sheets. Joy-Ann looked on with horror as her friend's immaterial body began, visibly, to decompose.

CHAPTER
46

"Giselle?" said the frog, blinking up into the branches of the willow. "Are you there, Giselle?"

In the sleep that was not sleep, in the grave that was not a grave, she stirred.

"Giselle? It's me, John Berryman. I brought you back your ring."

She seemed to be in bed beside her husband. He was trying to wake her. She did not want to be awakened. "Go away."

"First you have to kiss me," said the frog, and chuckled.

"No," she said, curling into the whorled wood as into a cocoon of blankets on a heatless winter morning. "Go away, I'm asleep."

With its webbed feet the frog scrabbled at the loose dirt at the foot of the willow where the red-checked potholder had been buried. It was not buried deep. The frog gripped its hemmed edge in his mouth and tugged.

"Stop it," Giselle protested. Then all at once (as the potholder came free of its little grave) she was fully awake and aware of yet another impossible situation. "You're a *frog?*" she inquired skeptically.

"If you can be a tree, I don't see why I shouldn't be allowed to be a frog. It's just as traditional."

"Am I a tree?" she marveled, turning herself around in the slim trunk of the willow as she might have turned before a mirror to model a new dress. The wind shivered her half-budded leaves. Her roots curled solidly in the clayey mud. She *was* a tree, and she felt terrific!

"In fact," said the frog in a rather pedantic tone, "you're not a tree, precisely. You're a hamadryad—which is to say, a wood nymph."

"I *feel* like a tree. And it's a comfortable feeling."

"For my part, too, I'm much more comfortable as a frog than I was as myself the last time you saw me. If you remember any of that."

The leaves shivered, and she let her mind go completely blank. It was something one could do much more easily as a tree than as a human being, or even as the ghost of a human being. Thinking was no more than a kind of tune she could hum or not hum as she chose. The frog had begun talking again, but she didn't pay it any attention. Ought she to? There was something so pleasant about having no thoughts at all. Rather like swimming under water, but without the need to hold her breath. Yet in a way she *was* thinking. Even this slow subaqueous drift of dim pleasure was a *kind* of thought, a tree's thoughts, a way of swaying in the breeze and going nowhere.

"Giselle!" the frog croaked patiently, over and over. "Giselle, please pay attention! Giselle!"

"Please," she said, rising briefly above the surface, where his words became meaningful again. "Can't you leave me alone? I'm thinking. I'm thinking about thinking."

"You're in danger," the frog explained patiently, "of simply sinking out of existence. It can happen. Spirits aren't indestructible. Adah Menken explained the whole system to me. You've got to stir yourself. Are you listening to me?"

"There's such a lovely breeze," she observed. "Do you feel it?"

"There are different levels of existence, and when you die you can rise to a higher level or sink to a lower. Or for a while you might just hold steady, which is what ghosts do. But right now, Giselle, you're sinking. First to a vegetable level of awareness. Then, after that, you could end as a stone. As salts leeching into groundwater. You could end up just being part of the soup of the sea. There's *no* awareness at that level, Giselle."

She sighed.

"I'm not asking you to tear yourself up by your roots. Just talk to me, huh? Give me some sign of consciousness."

"Why do you want to bother me?" she asked. "What difference does it make to you?"

"Oh, don't ask me about my motives. Let's say I owe you a favor—or owe one to your mother. It seems that after my unfortunate experience of midwifery, she actually got Adah to admit that she'd been unfair all this time in keeping me and certain other poets out of heaven. I have no idea how she did it. Adah Menken isn't an easy person to persuade."

"So now you're free to go to heaven?"

The frog nodded happily, puffed up its cheeks, and croaked.

"Then why don't you go there? Why are you being a frog?"

"Sheer magnanimity, my dear. I intend to rescue you from

a fate worse than death. Also (it's true), Adah did ask if I'd help. Or did you mean why have I chosen to be a frog in particular? Well, the answer to that lies in this." He held up his right forelimb to show the tiny gold ring on his webbed finger. "The ring only lets me shift my shape into one that's locally available, and here in suburbia there's not a wide range of choices."

"But why not just be yourself?"

"One reason is because this way I can see. Adah wasn't able to cure my blindness—I guess because at some deep-down level I really want to be blind. And the other reason is so as not to *be* seen by your son the demon."

It was the wrong thing to have said. Giselle, reminded of the halfling, let her mind be resorbed into the bole of the tree. As a hamadryad she had the option, at any time, of simplifying herself into wood.

The frog went on croaking all that afternoon and far into the night at the foot of the willow, but the willow refused to listen. Its leaves stirred in the wind, and tiny droplets of drizzling rain trickled down their veins to form larger droplets at the tips of the leaves, thence to plunge to lower leaves, to the matted grass, to the surface of the little pond.

CHAPTER
47

"Boy," said Jack, sitting down and helping himself to the granola, "you would not *believe* the grotesque thing that happened yesterday at this fishing resort up north."

"They caught Godzilla," Maryann suggested, not looking up from "The Rime of the Ancient Mariner" on which she was to be tested in her first-period class.

"Oh, don't encourage him, Maryann," said Judy, darting her brother a look of sincere malevolence. Her experiences in combating abortion had lately confirmed in Judy Sheehy a natural predisposition to blame the male sex for everything she found disagreeable. As the member of the male sex whose presence she was most often forced to endure, and a person, moreover, inherently disagreeable, her younger brother aroused in her an antipathy that amounted, especially at mealtimes (she being a finicky eater), to horror.

Jack sloshed milk from the carton into his cereal bowl and reported the rest of his news story through mouthfuls of moist granola. "No, honest, I'm not making this up. It was in this morning's paper: BIZARRE TRAGEDY ON RUSH LAKE. There was this Vietnam vet, see, who was out fishing in this boat, and half of his body is prosthetic. Well, he's standing up in the boat and casting, and then comes the weird part. This heron flies overhead and grabs the fishing line in the middle right while he's casting, and the hook at the end of the line swings back and hooks itself right into the guy's eyeball! So naturally he staggers back, the boat tips over, and he *drowns.* Isn't that incredible?"

"Oh, you are so disgusting," said Judy. She got up from the table and began to buckle on her yellow rain slicker.

"Hey, it was in the newspaper. I didn't make it up."

"But if I know you," said Maryann knowingly, "you're sorry you weren't there to see it happen."

"Judy didn't eat any breakfast," Jack reported in a neutral tone, so as not to seem to be tattling.

"Oh, Judy, you shouldn't neglect your breakfast," said Mrs. Sheehy dully. She was standing propped against a kitchen counter watching the coffee trickle down through the Mr. Coffee.

"I'm not hungry," said Judy, "and I don't want to have an argument about it."

"She thinks," said Jack, "that anorexia is a status symbol. It said on that TV program she watches that only girls from very well-to-do families become anorexics. Right, Judy?"

"Oh, why don't you go *fishing!*"

Maryann laughed, spluttering milk across the table.

Mrs. Sheehy sighed. "Maryann, you better get your coat on. You're going to miss the bus again, and I won't be able to drive you. The Toyota's getting fixed."

215

"Right, Mother." She slammed her textbook closed, looked up at the spider plant hanging in a macrame web above the table, and declaimed:

> "Alone, alone, all, all alone,
> Alone on a wide, wide sea!
> And never a saint took pity on
> My soul in agony.
>
> "The many men, so beautiful!
> And they all dead did lie:
> And a thousand thousand slimy things
> Lived on; and so did I."

Jack smirked (it was poetry) but applauded out of respect for his sister's histrionics and the scuzzy details. Judy stalked out of the room with an accusing glance at her sister, who ought to have known better than to offer Jack aid and assistance in his endless efforts to lower the tone of the Sheehy household. Mr. Coffee blinked a red light to show that he had performed his first task of the day, and Mrs. Sheehy poured herself a cup of coffee.

Jack had ten minutes' leeway between the time his sisters left to catch their school bus and when he had to set off for his. This morning, seeing that his mother was hung over and unavailable for small talk, Jack passed the time working on areas of rooftops and trees in the jigsaw puzzle of Berchtesgaden presently in progress in the family room in the basement.

At precisely 8:12 Jack's digital watch bleeped. For a moment divine grace offered him a detour around the fate awaiting him in the back yard, but Jack misinterpreted his impulse to finish the jigsaw puzzle with no more delay as a simple temptation to play hookey. But what would be the good of that? Dull as school could be, it was more fun than moping around the house and watching his mother watch TV. So, ignoring God's little hint, Jack put on his plastic rain poncho and went out the back door and across the commons to the school bus stop on Pillsbury Road.

He'd not gone many steps beyond the Sheehys' own lot when he was brought up short by a sight that surely had not been seen in Willowville since it had ceased to be a swamp. High up in the top branches of the willow overlooking the concrete pond in which Jack had daydreamed of breeding lobsters there was a large blue heron. At least that's what Jack assumed it was, for it was that general color and had long legs and a long pointy beak of the type he knew herons were supposed to have. While he watched, the heron spread its wings and glided on a long spiral down toward the pond, where, without ever landing, it made a jabbing motion with its beak, as though trying to spear a fish.

A heron—here in Willowville! It went beyond being a mere matter of interest: it was a news event. Jack's father kept an old 35 mm camera loaded with film on the principle, now proven, that you never knew when something amazing might happen. While the heron circled the tree and glided down over the pond for another grab at whatever it had its eye on, Jack dashed back into the house, taking care not to slam the door or otherwise alert his mother to his return. She'd already settled down in front of *Good Morning, America* to listen to celebrities discuss the problems of success. The camera was where it was supposed to be, in the lower right-hand drawer of the china cupboard in the dining room. Back on the commons, Jack slipped the camera out of its leather case, removed the lens cap, and framed the heron, now standing in the pool, in the viewfinder.

The heron was too far off for a good picture. Jack snuck up to it little by little, always keeping it in the center of the hairline bull's-eye, adjusting the focus the nearer he got. It was going to a super picture.

And there, hopping out of the pond, was the heron's destined prey, a green frog. The frog obligingly zigzagged through the tulips and across the lawn right toward the camera, and the heron wobbled along after him, hot in pursuit, jabbing at him with the long skewer of its beak. Already Jack could see the caption under his picture: Shish-Kebab for Breakfast!

Only ten feet away the heron stopped in its tracks to cock its head sideways and give Jack a long, level stare. Jack made one last adjustment for focus, then snapped the shutter. At that moment of alignment between the eye of the heron, the lens of the camera, and Jack's perfect and entire concentration, the halfling slipped across the diaphanous psychic barrier between bird and boy and took possession of his physical being.

At first the halfling's control was less than complete. Jack resisted the halfling's will along whatever channels of volition remained open to him. He attempted to scream; the halfling constricted the muscles of his throat, and the scream became a dry little cough. He fought the halfling for control of his legs and fell sideways on the dewy grass, alarming the heron, which, regaining its autonomy in the instant Jack lost his, took to the air with a yawp of fear.

The heron's flight was the last image to reach Jack through his own eyes. One by one the halfling sealed off the avenues of sense. Jack felt himself plunged into the black well of his unconscious. Struggle was useless. The waters closed over him, and his mind drifted in a confusion amounting to terror, in a featureless void, a mote of uncomprehending consciousness in an ocean without surface or shore.

CHAPTER
48

Mr. Beck did not suppose he was dying. If his doctor, his wife, or his daughter Dorothy had told him they knew him to be dying, he would have refused to believe them. For some patients it was enough to have been brought to the hospital for the fear of death to be set jangling; for others it was more like getting the cap off a particularly obdurate bottle of syrup; but for those like Mr. Beck, nothing would serve the purpose short of death itself. It was not that Mr. Beck possessed any superabundance of faith or *joie de vivre*, nor was it stupidity, precisely. If his insensibility on the subject of death could be ascribed to any cause, it would have to be good manners. Death was not something one spoke of, except after the fact, to extend one's sympathy to those presumed to be bereaved.

Mrs. Beck and Dorothy entirely approved of Mr. Beck's deportment in these potentially embarrassing circumstances. They would have been very much at a loss for words, should his spirit have awakened from its lifelong enchanted slumber. In his hospital bed he could slumber on right to the end, which need not, therefore, be bitter. He was well insured. The mortgage was paid. Admittedly, no money had been set aside for tuition, but Dorothy made it clear that she regarded college in much the same way her father looked on the afterlife—a place she knew of by hearsay but did not intend to go to.

On the Tuesday that Mr. Beck was murdered, Mrs. Beck came to the hospital at 10 A.M. and sat by her husband's side for forty-five minutes. Before she took up her knitting, and he his copy of the *Tribune,* she asked him if he had slept well. He said he had. In fact, he had been having nightmares ever since, on Sunday, the man with the bandaged head had been moved into the other corner of the room. It was not a private room (Mr. Beck's hospitalization did not allow for that degree of luxury), and so he had no right to complain. But he did not like to look at the man, inert in his bed, and he knew that his presence was somehow connected with these nightmares. But how could he have explained this to his wife? The dreams were forgotten within moments of his waking, all but the lingering sense of straining for breath.

Sometime after his wife left, the priest, who had come by yesterday to sit beside the man with the bandaged head, came by again. He asked Mr. Beck if his friend—that is, the mummified Mr. Anker—had showed signs of consciousness yet. No, said Mr. Beck, he hadn't. Then he asked Mr. Beck if there was anything he could do for him, and Mr. Beck said yes, would he be so kind as to draw the room-dividing curtain about his corner of the room and would he also turn the

220

television set on. It was time for *Bowling for Dollars* on Channel 7. The old priest obliged him in this, and for several minutes Mr. Beck watched contentedly as one after another of the contestants failed to bowl so much as a single strike. Behind the double screen of the shimmery blue curtain and the noise of clattering pins and the boisterous announcer it was possible to ignore the old priest as he muttered over his rosary. Then, as Doug Koskinen of Rochester, Minnesota, was preparing to pick up a spare, the priest could be heard to shout something, and this was followed by bumpings and thumpings. On the TV screen four of the five needful pins went sprawling, and the audience made a sympathetic groan of disappointment.

"Is something wrong?" Mr. Beck called out. Whereupon the curtain screening Mr. Beck's corner of the room parted—or more exactly was torn down from its runners—and the old priest, clutching the curtain in both hands and bleeding over it profusely, fell across the foot of Mr. Beck's bed. The blood came in spurts from a wound in his throat.

So alarmed was Mr. Beck by the sight of the bleeding priest that he did not even notice the lurch of his bed as it was pushed out from the wall. Nor did he think, until it was too late, to reach for the button that would have summoned the nurse. He became aware of the cord about his neck only as it was drawn tight, just as it had been drawn tight in his forgotten—and now remembered—dream.

For the first time Mr. Beck knew that he was dying, and he could feel, at last, an appropriate response. "No!" he screamed, "Please! Stop!" as fear and terror shattered his fragile and unevolved soul into a million and a million silvery particles, shards of an order that would never be restored. Before his lungs had drawn their last breath, before his heart had stopped beating, Mr. Beck had ceased to be.

CHAPTER
49

The name of the cemetery—Elysian Fields—was spelled out in curlicue wrought-iron letters over the entrance gate. The cemetery itself was so beautiful it took Joy-Ann's breath away. There were marble statues of angels, immense flower beds, geysering fountains, ivy-draped chapels, and lovely white temples, like miniature banks, on the faraway hills. Beyond those hills, in the mistier distance, were other hills, and even a hint beyond that mistiness of further expanses, as though the cemetery were limitless, as though no one had ever come to heaven except to be buried here in heaven's infinite cemetery.

Carrying her tribute of red roses mixed with white, Joy-Ann followed Adah Menken down the gravel path to the grave of her friend and former neighbor, Alice Hoffman. Every time Joy-Ann thought of how she'd seen Alice at McCarron's Funeral Home crying her eyes out over Joy-Ann's own corpse, she would get misty-eyed and mournful, but when she tried to elicit other memories of Alice from the deeper past, memory would not oblige her with suitable mementos. Ungratefully, her thoughts would be diverted from the grief she ought to have felt at Alice's demise to the general paradox of how people could still die even after they'd gone to heaven.

Pretty as the cemetery was, no effort was made to obscure the central fact on which all cemeteries are based, the fact that people die and must be tucked somewhere out of sight to decompose. When they reached Alice's plot they found that her casket had already been lowered into the neatly dug grave. At the side of the grave a blank headstone waited to be put into place: in eternity the dead are dispossessed even of names and dates.

Joy-Ann placed her roses in a vase at the foot of the grave, but Adah remained for a while in a pensive pose, clutching the flowers to her breast and shedding tears of all-purpose sorrow for the human condition. They couldn't have been for Alice Hoffman specifically (Joy-Ann reasoned), since Adah hadn't laid eyes on Alice till the night of the fatal séance. Yet it couldn't be denied that, whatever her inspiration, Adah mourned beautifully. With her roses and her monumental black gown she might have been the winning contestant in a funereal beauty pageant.

"I just don't understand," Joy-Ann said, as she had so many times before. "I just do not understand. Why did she come to heaven at all if she was only going to die when she got here?"

"Now I explained all that before," said Adah in the soothing, anchorperson tone she reserved for lecturing. "She hasn't died; she's been transmogrified."

"Into a hydrangea!" Joy-Ann protested. "What kind of life is that after you've been a human being?"

"I daresay I wouldn't want to become a hydrangea, and you wouldn't, but evidently it's what Alice was best adapted for. If she'd had a livelier nature, she might have been reincarnated as a cat or a dog. Or if she'd had a larger appetite, she might have become a pig or a shark. Or if she'd taken an interest in sex, she might have changed into a pigeon or a rabbit."

"But why must she be reincarnated at all? We weren't. It doesn't seem fair."

"Who ever suggested that heaven is fair? Is predestination fair, would you say? Or the gift of grace (so amply bestowed on you)? Is it *fair* that someone like John Berryman should be smothered in laurels while *my* poetry has never once been reprinted since my death? Is that fair?"

"But you did admit to me, finally, that you thought he had more sheer talent, a bigger imagination."

"And is that fair? Of course not, it's the greatest inequity of all. But there you put your finger on what it is that separates the sheep from the goats, and vice versa: imagination. Those who possess it have an afterlife; those who don't possess it, or in whom it has greatly atrophied, are reborn as plants or animals. It's as simple, and unfair, as that. You could almost say that heaven is no more than a fantasm generated by the excess energies of the pooled imaginations of the blessed. Surely that would hold true for *this* level. Higher up and nearer God, imagination becomes less important. Or rather it's taken for granted. But here in Paradise it is the *sine qua non*."

"The what?"

"The without-which-nothing. Without which your friend Alice was unable to imagine herself into a heavenly existence."

"In that case why did she come to heaven at all?"

"Because in the natural order of things Alice Hoffman

224

would not have died such a brutal death. She would simply have vanished into a coma in a comfortable hospital bed. So by way of remedying that departure from the norm she was allowed a second, more suitable death in Paradise with a friend at hand. Your daughter's case is rather similar. Not that she was destined to be reborn as a hydrangea. On the contrary, in the natural order of *her* life she was destined to become a saint."

"Giselle?" Joy-Ann laughed. "What kind of saint? The patron saint of casinos?"

"Saints are usually a little incongruous. But my point is that her career of sanctity was nipped in the bud, and before she can get where she was going—up in the higher spheres of heaven where saints congregate—she has to complete the job."

"How?"

Adah shrugged. "If I could tell you that I'd be a saint myself, and not the custodian of all these—" She made a broad, dismissive gesture that encompassed all the mellow, melancholy vistas of the endless cemetery. "—stage sets."

Joy-Ann shook her head in mild reproof of Adah's disparaging tone. To call this beautiful cemetery a stage set!

"You understand, don't you," said Adah, "that none of this actually *exists*. It's a function of our two imaginations; a work of collaboration, so to speak; a shared metaphor."

"Alice Hoffman wasn't killed by a metaphor. That demon, or whatever it was, got hold of poor little Sugar and took possession of him just like in that movie *The Exorcist*."

"Yes. Unfortunately in the spiritual realm it is possible to inherit acquired characteristics."

"There you go," Joy-Ann sniffed, "talking over my head again."

"Which is to say that the powers of the ring you gave to Giselle and which she was wearing through most of her pregnancy were passed on to her offspring. And since the thing was a kind of half-breed in any case, being fathered by

225

a living human being, I'm afraid its capabilities are rather extensive. Though not limitless. It could not, for instance, take possession of an *adult* human being. Sexual maturity acts as a kind of sealant."

"But what is to become of things down there with that creature going around murdering anyone it takes a fancy to? How can God *allow* something like that?"

Adah sighed and lowered a dark veil that had been piled in decorative billows about the wide brim of her black straw hat. "That, Joy-Ann, is a question you will have to address directly to the Almighty. I confess I've never been so near His throne that I could get a clear and unequivocal answer to any of the classic dilemmas. Why does He allow innocent children to suffer? Ask Him that!"

Joy-Ann sighed, but more by way of sympathy than from shared philosophical distress. "Well, it's a mystery to me too," she said in a tone that politely closed the door to further discussion. She looked across the cemetery, which had darkened to a deeper green as the sky had grown overcast. It was such a beautiful, restful, lovely place—the best of all possible back yards. She didn't understand how Adah could suppose it didn't exist. It obviously did exist. Joy-Ann was standing on it, and so for that matter was Adah. You couldn't stand on something that didn't exist. That was only common sense.

Poetry—there was Adah's problem. All that poetry had weakened her common sense. It wouldn't do to argue the matter with her, though. Best just to steer her away from subjects that got her speculating along poetical lines and concentrate on practical matters, such as how to get Giselle out of that willow tree she was stuck in and up into heaven where she belonged.

Joy-Ann turned to Adah and smiled a bright, cheerful smile. "Well, this was lovely, but I think we'd better be heading back, don't you? It looks like it means to rain."

CHAPTER

50

It was ten o'clock. The drapes were drawn and the lights burning throughout the house. Perhaps, if he had gone to bed, he might have been able to sleep, but he didn't want to. Sleep seemed dangerous. He needed to control his mind, and reading seemed ideal for that purpose, but when he had sat down to read, he'd been unable to make his eyes move along the lines of print. The television was out of the question: all this insanity had begun when he was watching TV.

Fear, a diffuse physical ache of fear, had spread through his whole body, like the ache of flu or fever. The thought of food nauseated him. His body stank with sweat. He kept thinking he was about to have the trots, but when he sat on the toilet he couldn't produce so much as a fart. And behind these several discomforts, like someone waiting with a knife behind a curtain, was the fear. What the object of that fear was he couldn't have said, except that it was out there in the real world, not just in his head, and it was out to get him.

Then the doorbell rang, and he knew that whatever he had feared was there at the door, demanding to be let in. He felt powerless either to bar the door or to answer it. Yet for all the intensity of his fear, he could not even now imagine whose hand it could be that was turning the knob of the door. A devil, a witch, a goblin from some children's story-book—nothing would have surprised him.

But when his caller stood revealed as the son of his neighbor, Michael Sheehy, he felt he'd been made a fool of. Fear could not reasonably take such a form as this.

The boy just stood there in the doorway smiling at him, a smile that seemed to imply some long-established under-standing between the two of them. He said nothing, and Glandier could think of nothing to say to him. Not "What are you doing here, young man?" Clearly, that would be inadequate, for in a sense he already knew what Jack Sheehy was doing here—in the sense that he could see, in the boy's eyes, so intently fixed on his own, that gleam of malice and complicity he'd seen in the eyes of Alice Hoffman's Scottish terrier.

"It's so bright in here," the boy said. He reached for the switch beside the door and turned off the overhead light.

"You shouldn't be here," Glandier at last brought out.

"No, I don't suppose I should." He flashed a smile that any advertiser of breakfast food would have been happy to print on his cereal boxes, it was that overdone and profes-sional. "Not so late as this. Like it says on TV: 'It's ten o'clock. Do you know where your children are?' They don't. But *you* do."

With a conspiratorial wink he disappeared into the kitchen. One by one he switched off each of the three kitchen lights and returned with a large bag of garlic-flavored potato chips. He took a seat in the corner of the sofa next to the lamp pole.

"I suppose," he said, reaching up, without looking, and turning off the lights on the pole, "that it's difficult for you to think of me as *yours*. It's all happened so suddenly, and there've been no written instructions. It was only yesterday that we took care of that creep out there on the lake. What was his name? I don't think I ever knew. No, wait—it's right here in my little memory bank: Nils Gulbradsen, right?"

Glandier nodded.

The boy grinned and ripped open the bag of potato chips. "How's that for data access, huh? Jack read that in the paper this morning."

"Read what?"

"Oh, come on, don't play dumb with me. You were there. I was there. And there were two other witnesses. What do you think, that you'll be arrested for attack-training a blue heron?" He stuffed a handful of potato chips into his mouth and chewed zestfully.

"This afternoon's another matter," he went on, spluttering half-chewed bits of chips across his plaid flannel shirt. "Of course, the very fact that I'm sitting here enjoying your hospitality is a sign that I didn't get caught. And I'm fairly sure there were no witnesses this time, except the sort of witness who tells no tales."

The boy went on eating potato chips imperturbably. At last Glandier had to ask, "What . . . happened this afternoon?"

"Didn't you watch the six o'clock news? It was the feature story, even before Reagan's budget. After all, how often does a Catholic priest get murdered in the Twin Cities? And so mysteriously."

"You *killed* a Catholic priest? Why?"

The boy nodded. "Father—" He swallowed a mulch of potato chips, cleared his throat, and enunciated syllable by syllable. "—Windakiewiczowa. As for why, he didn't leave me a lot of choice. You see, all I intended to do was finish the job on your brother-in-law before he makes trouble for you. I thought I was being so clever and efficient. I'd put a bottle of bleach into a box that a liquor bottle had come in, and then gift-wrapped it in paper that had *Get Well Soon* written all over it in little pink ribbony letters. It got me into the hospital like a charm, but first I had to wait most of an hour while the wife of the fat nerd in the same room was visiting, so I went down to the official waiting room and played Space Invaders until I ran out of quarters. Fascinating game. Anyhow—" He broke off to munch another handful of potato chips. "Anyhow, when I went back, there was this *priest* sitting by his bed with a goddamn rosary. As though heaven had posted a guard at the door or something. I *was* pissed off. Naturally, I didn't want to attract attention to myself by loitering in the corridor, so I had to think of a way to get the priest out of the room. So I knocked on the door and opened it a crack and said a priest was wanted in the emergency ward, which naturally he believed. So when he went off, I went in and moved a chair over to the other side of the bed and got up on it and made a slit in the top of the plastic bag that was feeding into his arm intravenously. And then I unwrapped the bleach bottle and started pouring bleach into the IV bag. There are probably deadlier poisons, but I figured that bleach in the bloodstream would do the job. And it would have, I'm sure, only what happened is that the old priest had left something in the room and came back for it, and so I was caught in the act. I'll tell you, Dad, I thought I was sunk. Do you mind if I call you Dad?"

Glandier shook his head.

The boy dug his hand into the potato-chip bag, then looked up with a camera-ready impish grin. "Hey, I've been hogging these all to myself." He held out the bag. "Here, you have some."

Glandier shook his head.

"You're sure?"

"How did you kill the priest?" Glandier demanded.

"It wasn't easy. I mean, think of it, there I was up on the chair, and like a *dummy* I'd dropped the razor blade I'd used to slice open the IV bag. What could I use as a weapon? Not the damned IV bag. But then I got inspired. I hopped down from the chair and tore off the tape that was holding the IV line to the guy's arm. The priest must have thought I was attacking the guy in the bed, because instead of running off for reinforcements, which he should have, he came after me with 'See here, young man, what do you think you're doing!'

"Which were his last words, because when he was near enough, I took the needle, which was still connected to the IV tube, and rammed it right into the old fucker's adam's apple. That did the trick, though he didn't go out quite like a light. He staggered around and finally fell down over the fat nerd in the other bed, which meant that I had to take care of him too. But that was easy. He didn't have any juice in him, and *did* go out just like a light. Which reminds me: Do you think you could turn off the lamp by your chair, or at least make it dimmer? It kind of hurts my eyes."

Glandier reached for the knob of the lamp reluctantly. There was no way to dim the light without first turning it off completely, and all the other lights in the house were out. He didn't want to be alone in the dark even a moment with an eleven-year-old homicidal maniac. On the other hand, he didn't want to annoy him by any kind of refusal. He closed his eyes and turned the knob through two clicks, so that the bulb was burning only 50 watts.

"Thanks, that's much more agreeable." The boy helped himself to more potato chips. "So, where did we leave off? I'd just killed Father Windakiewiczowa, right, and the nerd? Well, just to be sure they were both dead I hunted about for the razor blade I'd dropped and sliced open both their jugular veins—without getting a *drop* on myself, which is not that easy. And then, not forgetting my original purpose in coming to the hospital, I stuck the IV needle back in Bing Anker's arm and let nature—gravity, that is—do the rest of the job. Only I'm afraid I botched it. I missed the vein, and according to WCCO, no serious harm was done. For which you have my apologies."

Glandier nodded.

"Proud of me?" He flashed another sunlight-on-Shredded Wheat smile.

Was there, Glandier wondered, any way to approach this situation rationally? He was certain he wasn't having a hallucination. Michael Sheehy's son was actually here in his living room confessing to a double murder that he had probably committed. The wisest course, in ordinary circumstances, would have been to phone the boy's father and let him handle the problem. But that clearly was not a practicable solution. The boy knew too much. Glandier didn't dare risk offending him in any way. Furthermore, he seemed genuinely interested in helping Glandier—in his own mad way. So perhaps the wisest course would be to humor him and to suggest less compromising ways of being helpful.

"Of course," the boy went on, "you're worried about my long-term goals. I can understand that, but there's not much I can say by way of reassurance. You see I act . . . impulsively. There's no organized agenda, no game plan—just promptings. I wasn't even intending to pay you a visit tonight, until I saw the news on TV and started wondering if you were watching too and what you must have thought. I mean, I'm your son, true enough, but that doesn't mean my every waking moment is spent thinking about *you*. I have my own independent existence."

"There is a lot of this," Glandier said carefully, "that I don't understand."

"Don't try to. Just enjoy the ride."

"You say you're my son. . . . "

"Hey!" He looked up, eyes glinting with mischief. "You

wouldn't want me to say I was your *lover,* would you?"

Glandier blenched.

The boy laughed. "Just kidding, Daddy-O, just kidding. Anyhow, you would need a whole lot of loosening up before you'd be ready for child-molesting. Those are *deep* waters."

"I have *no* intention of ever . . . ever doing anything like that!"

"See what I mean? You can't even speak the dreaded word. Not to worry. I didn't come over here to seduce you, Pops. To be perfectly frank, sex is not one of my vital interests. Violence is another matter. I love violence. Really, I'm not that different from any other eleven-year-old these days. Just a little more open and straightforward."

"I would consider it a favor—" Glandier began, then broke off, afraid to say anything the boy might take exception to.

"You want me to go home, I'll bet."

Glandier nodded.

"I sensed that. And I'd do it—but I've got a problem: I can't sleep. It's the chief disadvantage of my situation. If I sleep, then young Jack can get back in the driver's seat. Not that he'd be able to do that much. I can resume control at will, I'm pretty sure. But why put it to a test? Anyhow, sleep is not one of my top priorities. For centuries I never existed, and after this sojourn in Willowville I may not exist for further centuries. So my motto is eat, drink, and be merry. Would you like to play cards?"

"But your parents—Jack's parents, that is. Won't they . . ."

The boy shrugged. "They think I'm in bed. If you don't like cards, how about backgammon?"

"I've never played backgammon," Glandier confessed.

"Cribbage?"

Glandier tried to think of a way to refuse. He couldn't. He went to the bedroom to get the cribbage board and a deck of cards.

CHAPTER
51

The light touched her leaves like a lover going off to work, not wanting to wake her but not wanting to leave without saying goodbye. Fibers of consciousness that sleep had strewn through the branches of the willow retracted and were concentrated in a single focused unwillingness to be awakened, and then, the light brightening, she woke to the sound of the poet, Berryman, croaking in her ear. "Wake up, Giselle! Wake up! It's morning. Listen to the robins. The breakfast grub is in the air. Come on, sleepyhead, wake up!"

"I'm up, I'm up," she grumbled. "So stop your silly nonsense."

"Then let me see you, huh?"

She sighed and made herself visible in human form, sitting—seemingly at her ease—at the lowest forking of the willow's trunk, some four feet off the ground. "You're still a frog," she observed.

He puffed out his cheeks complacently and blinked. "I like being a frog. The skin fits. How about you? What's it like living inside a tree?"

She closed her eyes and thought for a while before she answered. One of the advantages of a semi-vegetable existence was the different time scale. There was never any need to hurry.

"Sexy," she said at last. "It feels stupendously sexy. There are all these little yellow whatyamacallems."

"Catkins," Berryman suggested.

"If you say so. Anyhow, there aren't many of them left. A week or two ago when I was covered with the things it must have been incredible. Even now when the bees come at me it's as though each one were a little vibrator. But there isn't just one, there are hundreds—hundreds of little tiny orgasms all going on at the same time." She sighed. "Trees are *very* happy in the spring. It probably makes up for the boredom other times."

"It sounds like you're considering taking up permanent residence."

"The light feels good too," she added thoughtfully. "Not sexy, but good."

"What about blight, beetles, acid rain?"

She smiled. "What about death?"

"But you've survived death," Berryman croaked.

"Sometimes I wonder about that. You know that old song we had to sing in grade school?" She began singing the song in an effortless, rich contralto. "Row, row, row your boat . . ."

"Row, row, row your boat," he sang along happily (for the frog in him loved nothing so much as a round), as she continued.

"Gently down the stream . . ."

"Gently down the stream," sang Berryman.

"Merrily, merrily, merrily . . ."

"Merrily, merrily, merrily."

"Life is but a dream."

She had made her point and fell silent—never, indeed, to make another point that the poet would hear her speak or sing.

Giselle slipped from sight into the willow, and Berryman sang on alone, beside the concrete-bottomed pond, that briefest and solemnest of elegies, the invention of his melancholy predecessor, Mr. Poe. "Nevermore!" croaked the enchanted frog, as though given foreknowledge of his and Giselle's sundering. "Nevermore! Nevermore!"

CHAPTER

52

Toward five in the morning, Glandier stopped being able to count his cribbage hands. "Fifteen-two, fifteen-four, and a pair is . . ."

"Six," Jack Sheehy prompted.

Glandier pegged six points on the board.

"And another pair is eight," Jack pointed out, pegging these two points. He swept up the cards from the kitchen tabletop, tapped them into a neat pile, and shuffled them with stiff-fingered care.

The predawn light of another day was leaking into the house through all its uncaulked seams and cracks, making pencil lines of a lighter gray beneath the curtains and doors and turning the limp and long-unlaundered gauze about the kitchen windows to ectoplasm.

"Tell me," said Jack pleasantly, as he dealt another hand, "how did you know where your wife would be, so you could go there and kill her?"

The fear that the dawning light had quickened in Glandier's spirit now surged through all parts of his body, like sludge being stirred up from the bottom of a cesspool. Always until now he'd been able to refuse to imagine the darker possibilities that might issue from Giselle's murder, to look the other way from the punishments the law allotted to convicted criminals. A flood of self-pity pressed against his glazed, dry eyes as he imagined himself a prisoner among other prisoners—blacks, most of them, and crazed, even there in prison, with drugs. Sealed away with such scum from the world of everyday pleasures: no car to drive, no office filled with employees to command, with other businessmen offering him the ikon of himself mirrored in uniforms of cloth, speech, and thought. He would do anything before he would let himself be reduced to such abject shame—but what could he do? Kill the boy? Useless, for it was not the boy who was a danger to him, but something *inside* the boy. Glandier had killed Sugar when that same something had been in the dog, and what good had come of that?

"Hey," said Jack, snapping down the undealt cards in the middle of the table beside the cribbage board. "Wake up. We've got a game to play."

"Right," said Glandier. He began to arrange the cards in his hand.

"Didn't you hear my question?"

"Oh, yes, sorry. Mind's wandering. She called her mother collect once from Las Vegas. When her mother went into the hospital I took care of her bills for her. The Las Vegas number was on the phone bill. I knew she didn't have anything to do with her son, so who else was it likely to be? I called the number. It was a motel." He looked at the cards in his hand. They made no sense. "I don't think I can play cribbage any more. My mind is . . . I mean, I need sleep."

"So sleep," said Jack.

"It's almost day. Your parents will be getting up soon. You'll have to go home. They'll become alarmed if you're not there."

"Right," said Jack, without stirring.

"What are you?" Glandier asked, surprising himself as much as the boy, whose gaze lifted up from the cards in his hand like a cobra rising from a basket.

"Don't you mean *who* are you? People are usually whos, not whats."

"But you're not a person. What else is there? Devils? Are you a devil?"

"Do *you* believe in devils?" the boy countered with a sneer.

"You're not answering my question."

"And you're not answering mine. But no, *I* wouldn't say I'm a devil. Unless you want to say that tumors are devils, or bombs, or gamma rays, or tornadoes. The idea seems to be, if it hurts, call it a devil. But I haven't hurt you. Have I? Have I?"

Glandier ignored the question. "When I dream . . ." He didn't know how to continue.

The boy nodded, smiling encouragement, like a teacher drawing out a slow student. "That's warmer, yes. I'm there then, in a way. I'd even say that's when we're closest. Closer than this, certainly. When was the last time you saw yourself in a mirror?"

"I suppose the last time I went into the bathroom."

"No, I mean really saw yourself, saw behind your eyes and

inside your head. Because in a way that's me. A reflection, but free from the mirror, so I don't have to behave like your fucking monkey."

"If I . . ." But no, he wouldn't ask that question.

"If you were to die? I suppose I'd just gradually fade away, like the smoke in those ads for air purifiers. But that's only my guess. I'm no fortune-teller." He grinned with new ferocity. "Hey, is that what you'd like? Me to read your fortune? Why not." He picked up the deck of undealt cards from the table and fanned it out clumsily. Cards dropped to the tabletop: the six of hearts, the jack of clubs, the queen of spades. "Pick a card, any card."

"No." Retreating into the living room. "Honestly. I've got to get some sleep now. I'm falling to pieces."

The boy laughed, "So good night. Unless you want me to come and tuck you in?"

"Why are you doing this to me?" Glandier groaned.

"To you? What have you got to do with it one way or the other? Do you think the reflection in the mirror cares about what it's reflecting? It just wants to get loose, that's all. Go to sleep."

Then there was an interval Glandier could not account for. He was in the bedroom with no memory of having left Jack Sheehy alone in the kitchen. He was lying in bed, still dressed, except for his shoes. He was dreaming, and yet he was not properly asleep. There were dots of phosphorescent color flickering on the blank screen of the ceiling. The colors coalesced into a long rectangle of lawn, just as though a strip of sod had been unrolled across the ceiling. Dew flashed on the blades of grass as the first rays of daylight raked the ground. Jack's sneakers darkened with dampness as he advanced across the lawn toward the bleating of a solitary frog. He swung a long-handled ax in his right hand, scything the dew with each broad sweep of the blade. The ax had come from Glandier's cellar, one of the relics of his youth that he'd kept back from the sale of his parents' effects after his father's death. Once, at the age of eight, Glandier had spent an entire frantic afternoon hacking away at a half-rotten apple tree with that same ax. Jack ought not to have taken the ax from the cellar, but Glandier was helpless to prevent him. He could not call out *Stop!* or whisper *Please.* The dream went on, indifferent as a TV program to what he might hope or dread. The blade of the ax paused, assessingly, by the bark of a large-boled, low-forking willow, then drew back and reared up and swung down and struck the tree trunk, leaving a long incision in the bark. Again the blade bit into the tree, this time at a slightly sharper angle, so that a small almond-shaped wound of whiteness was formed by the two strokes. The blade was lifted a third time, but now a voice called out *Woodman, spare that tree!* and Jack Sheehy turned around, ax handle balanced on his shoulder, to scan the grass for the source of this sudden prohibition. There he stood, at the edge of the artificial pond, a green frog with one good eye and one eyesocket empty and bleeding. The frog, when Jack had seen him, swelled his cheeks, as if in scorn, and croaked another line of the old poem: *Touch not a single bough!* To which the boy replied, *The fucking hell I won't!* and swung the ax at the frog. The frog jumped away, and the ax hit the concrete with a loud, edge-dulling crack. Then the frog leaped across the lawn with Jack in pursuit. The frog would croak derisively, and Jack would swing the ax into the still dewy lawn, gouging dark holes where bugs and angleworms squirmed with dimly apprehended fear to find themselves exposed to the sun's withering heat and the eyes of predators. The frog leaped through a bed of tulips Mrs. Kendall had forced to early bloom. Jack pursued him, oblivious of the flowers. The frog zigzagged about the Mertons' lilac bush, and Jack pursued. He hid in the shadow of a lawn chair, but Jack spied him there, and the ax came swinging down, missing the frog by less than an inch. The frog fled down the narrow corridor between the Mertons' and the Gallaghers' garages, veered to the left around the black-faced jockey holding up a lantern at the foot of the Mertons' asphalt drive, and took refuge beneath the thick prickly branches of the ornamental junipers that graced the fieldstone-trimmed facade of the Gallaghers' house. As it happened, Mrs. Gallagher, an early riser, was standing by the picture window at the moment that Jack Sheehy pursued the frog into her junipers. Glandier could see her, through the window, dialing and then speaking into a phone, all the while Jack continued, in an ecstasy of rage, to attack the shrubberies, screaming *Little fucker, I'll get you yet!* Glandier wanted to warn him, to tell him he must stop, but in the trance of his dream, speech and motion were denied him. He could only lie there, sweating, and watch as Jack's father stalked from the Sheehy house and across his lawn and the Gallaghers' driveway, to stand behind his son, who still raged on, laying waste the junipers. *What in the name of God do you think you're doing?* Mr. Sheehy roared. The boy stopped at last, looked up at his father, seemed to take a firmer grip on the handle of the ax, as though he meant to . . . But no, he lowered it, and said, mildly enough, but not at all apologetically, *I'm trying to kill a frog.*

Glandier woke then, buttered in his own sweat. I've had a dream, he told himself; that's all it was, a dream. But his heart was thudding in his chest as fast as if he'd just got through an especially strenuous fuck, and he refused to get up and go to the front door and look out to see whether indeed it had been only a dream.

He was not, in any case, to be spared the knowledge. The doorbell rang. He got up from the bed, groaning, and looked at himself in the mirror. His pants were rumpled, his shirt soaked with sweat, and his sparse hair was pasted to his forehead higgledy-piggledy, like fracture lines in a broken windshield. The doorbell rang again. He toweled his face with a terrycloth bathrobe, then slipped the bathrobe over his clothes and went to answer the door. It was Jack's father. He was carrying the ax. His face had gone beet-red with anger.

"What is it?" Glandier asked.

Michael Sheehy held up the ax. "Is this yours?"

"It could be, I suppose. But mine should be in my basement. Why?"

"Then this is yours. Would you take it please."

Glandier opened the screen door separating him from Michael Sheehy and gingerly accepted the ax. "I still don't understand," he said, when the door was closed.

"I can't say that I do either. My son told me he stole this ax from your basement. Would you know anything about that?"

Glandier made his face into a mask of puzzlement—brow furrowed, lips pursed—and shook his head. It was soothing to be able to lie. Glandier took an almost professional pride in his ability to deceive other people.

"Don't you keep your doors locked?" Sheehy asked, looking for a way to put Glandier in the wrong.

"Of course not. Do you? I never supposed it was that kind of neighborhood."

Sheehy bit his lip. "Well, maybe it would be better if you did. I'm sorry about this."

Glandier couldn't resist giving the thumbscrew another little twist. "But what was your boy doing with the ax? It looks as though—" He held the blade up and saw a long liquid streak across the gray steel. "—as though he tried to dig up the sidewalk with it."

"He killed a frog," said Sheehy.

"A frog?" Glandier repeated.

"There's really nothing more I can tell you." Sheehy turned away.

Glandier was almost overpowered by a feeling of wild hilarity. He wanted to call out after Sheehy, to jeer at him, to take a Polaroid picture of the man's face stained with shame.

He looked at the blade of the ax. Was that really blood on it? Why had that boy (who was not, of course, a "boy") been so determined to kill a frog (which was not, in all likelihood, a "frog")?

As though the answer might be coded to its taste, he lifted the ax blade to his mouth and touched the tip of his tongue to the smear of blood. It was salty and . . . something else. He licked up the whole smear with the full stretch of his tongue as if it were a drip running down the side of an ice-cream cone. The strange taste awakened familiar pangs of hunger. Breakfast beckoned from the kitchen, sacramental with its promise of an ordinary life. He propped the ax against the doorjamb and stumbled toward the kitchen. He would make bacon and eggs, coffee and buttered toast. Juice too, if there was a can left in the freezer compartment.

But when he went into the kitchen there was the table covered with cards. With a single unconsidered sweep of his hand he swept them off the table. Damn, he thought the moment after he'd done it, for now he would have to pick them all up.

The doorbell rang.

Fear froze Glandier to the spot. The early sunlight spilled across the kitchen floor, exposing the months of unmopped stains, the helter-skelter cards, almost all of them face up, spelling out a fortune he could not read. The clock face, a white disc in a walnut skillet, gave the time to be 6:03.

He heard the front door open—and close.

"Anyone home?" asked a voice. A voice that was not, to Glandier's immense relief, that of Jack Sheehy.

Then, that doubt allayed, he was able to feel the luxury of indignation: for who the fuck could walk in the front door with no more than "Anybody home?" Glandier strode out of the kitchen ready to berate the unknown intruder—but there was no one there. He was certain he'd heard someone come in. Could whoever it was have already gone down the hall to the bedroom?

There was a burst of light from the shadowed hallway, like the last flare from a bulb as it burns out. But when Glandier looked down the hallway, again there was no one there.

Then, just behind him, in the living room, that same voice called his name: "Bob?"

He turned around and saw, with a horror tempered by sheer disbelief, the statue of the nigger jockey that belonged at the foot of the Mertons' driveway. It held aloft its iron lantern so that the light from it was at a level with Glandier's eyes: a brilliant light, so intense that looking at the statue's features was like driving straight into the sun. But he could see that its wide crimson lips *moved* when it repeated his name, and from this he reasoned that he must be hallucinating. Yet he stood there immobilized, unable to act on this awareness as reason further demanded, to return to the kitchen and begin making breakfast, ignoring the presence of this apparition until it faded in the light of day.

Instead, he asked, "Who are you?" and the statue, as though this question were the permission it had been awaiting, lowered its lantern and lifted the visor of its purple cap to stare at him with its one good eye. From the other eye socket, blood flowed down the statue's black face, crimson as its painted lips.

"Berryman's the name," said the statue, grinning, "and poetry's the game. And you must be Bob Glandier, right?"

Glandier said nothing.

"Of course that's who you are. I wouldn't be visible to anyone else. Ghosts only appear to people wired to receive them. It's like cable TV. And that's what I am, sure enough, a ghost who's come to haunt you, round the clock, twenty-four hours a day. Properly speaking, Bob (do you mind if I call you Bob?), this is a job that your wife should handle, but because of your offspring's nasty little trick with that ax (to mention only one of his nasty tricks), Giselle is stuck inside that tree until the wound in the bark heals. Like a genie in a bottle with a stuck cork. Who would have thought the after-life had so many *rules*, eh? Or, for that matter, who would have thought there *was* an afterlife?"

If (Glandier reasoned) it were a hallucination, its only re-ality would be mental, not physical. So that if he stepped forward and put his hand out where the statue seemed to be, then his hand would pass right through it. Wouldn't it?

"I doubt," said the statue, "that you've ever read Thomas Lovell Beddoes, a wonderful and much undervalued poet of the early nineteenth century. There's a scene in *Death's Jest Book*, his immensely long, often silly, but more often sublime closet drama, that is very apropos to our situation. The Duke, who has murdered Wolfram, sees his ghost and starts to rant:

> " 'Lie of my eyes, begone! Art thou not dead?
> Are not the worms, that ate thy marrow, dead?
> What dost thou here, thou wretched goblin fool?
> Think'st thou, I fear thee? Thou man-mocking air,
> Thou art not truer than a mirror's image,
> Nor half so lasting. Back again to coffin,
> Thou baffled idiot spectre, or haunt cradles:
> Or stay, and I'll laugh at thee.'

"It's wonderful fustian, and you must forgive me for tak-ing what ought by right to be your lines. In the fullness of time, perhaps, we'll be able to do the scene together. For, like Wolfram in the play, I don't mean to go away."

"You're not real," Glandier insisted. "None of this is real."

"To which objection," said the statue, "the ghostly Wol-fram replied: 'Is this thin air, that thrusts thy sword away?' That's to say: Touch me if you don't believe I'm real. Take the Doubting Thomas finger test." To illustrate, the statue stuck its forefinger into its bleeding eye socket and drew it out, dripping. "This, for instance, is the highest quality Velva-Chrome Chinese Red Enamel." The statue offered its finger for Glandier's closer inspection. When he backed away, the statue went to the recliner, on which Glandier had draped the rumpled jacket of his gray pinstripe suit. It scrawled a large M on the back of the jacket. "There," it said with satisfaction, wiping its finger on its yellow riding breeches. "Just like the movie."

"Get out of here," Glandier said, without notable conviction.

The statue grinned at him; then, fluttering three fingers over its lower lip, made a burbling sound.

Glandier closed his eyes.

The statue said, "Gibber, gibber? No? Still no response? Then how about some poltergeistry?"

Glandier opened his eyes in time to see the statue toss toward him a bulb it had unscrewed from the lowest of the lamps on the lamp pole. "Catch!" it shouted, as Glandier lurched for it. He was too slow, and the bulb shattered at his feet.

"That is just a sample of what it's going to be like to be haunted, just a sliver of the whole big cheese. Some of the effects, admittedly, are only stage magic. Like this." The statue adjusted a knob on the base of the lantern, and the light within flared to an eye-searing, furnacelike brightness. "But, as witness that former light bulb, some of my tricks pass well beyond the subjective. One idea I want to try out right away is to see what I can do with the plumbing. I was never much of a handyman along those lines in my own lifetime, but sabotage is always easier than fixing. Of Sleep's two gates you may be sure that you shall pass through neither."

Keeping his eyes warily on the statue and his back to the

wall, Glandier began to edge around the room.

"But there is one way you can persuade me to leave off. Two ways, in fact. Do you want to know how?"

"How?" said Glandier, trying not to look at the ax where it leaned against the doorjamb, trying not to think of it for fear his thoughts could be read.

"The first way, and the one I recommend, is to follow my own example of some years past: kill yourself. I jumped off the bridge by the U, but there's no need to exert yourself to that degree. Just roll down the garage door, start the motor, and breathe deeply. Or if that seems not quite manly, try the Hemingway technique, a shotgun blast into the soft palate. Guaranteed to be effective. However, you may share Hamlet's scruples about the afterlife and not want to head off for undiscovered countries—in which case I can also be persuaded to leave by the simple expedient of confession. There's the phone. Just dial nine-one-one, ask for the police, and ease your soul. Those are your alternatives. Now what do you say?"

"What I say," said Glandier, bending sideways to grasp the handle of the ax, "is you can go to hell!"

As Glandier advanced across the living room, the statue held up its lantern as though to fend him off. Squinting against the lantern's glare, Glandier swung the ax with all the strength in his back and shoulders. There was a satisfying whack of connection. The lantern fell to the carpet. Crimson gouts spurted from the stump of the statue's arm.

"I shouldn't have to explain anything so obvious," said the statue, "but it is simply not possible to *kill* a ghost. You can only—"

Glandier swung again, taking more careful aim. The statue's head parted from its shoulders at a single blow. The instant it was severed, even before it hit the carpet, the black jockey's head metamorphosed into a fully human but

248

more horrible form—a man's head, grizzle-bearded, blind in both eyes.

The severed head continued calmly to berate Glandier. "You can only delay retribution, you know. Meanwhile you will surely sink deeper into guilt, become more entangled in the snares of your tempter. For it is not I who represents your gravest danger; that springs, rather, from the creature you spawned, the thing that twice attacked me on the lawn—first as a heron, then as your neighbor's son. He *thought* he'd got me; instead he killed a poor scapegoat of a frog, while I shifted my shape to *this*—or should I now say *that*?—in the course of his pursuit."

One more blow of the ax (Glandier thought) would split the skull of the jabbering ghost like a log split for firewood. But when he swung the ax back over his shoulder to take aim, the head of the ax flew from the handle and smashed through the picture window.

"You can't say," said the severed head, "that I didn't warn you."

In the kitchen there was a crash even louder than the shattering of the window. Glandier dropped the ax handle and ran to the kitchen door. The Frigidaire had been overturned, its opened door broken from the hinges. A kind of cold soup compounded from various broken bottles oozed out across the linoleum. Just behind the capsized icebox the decapitated statue groped about the surface of the counter with its one good hand. It waved the stump of its other arm in Glandier's general direction, as though warning him to stay back. Droplets of blood looped up, as from a lawn sprinkler, and spattered down over the counter, the cupboards, the floor. The knife drawer, Glandier thought, but before he could take a step toward it, the statue found the flour canister and hurled it at him. It struck the doorframe and exploded in a blizzard of powdery whiteness. Glandier felt his defiance crumble into fear; felt, at the same instant, his bowels loosening. He fled from the mayhem in the kitchen, through the living room, where the blue flames licked at the carpet all about the fallen lantern, and down the hallway to the bathroom. Even as he fumbled with the buckle of his belt, he could see the madness of it—that amid all these other horrors he should feel the keenest panic at the threat of shitting his pants. Yet the reality of his own physical existence was an anchor for his sanity. Even as his sphincter spasmed with fear, he felt a kind of gratitude for its being solid and real. He pushed down his pants and his fouled briefs to his knees and collapsed, squittering liquid shit, onto the toilet seat. The blessedness of relief forced tears from his eyes—but only for a moment. Then, still diarrhetic, he rose from the toilet screaming and tearing at the fingers of the severed hand that had grabbed hold of scrotum and balls.

"Will you confess now?" shouted the severed head from the living room. The hand squeezed his balls. It could not be pried loose. "Will you confess?"

"Yes. Only make it stop. Please make it stop."

"Then go to the phone. Call the police."

Dusted with flour, spattered with shit, Glandier crawled on his hands and knees into the bedroom. He picked up the phone and dialed 911. After four rings a voice said, "Emergency Service. Can we help you?" He asked to talk to the police.

"Where are you calling from?" the voice asked.

He realized he might still hang up. He had not yet confessed; the police would not be tracing the call. With his left hand he felt to see if the hand were still there. At his first touch, it gave another squeeze. He shrieked into the receiver. Without further questions, the operator put him through to the police.

"Willowville Police," said a man's voice. "What's the problem?"

"I've called to confess . . . a crime."

"Give me your name, please."

"Robert Glandier."

"Where are you calling from?"

"My home."

"Your address?"

"Twelve-thirty-two Willowville Drive."

"And when was this crime committed, Mr. Glandier?"

"A year ago. Longer."

"And the nature of the crime?"

"I can't say now." The hand at his crotch squeezed and twisted in a single motion. "I—murdered—my wife."

"Are you at home now?"

"Yes."

"Please stay there till someone from the department arrives. In the meantime I have some further questions—"

Glandier replaced the phone in its cradle. As he did so the fingers of the severed hand loosed their grip and fell to the soiled carpet. The hand scurried, spiderlike, toward the bathroom door, where the statue stood, holding not the lantern but the poet's severed head.

"There," said the poet, with a mocking smile, as it knelt to allow the severed hand to clamber up its shirt sleeve. "Now *that* wasn't so hard, was it?"

CHAPTER
53

Though he rarely indulged in the beverage himself, or in any other form of alcohol than wine, Dr. Samuel Helbron would describe himself, in moments of candor, as a "whiskey psychiatrist"—a psychiatrist, that is, who, like a whiskey priest, no longer believes in the faith whose external forms he continues, with cynical resignation, to observe. With the advent of effective psychotropic drugs, Dr. Helbron could think of no legitimate purpose to be served by encouraging suburban matrons and garrulous businessmen to indulge in the rigmaroles of secular confessions. People must be made to tow the line, and that was that. He regretted now not having majored in public administration. He would have liked to run a hospital, or a prison, or a police station—institutions that performed essential social services. But here he was with two rooms of teak furniture on the eighteenth floor of the Foshay Tower and an appointment calendar replete with the names of psychological cripples who used his bland and nonjudgmental presence as placebo, crutch, or scapegoat, according to their ever-shifting moods. He despised them for being rubes and himself for being a con man, but he was more than content to contend with such feelings for an income edging close to $100,000 a year.

Practiced as he was in maintaining an inexpressive demeanor, Dr. Helbron nevertheless found it difficult not to seem alarmed when a former patient—Robert Glandier, an executive with Techno-Controls—appeared at his office fifteen minutes before the first scheduled appointment in a state of manic animation bordering on hysteria and looking like he'd been dredged in flour. In such circumstances one did not insist on ordinary protocols, such as the need for a prior appointment. Helbron invited Glandier into his inner office and asked him what his problem was.

The man was not immediately forthcoming, but after some display of gruff impatience by the doctor, it developed that Glandier (after, in all likelihood, a bout of drinking) had phoned the Willowville police and confessed to his wife's murder. Dr. Helbron had formed the glimmering of such a suspicion when he had treated him the previous year and had then rather admired the man's self-possession. Too often clients insist on using their therapists' offices as psychological changing rooms where Dr. Jekyll can slip on the persona of Mr. Hyde. Glandier had never been like that. Even now he maintained that his confession had been "a mistake." He had been troubled, he said, by unusual nightmares. He feared he might be having a nervous breakdown and wanted Dr. Helbron to recommend an accredited convalescent home to which he might go to recuperate. But *not* a mental hospital: all he needed was a week or so of rest. He wanted, further, for Dr. Helbron to phone the Willowville police and explain that his own earlier phone call, confessing to his wife's murder, was not to be taken seriously. The doctor might tell the police it had been a drunken prank. As to the content of the nightmares that had troubled him or why he was covered with flour, these matters Glandier refused to discuss.

All in all, a singular performance, and one that Dr. Helbron would have willingly seen enlarged upon over a longer term of therapy. But the man was evidently out of control and very likely dangerous. There really was no way to deal with him but to turn him over to the civil authorities. First, however, he had to be persuaded to leave the office peaceably. As he adamantly refused to return to his home in Willowville, Dr. Helbron suggested that he check into the Raddison Hotel, get cleaned up, and wait for Dr. Helbron's all-clear signal.

Once Glandier had agreed to follow this advice and had departed (astonishing Mrs. Alden in the outer office), Dr. Helbron phoned Captain Maitland of the Minneapolis Police Department, his college friend and sometimes dinner companion, and informed him of what Glandier had told him and where he was to be found. Captain Maitland thanked him for his cooperation and arranged, in a spirit of good fellowship, to have dinner on Thursday of the following week.

Sad to say, Dr. Helbron and Captain Maitland were never to enjoy that engagement. Within minutes of Glandier's departure, Dr. Helbron received a phone call from the wife of another Techno-Controls executive, Michael Sheehy. Mrs. Sheehy was alarmed by the behavior of her eleven-year-old son Jack, who had attacked a neighbor's shrubberies with an ax while in pursuit (the boy claimed) of a frog. Since the incident with the shrubberies, the boy had kept to his room, refusing to speak with either of his parents. Mrs. Sheehy believed that drugs must be responsible for such behavior, and she wanted Jack to see Dr. Helbron while her suspicion was still verifiable. Dr. Helbron arranged to see Jack on his lunch hour.

At 12:05 the Sheehy boy arrived (not, however, accompanied by his mother, who, the boy said, was taking advantage of the trip downtown to do some shopping). Since Mrs. Alden had gone to lunch, Dr. Helbron led the boy into his inner office and offered to take his jacket, which he was carrying rolled up in a tight bundle. The boy said he would prefer to keep it by him. He sat with it in his lap.

Dr. Helbron then affected to fuss with his pipe. With younger patients it was a good rule-of-thumb to seem not to be scrutinizing them too intently in these first awkward moments. Today this deliberate inattention gave Jack Sheehy an opportunity to unroll his bundled jacket and, unperceived, take out the pistol (his father's) with which he had just murdered his mother.

Dr. Helbron finished lighting his pipe, spun his chair around smartly one quarter-swivel to the left, smiled in a manner calculated to inspire confidence, and asked, "Well now, Jack, what seems to be the problem?" They were his last words.

CHAPTER
54

It came almost as a relief to be arrested and put in jail. He was safer here, certainly, than he would have been anywhere else he could think of. No doubt the police had thought it strange that he didn't ask about bail and that he'd shown so little impatience when he'd been unable to get hold of his lawyer. For the time being he was better off without a lawyer, since there were so many questions for which he had no answers. Such as: Why had he phoned the police that morning? How had his house got wrecked? And the real poser: Who (if not he) had murdered Dr. Samuel Helbron? Glandier had his own idea of who it had to have been, but try and convey that idea to an arresting officer: "You see, my neighbor's got this kid who's possessed by a devil, who is also my son by my deceased wife, and this devil insists on knocking off anyone who may pose a threat to me, just to be nice."

So here he was, safe behind bars, charged with a murder he hadn't committed, mortally tired and unable to sleep. The cot sagged under his weight like a hammock. The sheet and blanket were too narrow to cover him. There was no way of shielding his eyes from the glare of the fluorescent fixture in the corridor outside his cell.

Sleep, he told himself. Now, while you can, sleep!

The policeman who'd fingerprinted him last night appeared at the door of the cell and told him he had a visitor.

—Who is it? he asked. —What time is it?

—Never mind, said the policeman. —Just move your ass.

He unlocked the cell and led Glandier along a shadowless corridor and into a small featureless room.

—Wait there, said the policeman, indicating one of the wooden chairs on either side of the Formica-topped table. The policeman left the room, closing the door behind him.

A moment later Jack Sheehy entered at another door. He took the chair on the other side of the table.

—We meet again, said Jack.

—I'm under arrest, said Glandier.

—I can see that.

—For a murder I believe *you* committed.

The boy grinned. —Which one?

—Dr. Helbron.

He shrugged. —So what do you want me to do? Go down to the desk and say, "Officer, I cannot tell a lie. *I* am the murderer. Robert Glandier is innocent." That would sure be dumb. Anyhow, who says you're innocent? You killed your wife; that's how this whole mess got started.

—This is a dream again, isn't it? They wouldn't have let you visit me.

—By now, Father dear, I would have thought you'd have

started paying attention to what happens in your dreams.

Glandier pressed his eyes tight-closed, then opened them.

—Am I still here? the boy asked sarcastically. —Tell you what, I'll make a bargain. I'll get you out of jail, no charges, your virtuous reputation restored. On one condition.

Glandier waited for him to name the condition.

—On the condition that the next time we encounter each other, I can take you off with me to hell. Is it a deal?

Glandier equivocated. —Am I really in jail? Is that much not a dream?

—Oh, you're in the clink all right. And unless you want to stay there a whole long time you better dip that fountain pen of yours into your own red blood and sign on the dotted line. Before they turn the lights on, and you wake up, and it's too fucking late.

Glandier stared at the Formica tabletop just in time to see a cockroach scuttle over the edge out of sight.

—Tell you what, to sweeten the deal I'll throw in a premium. You want to get rid of your wife's ghost permanently? And that other one, the poet who dresses up like a hitching post? I'll tell you what to do so that neither of them ever troubles you again. You'd like that, wouldn't you?

—Yes, certainly. But . . .

—But what? But you don't want to go to hell? You should have thought of that when the twig was bent. Around age three and a half, in your case. So what's it going to be? You better decide before you wake up.

—It's a deal, said Glandier.

What choice was there, really?

—Shake on it, said the boy, holding his hand out over the table.

Glandier shook his hand gingerly. The sensation was at once dry and squishy, as though the boy had been able to conceal a handful of cockroaches the moment before his hand was shaken.

At that moment Glandier felt a hand on his shoulder, shaking him awake. "No." Glandier groaned. "Not yet—he hasn't told me about my wife."

"Hey, mister, wake up. You're going home. Seems as how we've made a mistake. Here's your belt back, and your shoelaces."

"What! What's happened?"

"We'll tell you all about it in the D.A.'s office. Your lawyer's there now. You didn't want to discuss anything without him being there, remember? Well, that works both ways. But believe me, it's a lulu."

CHAPTER
55

As the two Sheehy girls, Judy and Maryann, walked home from the school bus stop on Pillsbury Road, Berryman, in the form, once more, of a black jockey carrying a lantern, ran ahead of them, or followed at their side, trying ineffectually to warn them against going into their own house. But for all the practical dread he was able to communicate he might as well have been one of his own books gathering dust on the highest shelf of the darkest stack of the most provincial library in the state of Minnesota. They were oblivious.

Berryman placed his hand on the back of Maryann's neck. "Come on, you've got to feel *something*—a shiver, a premonition. If you go in that house now you're as good as dead. *Listen* to me, will you?"

But Maryann experienced not so much as a goose bump. She continued to insist, over Judy's objections, that Jessica Breen was not a nerd, despite a few undeniable personality defects. However, Maryann maintained, if Jessica Breen wasn't perfect, neither was anyone else—a line of defense that Judy chose to interpret as a veiled criticism of herself.

"Listen," Berryman pleaded, tagging behind them, "will you please *listen!* Your brother's in there waiting to murder you. He's already shot your mother. He drowned your father when he came home from work after he'd knocked him unconscious with a croquet mallet. The boy has run amok. He's Charlie Manson writ small. Run away from home. Go to a pajama party. Do anything but go inside that house."

All unheeding, alas, the two sisters walked homeward through the sprawling communal back yard where earlier that day their brother had pursued the poet, John Berryman, in the frog stage of his metamorphic existence. Whether cued subliminally by the poet's warnings or simply reminded by the gouges the ax had cut into the sod, Judy observed, "Wasn't that a weird thing this morning?"

"Wasn't it," Maryann agreed.

"Did you ever find out *what* Jack thought he was up to?"

"According to Mom, he said he was chasing a frog. But with an *ax?* Apparently he wrecked the Gallaghers' shrubs in their front yard. I haven't actually seen what he did. I mean, it would have been pretty *obvious* if I'd walked around the front of their house to inspect the damage. Why would he do something like that? I mean, all right, we both know he's disturbed. *All* kids are a little weird at that age."

"*You* were going to commit suicide when *you* were twelve," Judy observed with malicious complacence.

"I never!" Maryann protested.

"You read the note *aloud* to me."

"That was a literary composition. I never seriously intended to commit suicide. And anyhow that was two years ago. It doesn't have anything to do with Jack being crazy."

"Who said Jack is crazy?"

"Well, what would you call it: normal?"

"No, but the important thing for us to remember," Judy said, "is to act as though nothing at all strange has happened. No remarks, no funny looks. Just pretend that nothing happened."

"Really?" Maryann looked dubious. Her hand rested on the handle of the back door of the Sheehy house. "Don't you think it might be better to reach out and try and *communicate* to him? I mean, you saw *Ordinary People*. The problem there was that people refused to discuss their problems."

"Oh, I'll discuss Timothy Hutton's problems with him any day. But I'm not going to discuss frog-killing with Jack, not if I can help it."

Berryman put his hand over Maryann's, trying against the irresistible pressure of her solid flesh to keep the door from opening. But the door opened, and one after the other Jack's destined victims walked inside to their slaughter.

"You did your best, John," said a voice from nowhere.

It was, he realized, Adah Menken's voice, and with that realization she appeared by the Sheehys' back door, wearing her costume for the role of Mazeppa—a white *broderie* bedspread cinched at the hips by a broad leather belt, another hunk of the bedspread wrapped about her head, a magnificently betasseled bolero jacket, and flesh-colored tights with white wrestling boots.

"I suppose," he said dourly, "I should go in there."

"No, John, it's gone beyond the point where we can hope to help them. I'm not a believer in predestination, but there is such a thing as the point of no return."

There was a longish silence as the two poets contemplated the mute siding of the house. Then Maryann let loose a blood-curdling scream as she went into the bathroom and discovered her father's dismembered torso in the bathtub.

"And Giselle?" Berryman insisted, turning his back on the Sheehy residence, resigned to the extinction of that family. "Don't try to tell me there's no way we can help her."

Adah looked down at the grass, abashed. "In some ways, I'm afraid, Giselle has already passed beyond our help—or out of our ken. Beyond, at least, the reach of language."

"But she's alive still," Berryman insisted. "In the sense that we are?"

"Oh yes. Alive as that tree. Which is why (you remind me) it would be wise if we took a shoot, or a clipping. *It* knows now where she is and how she can be attacked. We had better forestall such a possibility."

There was another scream (Judy's) inside the Sheehy residence, and then the sound of a banister railing snapping. (But not the ensuing thud of a body to the floor below that one might have expected, for Judy had taken a firm grip on a supporting baluster and was bludgeoning her brother's head with it.)

Berryman and Adah crossed the lawn to the willow by the ornamental pool, there to strip from it some dozen of its switchlike branches and weave with them a kind of garland.

Maryann, meanwhile, locked inside the bathroom with her dismembered father, continued to scream and to beat at the door.

"Now," said Adah, in her most authoritative tone, "it is time that I returned to Paradise, and I intend to take you with me. But first, John, you must give me back that ring. There'll be no more shape-shifting. You can't enter heaven looking like a refugee from a Hammacher-Schlemmer catalogue."

Berryman surrendered the magic ring and became in that instant himself again, a blinded poet in a shabby, blood-stained tweed jacket. "How do we get there?" he asked.

"We'll have to climb. And as there are no ladders in the immediate vicinity, I suggest that we climb this tree."

Berryman laid his hand on the tree's bark. "Will she feel us climbing?"

"Not in any very human sense. But never mind *her*. Self-help begins at home. Find the lowest cleft with your fingers—so. Now lift your left foot and put it in the stirrup I'm making with my hands."

Berryman followed her bidding, and soon he was climbing from limb to limb of the willow, which bent and bounced and swayed under his weight but always went on and up, like the proverbial beanstalk.

Jack Sheehy, meanwhile, had at last succeeded in gouging out the eyes of his elder sister and was now dousing the carpet of the upstairs hallway with gasoline.

Maryann, in the bathroom, was pounding a bottle of mouthwash against the glass of the Thermopane window, which Jack had earlier sealed shut with quick-bonding glue. The bottle shattered, and Maryann fell to the floor weeping tears of despair.

Wisps of smoke from the burning wool-and-acrylic carpet seeped in under the bathroom door.

"Are you still behind me?" Berryman called out, and Adah replied, reassuringly, that she was. "It seems we've been climbing longer than there could possibly be a tree to climb."

"We'll be there soon," she promised.

He reached up into the void and felt for another branch of the willow and wrapped his fingers about it and pulled himself some inches higher, feeling with his right foot for a lower branch. Ahead of him he could sense a difference in the enveloping darkness, a kind of flickering below the spectrum of visible light, and a coolness rippled up from his feet and along his spine, then bounced from brain to fingers in patterns ever more quick and complicated, like the wave patterns at the bottom of a pool as a rainstorm begins. "Are we there yet?" he demanded.

"Any moment now," she soothed.

Meanwhile, in the Sheehys' burning home, Jack opened the small window near the ceiling of the family room in the basement. He reached into the birdcage that he had bought only that afternoon at the Willowdale Mall, trying to encourage the parrakeet within to hop onto his finger. The parrakeet refused to cooperate. It hopped from its perch to the floor of the cage, then up its feed dish, squawking angrily, determined *not* to light on Jack's insistent finger. The room was filling so quickly with smoke that Jack could scarcely see what he was doing from the smarting of his eyes. At last he thought to lift the cylinder of metal bars up from their plastic base and upend it. After its most dire protest, the bird flew free of the cage, circled the room twice in confusion, and then as the halfling fled his body and Jack collapsed, asphyxiated, to the floor, it found its way through the window and out into the evening air, where, in the distance, it could hear the first shrill ululations of the approaching fire engines.

CHAPTER
56

"I'm in charge of the entire earth?" Joy-Ann marveled. "That's hard to believe!"

"Somebody has to do the job," said Adah, "and I've been at it since 1868. Surely that's long enough."

"But why me? I was never anything but a housewife."

"Well, you know what Christ said in the Sermon on the Mount."

"What did he say? I was never very good at memorizing those things."

"It's there on the wall behind you."

Joy-Ann spun around her swivel chair and looked at the sampler that hung on the gray metal wall. It was the twin to the sampler that had been in her hospital room when she'd first awakened in Paradise, but instead of a rainbow and elm trees and flowers, this one depicted the earth as it appeared in NASA photographs, with all the names and boundary lines erased, its shadowed hemisphere hazing into night, its blue oceans marbled with cloud. Springing up from the immensities of its land masses were stupendous spiral staircases, ornately carved and thickly encrusted with precious stones, by which a myriad blissful souls ascended and descended. Arching over all, in letters that twinkled like stars, were the words of the Third Beatitude:

BLESSED ARE
THE MEEK
FOR THEY SHALL
INHERIT THE EARTH.

"Meek!" Joy-Ann shrieked. "Why, I'm the last person anyone would ever call meek!"

"There's one other qualification for the job: it has to go to someone who enjoys what the earth has to offer. You'd be surprised how many people get to Paradise and just want to scoot right along to realms of light. No nostalgia at all for what they're leaving behind. I thought for a while when Colette died— Are you a reader of her books, by the way?"

Joy-Ann shook her head. Colette who? she wondered. Somehow she knew better than to ask.

"Well, I thought that she, of all people, would agree to relieve me of the job. But no, she just wanted to ascend onward and upward. Candidly, at *that* time, I didn't particularly want to go into retirement."

"What's changed your mind since then?"

"This business with the Sheehy family. The *injustice* of it! I don't ever want to be mixed up in that sort of thing again."

Joy-Ann nodded. "That's pretty much the attitude the Sheehys take themselves, that it was terribly unfair. But they blame Jack. I've tried to explain to them that Jack wasn't responsible for anything that happened, that he did the bad things he did because a terrible demon had got hold of him. But his father seems to think I'm inventing excuses. The boy's mother just sits there crying, and the two girls give me stony looks. As though it were *my* fault! I told them they're not going to leave that waiting room until they at least agree to *talk* with the boy. He's so upset, poor thing. He had no idea of anything that was happening till the moment he woke up in the burning house. Then a few moments later he was dead. You'd think they'd feel sorry for the little fellow."

"You have a waiting room?" Adah asked in a tone of commendation. "Where is it?"

Joy-Ann indicated the door Adah had entered by. "Right there. At first I tried working at home, but I found that that made most people uncomfortable. They're used to dealing with institutions, and when they come here, where everything can be so strange at times, the shock isn't so great if they find themselves in an office-type environment. Also, just from my own personal point of view I like it better this way. I realized, when you asked me to pinch-hit for you, that what I'd really always wanted was to have a career: a desk, and an office with my name on the door, and responsibilities. Of course, at first it was a little daunting. There are millions and millions of people dying every year, and while not all of them need special attention, a lot do. But then I thought of what you told me about eternity and there being no need to rush. So I just take my time, and eventually it all gets done." She smiled. "Knock on wood." And rapped her knuckles on the veneer of her immense desk.

"Oh, one last thing before I forget." Adah bent over and removed from her carrier bag the garland of willow branches, now unwoven and wrapped in crinkly florist's paper. "These. Keep them watered, and see that they get a bit of sunlight from time to time, but don't overdo it. And when they're quite healthy, take just a teeny-tiny piece out of one leaf and plant it in an embryo from the list of available embryos. And that should do the trick."

"What trick will it do?" Joy-Ann demanded, with some alarm.

"It's a way for Giselle to be reincarnated."

"You mean she has to go through another entire life?"

"I'm afraid so."

"Will she be able to remember anything from her first life?"

"She's left all that behind already, I'm afraid."

"Not even her name."

"No. But her soul is still her own and no one else's."

Joy-Ann regarded the posy of willow branches sorrowfully. She sighed. "I suppose I should get a vase for it."

Adah nodded. She held out her hand in farewell.

"The ring," Joy-Ann reminded her.

"The ring, of course. I almost forgot." She wiggled a finger down into the bodice of her tight-fitting bolero jacket and retrieved the magic ring. She handed it to Joy-Ann, who put it on her own left-hand ring finger.

They shook hands and then, more affectionately, kissed each other's cheeks.

"Goodbye," said Joy-Ann. "Have a *nice* time in heaven."

"Goodbye. Enjoy yourself. Don't work too hard."

"Oh, I will, and I won't. Which reminds me: when you go out—"

"Yes?" Adah stood by the partly opened door.

"Ask the Sheehys to come in here again. They've been waiting so long, and there aren't any magazines out there. I've looked all over, but I can't find a newsstand anywhere."

"There are books in Paradise," Adah explained, "but no magazines. I'll send them in."

She stepped into the waiting room and smiled at the Sheehys. "You can go in now," she told them.

269

Mr. Sheehy scowled at her, and Mrs. Sheehy dabbed at her tearful cheeks with a Kleenex. Both girls made disdainful smirks at the Mazeppa costume.

Thank God, Adah thought, I am quitting this job forever. She left the waiting room with a little sashay of liberation— and almost collided with John Berryman (no longer blind but very nearsighted), who was waiting in the outer corridor.

"Ready?" he asked her.

"I couldn't be readier."

"Then it's up, up, and away!"

"Excelsior," she concurred.

CHAPTER
57

While he waited for Giselle's remains to be brought to the Dove Room, Glandier spent his time in one of the larger enclosed courtyards upstairs, listening to canned music and reading a promotional brochure for Schinder's Memorial Gardens. This courtyard was devoted to a single sculpture by Helmut Vliet that looked, to Glandier's untutored eye, like the aftermath of a bombing raid on a used-car lot. The tortured shapes of particolored steel were somewhat softened by the addition of potted ferns and a central fountain. From an esthetic point of view Glandier abominated Schinder's Memorial Gardens, as he abominated any art that was not clearly subordinated to commercial purposes, but he had been unable to persuade the management of the cemetery where Giselle had originally been buried—or rather, mis-buried—to cremate her exhumed body. They would only re-bury it in the plot for which it had originally been intended. Whereupon Glandier told them he would take his business elsewhere. After several telephone inquiries, Schinder's had been the only mortuary willing to provide the service Glandier required.

Schinder's (the brochure explained) represented a twofold evolution in the funeral industry. First, with regard to the practical business of interment and cremation, Schinder's offered facilities that were efficient, thrifty, and free of the tasteless pomp and ostentation of conventional funeral arrangements. Secondly, with respect to the more intangible values associated with the commemorative function of a cemetery, Schinder's philosophy was to create, as much as possible, the ambience of a museum of contemporary art. Not (the brochure insisted) a mere potpourri of casts and copies, the originals of which were to be found only in European collections, but a tribute to the achievements of America's greatest contemporary artists, the artists who had brought Modernism to the New World and here made it yield its richest harvests.

To achieve this visionary purpose Graham Schinder, the sole heir of the Schinder meat-packing and milling fortune, had spent more than $65,000,000 over a period of twenty years, assembling a collection of American art of unique refinement and importance. The gardens, courtyards, and pavilions of the Memorial Gardens displayed notable paintings by Mark Rothko, Barnett Newman, Jasper Johns, Helen Frankenthaler, and Morris Louis, as well as the most extensive collections in the world of the sculptures of David Smith, Louise Nevelson, Marisol, and Helmut Vliet. (Vliet, the brochure noted, had been a close personal friend of Mr. Schinder and had contributed to the conception and design of the Memorial Gardens.) The Gardens had been cited by the Academy of American Architects as the most innovative and distinguished cemetery of the twentieth century.

What all the brochure's PR added up to, for Glandier, was a price tag four times greater than he'd had to spend for Giselle's previous plot. In return, Giselle's ashes would be accorded some few cubic inches of elbow room in the Nevelson Cinerarium and her memory honored by the never-to-be-noticed tribute of having her name engraved on the long brazen list of the Remembered that graced its entrance. Glandier thought that Schinder might more aptly have been called Swindler, but even so he was grateful for the opportunity of having the remains of his wife's body burnt and pulverized. Only a countervailing wish to avoid an argument with Joy-Ann (who had thought cremation sinful) had prevented Glandier from having his wife's body cremated the first time around. Most murderers would express a similar preference for cremation, as it affords a sense of closure that mere burial can never equal.

At last a blond girl in a dark dress, whose name he forgot as soon as she introduced herself, led Glandier down two flights of stairs, along a dim-lighted corridor, and into the Dove Room, which was the most nondescript mortuary chapel he'd ever seen. There were some four or five small pictures on the walls, and the few pieces of furniture looked like they'd come from a garage sale.

"Where are the doves?" he asked.

"The paintings in this room are all by Arthur Dove," the blond girl explained, without the trace of a smile.

"Oh."

"Here," the girl explained, in the manner of an airline stewardess performing the incantations of a takeoff, "is the sound system. There are nine channels, and the musical selections are noted on this card. Here—" She touched a black plastic button that put Glandier in mind of the pin-reset button at a bowling alley. "—is this switch that activates the trolley on which the casket—" She placed her hand gently on same. "—will travel into the crematory chamber. And now, as I understand that you've requested to make this last farewell privately, I will leave you with your wife. The room is yours for the next half-hour. Please accept my sincere sympathy."

Glandier wondered if he ought to tip, but she'd gone out the door before he could reach for his wallet.

Alone with his wife's corpse, he allowed himself a moment to gloat before he punched the button that would send her into the flames. Already he had seen to the disposal of the wood from the willow tree that he had paid to have cut down, as per the instructions left him (in an envelope tucked under the bedroom phone) by Jack Sheehy. Good to his promise to instruct Glandier in the means to prevent his further haunting either by his wife or any of her otherworldy delegates, Jack had told him to burn both her fleshy remains and her etheric body (contained within the willow's wood). Then, having delivered that note, he had accomplished the slaughter of the Sheehy family, which (with its attendant relevations) had sprung Glandier from jail.

Glandier checked the musical offerings listed on the card and chose the Mormon Tabernacle Choir singing "Nearer My God to Thee."

A preliminary flourish of organ music drowned out the chirping of the robin that had hopped onto the sill of the Dove Room's single window. From the sill the robin dropped to the forest-green carpet, and then in a few hops it crossed the room to the foot of the trolley (as the attendant had termed it, though it more closely resembled a simple conveyor belt) on which the casket had been placed. Thence, with a flutter of its wings, it rose to perch upon the casket itself.

Glandier at last noticed the robin, and remarked, "What the fuck." He walked over to the casket and took a swat at the bird, but the robin proved more agile, and its parrying peck drew blood from the back of Glandier's hand.

Only then did it occur to him that this might be no ordinary robin. Ordinary robins would not peck at the silver cross that decorated the lid of a casket. ("Silvery," rather, for the cross was only a piece of paper glued over a thin shell of molded plastic. Schinder's, true to its advertising claims, did not waste their clients' money on needless pomp.) No, this was a robin only in the illusory sense that the heron at Rush Lake had been a heron. Yet in another sense it *was* a robin, at least until it could change to some larger and less vulnerable form. Now, if ever, was the moment to see to it that it underwent no further metamorphoses.

With conscious slyness and with a sense of delight born of that slyness, Glandier slipped off the jacket of his coat and, holding it up, netlike, in both hands, pounced upon the robin. But, being ponderous at the best of times and especially awkward in this particular, he pounced too hard, and the plastic casket, weakened by the robin's pecking, split apart at the seams the silvery cross had concealed. In the same instant the halfling leaped across the infinitesimal interface separating the animate tissues of the robin from the inanimate remains of the corpse.

Glandier had lost his balance, so that both hands and most of his weight were resting on the slick surface of the body bag within the sundered casket. As he struggled to push himself upright, and as the reanimate corpse within tore at this last confining membrane, the black plastic ripped and a noxious odor filled the air of the Dove Room to mingle with the triumphant strains of the Mormon Tabernacle Choir.

Bony fingers knotted about Glandier's silk rep tie. As though he'd received a blow to the solar plexus, Glandier doubled forward. In an instinctive gesture of self-protection, he lifted his right knee. It touched the button that triggered the casket's journey to the crematory chamber. Two doors of polished brass opened at the end of the short conveyor belt, and the casket was propelled toward the opening.

Glandier's screams, as he was pulled by his necktie down the metal-rollered incline beyond the double doors (in much the way a carton of canned goods enters the basement of a supermarket), could not be heard above the hymn's joyous conclusion. The doors closed behind him, and for a moment all was blackness. Then through the grating of the grille on which he lay he saw the hundred blue flames of the crematorium winking on, row upon row, as his wife's grinning, fleshless mouth rose toward his to seal their union with a final kiss.

CHAPTER
58

They walked along an infinite path through a boundless prairie toward a horizon that seemed always just fifty or sixty feet ahead. He had taken off his tweed jacket and left it on a scarecrow. His sleeves were rolled up, and his feet were bare. She too had thrown away her wrestling boots, though she still wore the rest of her Mazeppa costume, except for the cumbersome, sweaty turban. They talked about politics and the folly of the nuclear arms race, about Paris and New York, but mostly they talked about poets and poetry. She was full of wonderful gossip about Whitman, whom she had seen cruising Manhattan's primal beatniks at Charley Pfaff's beer cellar on Broadway and Bleecker, and about Swinburne, whom she had tried to vamp for £10 at the request of

277

his friend, Gabriel Rossetti. She was able to compare the sexual staying power of Dickens to that of Dumas *père* (the latter excelling, she insisted, in strict proportion to his greater girth). Berryman told tales of Roethke and Lowell and Delmore Schwartz, to all which she listened with remarkable patience and attentiveness, considering she knew nothing about them and had never read their work.

At last, when his reminiscences had wound down and she judged him to be in his mellowest mood, she proffered the suggestion she had been reserving all the while they had been journeying. "Do you know what would be wonderful?"

"What?"

"A workshop."

"A what?"

"A poetry workshop—in heaven. Not in the Empyrean, perhaps. In the higher reaches, I suppose, one loses interest in poetry—and in prose. But Dante *does* put Homer and the other classical poets in the very first circle—"

"Of his *Inferno*," Berryman noted.

"Yes, but they're not *suffering* there. They're discussing poetry, just as we were. And there are probably millions and millions of souls in heaven who'd like to take a workshop with the great John Berryman. Your reputation with your students stood very high, you know."

"And would these millions of celestial poets sit and listen while each of the others read his or her poems aloud and then had them critiqued? That could take rather a long time."

"Well, we'll be there for all eternity. It was only a suggestion."

"I thought that once we arrived in heaven we'd be in a state of permanent mindless ecstasy. When *do* we arrive, by the way?"

Adah looked down at her forearm, as though consulting a

wristwatch, though she wore only bangles. "It's not much farther." She was pouting.

"I didn't mean to seem slighting."

"Your problem, John Berryman, is that you're an elitist."

He shrugged.

From behind them there was a voice, hailing them by their names: "Hey there, Mr. Berryman! Mrs. Menken! Wait up!"

It was the Sheehy boy, riding toward them (with some difficulty, owing to the bumpiness of the path) on a bicycle.

"Puck!" Berryman saluted him with a wave of his arm.

The boy braked to a stop beside them. "It's Jack," he corrected, in an aggrieved tone. "Jack Sheehy. You probably don't remember, but I tried to kill you a few days ago."

"Oh, we remember, certainly," said Adah. "Mr. Berryman was just giving you a kind of nickname. Do you already have a nickname that you prefer?"

"Not really."

"Well, now you do!" she said brightly. "Puck was the hero in a play by William Shakespeare. In case you didn't know."

Jack seemed unsure whether he was being made fun of, and then decided it didn't matter. "Here," he said, reaching into the basket of his bicycle. "Mrs. Anker told me to give this to you as a bon voyage present." He presented Adah with a bouquet of bloodroot, bluet, and bridal wreath. "And this is for Mr. Berryman." He produced a bottle of New York State champagne.

"Isn't that nice of her," said Adah. "Do give Joy-Ann my thanks, and a big kiss from me." She stooped to kiss Jack on the forehead. He grimaced.

"She didn't think to send glasses with the champagne, did she?" Berryman asked.

"Right here," said Jack, and reached into the basket to produce two wineglasses of blue cut glass.

279

Berryman thumbed off the cork of the bottle, which, under the open sky of the endless prairie, did not make much of a pop, but the champagne itself foamed out of the bottle quite dramatically, thanks to the bumpy ride it had enjoyed in the bicycle basket.

"Look," said Jack, just as they'd lifted their glasses to each other in a wordless toast. "Up there—a blimp!"

And so there was; in the western sky, where the sun was sinking into banks of apricot and cantaloupe clouds, a silvery dirigible covered with winking lights approached.

"Can you read what the lights spell out?" Adah asked.

"My eyes were never that good," said Berryman. "It's still a long way off."

They strolled down the path, sipping the champagne and admiring the joint spectacle of the sunset, which was a supremely beautiful sunset, and the blimp's approach, which was ponderous but also, in its own way, sublime. Jack followed, wheeling his bicycle.

After a very short time the path came to a stop at the edge of a cliff. Below them a river of awesome breadth wound from north to south, bisecting the infinite prairie. The sunset slanted down into the mirror of the river and leaped up in glory.

"That can't be—" Berryman began. "No. Impossible."

"What's impossible?" asked Adah.

"That isn't . . . the Styx?"

"Of course not!" Adah said indignantly. "The Styx is off in Greece or some such place, a perfectly insignificant river. This, surely, is the Mississippi. Not the real Mississippi, perhaps: the Spiritual Mississippi, one might better say. Americans do some things better, you know, and size is definitely one of those things."

As though to prove her point, the dirigible had now drawn near enough for them to make out both its individual markings and its overall size. The latter was expressed succinctly by Jack, who declared it to be at least as large as the mother ship that lands on Satan's Bluff at the end of *Close Encounters.* Its vast bulk was given over to a complicated array of blinking lights that alternated the single, cheery exclamation

SAVED!

with explosions and geysers and pinwheels of shimmery color, each of them an advertisement and a promise of heavenly bliss.

"Wowee-zowee!" said Jack (for Adah and Berryman were speechless). "Will you look at that! *That* is something special."

The blimp, as it neared the cliff from which they were regarding river, sunset, and light show, began to descend, until at last the cabin slung underneath the ship proper was brushing the grass and its shadow had darkened the meadow for acres about. A door opened, and a figure stepped from the cabin.

It was Jesus Christ, wearing the uniform of an officer in the Salvation Army. He strode across the meadow grass with his arms outstretched, smiling the friendliest of smiles.

"Hi there," said Jesus. "You must be Adah Menken." He took her hands and beamed. She blushed. He squeezed. She smiled. He laughed and, without releasing her hands, turned to Berryman. "And you're John, the same as my beloved disciple. Good to meet you, after all I've been told. But who—" He took off his visored cap and hunkered down to be face to face with Jack Sheehy. "—is this? Are you coming back to heaven with me too?"

"No, sir, I'm sorry but I can't. I'd love to have a ride in your dirigible, but I promised Joy-Ann—Mrs. Anker, that is—that I would go to Tanganyika and help her daughter get reincarnated there. She's going to be a Masai warrior in her next life. All I have to do is plant this—" He showed Jesus the protoplast taken from a leaf of the willow that Berryman

281

had brought to Paradise. "—in the uterus of her mother-to-be. Or I guess I should say 'his.' "

"A Masai warrior!" Adah marveled. "What a strange choice."

"It was either that," Jack explained, "or the eighth daughter of a Polish miner with Somebody's syndrome as a birth defect. I don't know how it worked out to just those two possibilities. A computer does all the astrological calculations. Anyhow, Joy-Ann decided that Giselle should start off her next life from a new angle."

"Sounds like a good idea, though I hope it won't take her a whole lot longer to join the rest of us here." He stood up. "Well, time to be on our way. Sorry you can't come along with us today, Jack. Maybe next time?"

"Actually," said Jack, "I'm in a kind of apprentice program right now. Eventually I'm going to be Mrs. Anker's assistant, in charge of everything to do with sex and stuff like that. There's some kind of connection between sex and death."

"I know," said Jesus. "Though *we*—" His smile embraced (almost, it seemed, quite literally) Adah and John. "—have passed beyond all that."

He offered his hands to them, and like children in a calendar picture they took, each of them, one of his hands and followed him back to the dirigible.

Jack watched till they were safe inside and the dirigible was back in the air high above the Spiritual Mississippi. Then he turned his bicycle around and started pedaling east to Tanganyika.

CHAPTER
59

"Another *quennelle?*" Bing urged. "Or some more *soubise?*"

"Thank you," said Father Mabbley, "but I've already had a genteel sufficiency. Quite seriously, dear boy, such gifts as yours ought not to be wasted on the desert air."

"These days, Father, Julia Child is universal, and in any case the desert is *your* home. Here in the cities of the Great Plains, milk and honey and butter and eggs and all the other sources of cholesterol have their source. In due course Minnesota shall be the Normandy of America. But I'm glad you enjoyed your dinner. Now, shall we repair to the drawing room for our coffee?"

"What I meant to say," said the priest, pushing back his chair and rising from the candlelit table, "is that we've missed you, Bing dear, simply that. And I *do* find it hard to understand how you can want to stay on here in St. Paul a day longer than need be. After all you've been through."

Bing snuffed out the candles with his fingers and followed his guest into the "drawing room," which differed from the living room it had been in Joy-Ann's time only with respect to the installation of new drapes and the banishment of some of the tackier furniture to the basement. The drapes, however, were spectacularly *au courant* and opulent, a cream-colored silk damask of so monumental a pattern that in their fullest extent they seemed but a swatch snipped from a bolt of gargantuan proportions. Their effect, when drawn, was to make the surviving furnishings seem somehow hypothetical, the furniture of a dollhouse or a stage set rather than of an actual house that people lived in. With that single alteration (and a change of name) Bing now felt entirely comfortable living as the custodian of the museum of his childhood.

Bing poured the coffee from a Royal Worcester pot that he'd bought on his first great spree after being released from the hospital. It had cost well over a hundred dollars, but it was truly the most beautiful of coffeepots, with orange lotuses blossoming on a field of bone white china, a coffeepot that could be counted as a friend.

Over their coffee Bing filled in Father Mabbley on the details of his strange good fortune, details too distressing to have gone into at dinner. First, as to Glandier's dark guilt: the Scrabble Ouija message Bing had received with Alice Hoffman had been confirmed from the unlikeliest of sources. The sister of a crippled Vietnam veteran who had died in a freak fishing accident had discovered among her brother's effects a confession of his having agreed to supply Glandier with a false alibi for the time of Giselle's murder, in consideration for Glandier's buying a lakeside cabin at a wildly inflated price. This, in conjunction with Glandier's subsequently retracted confession over the phone to the

Willowville police, had been enough to persuade Glandier's attorney and other relevant authorities to declare Bing to be Glandier's heir, ostensibly as next-of-kin.

"And so you have *two* houses," Father Mabbley marveled.

"And a cottage by a lake, *and* rather a large lump of money. Glandier's company lavished life insurance on its executives as though there were no tomorrow. I'm rich. Or *very* prosperous, anyhow. So long as interest rates stay above eight percent, I'll never have to work again. Though just to keep from going utterly to seed and forgetting all my professional training, I've volunteered to be the bingo caller for Our Lady of Mercy's Las Vegas nights."

"Ahhh!" purred Father Mabbley with a sanctimony delicately laced with sarcasm. "I'm glad to know that you don't intend to be wanting in your love for Mother Church. You realize, of course, that in some particulars the church here may not have quite the same enlightened attitudes as you've come to take for granted at St. Jude's."

"In that regard, Father, I intend to balance my benefactions. St. Paul is notoriously homophobic. There was a referendum here some years ago on the issue of gay civil rights, the result of which was that gays were told they were to have none. So, by way of showing gratitude for my various windfalls, I'll be letting THRUST, which is the most radical and outspoken of the various gay activists' groups in the area, use this house for their hotline. And the house in Willowville is going to be a hostel for gays who've had problems with their landlords."

"I wonder if that will sit well with the rectory at Our Lady of Mercy."

"If they choose to make an issue of it, I'll reveal that I am acting according to express wishes of Father Windakiewiczowa."

"Surely that would be fibbing," said Father Mabbley.

Bing pursed his lips and shook his head. "On my honor,

Father Mabbley, as a good Catholic. After all, the man did die at my very bedside. Who would know more about his last wishes?"

"It's that, of course—the murder of Father What's-it when he was visiting you at the hospital—that represents the most impenetrable mystery in the whole tangled skein. One can understand why a disturbed adolescent—"

"Jack Sheehy was not yet an adolescent," Bing corrected.

"Child, in that case: why a child might murder his entire family. Such things have been known to happen, alas. One can even conceive his shooting a psychiatrist he's been sent to, though it seems altogether too odd a coincidence that your brother-in-law should have visited the same psychiatrist earlier on the day of the murder."

"Yet there's no doubt at all that the boy was responsible, and not Bob. The keys to Helbron's office door were found in the boy's pocket. The gun had been registered in his father's name."

"But *why* would he go to the hospital room of a man he's never met, to *your* room, and try and kill you, and then in what seems an excess of high spirits actually murder two complete strangers? Why? It defies belief."

"Yet the police have established fairly conclusively that it was him. The wrapping paper left in the room was from a roll in the Sheehy house. A witness saw him playing Space Invaders in the hospital basement just before the murder."

"But *why?*"

Bing smiled mysteriously, as who would say, I know more than I'm telling. As indeed he did. For some weeks now he had been receiving Scrabble Ouija messages from a spirit calling itself Puck. These messages would have answered almost all of Father Mabbley's questions (and told him a great deal, additionally, about the domestic arrangements of eels and lobsters), but Bing was sworn to secrecy. In any case, Puck's explanation of all these events was several degrees stranger than the events themselves.

Besides, Bing liked to keep secrets. He teased Father Mabbley along, with will-o'-the-wisp cruelty, through a whole tangled forest of fruitless speculations, supplemented, when the gelatin had finally gelled, with a slice of Brandy Alexander pie.

Then, when he could endure the suspense no longer, Bing said, "Now that you're sufficiently mellow, Father, let me show you the rest of the house. I've taken much greater liberties with the upstairs rooms."

"By all means," said Father Mabbley.

"Mother's room," Bing explained, mounting the stairs, "is just a hollow shell at this point. That's where I mean to put the Hotline office. You'll be staying in the guest room, which used to be Giselle's. I've done it up in 1930s Hollywood-Moroccan. My own room is still in transition, and I need your advice about the canopy over the bed. But the *pièce de résistance*, so far, is the bathroom. *Voilà!*"

Bing flung open the bathroom door with a flourish, and Robert Glandier, stark naked, leaped up from the seat of the toilet and placed his hands over his genitals in the classic pose of post-lapsarian shame.

"Well, Father, what do you think?"

"Beardsley?" said the priest, in rather a stricken than a commendatory tone.

"I did them all myself," said Bing. "With ordinary house paint."

"I didn't know you had ambitions as a muralist."

"I'd never realized how easy it was to do until I read this article in *Family Circle* on how to paint enlargements of familiar cartoon characters on children's bedroom walls. I figured if it would work for Huckleberry Hound it would work with Beardsley's *Salome*. Admittedly, the execution is ragged in places. The ceiling especially. Ceilings are a bitch to paint."

"So it would seem."

Bing giggled. "On your honor, Father: what do you think?"

"Of this? On my honor? I would have to say I think it's appalling. But I gather it's *meant* to be appalling."

"Mm, yes, in a way that's so. Oh dear. Excuse me, but I fear the power of suggestion is proving too much. Would you mind interrupting the guided tour for a moment? I have to wee-wee something awful."

"That's quite all right, my boy. I'll take the opportunity to do what I earlier was threatening to do—the dishes."

"No, Father, really!"

Father Mabbley raised his hand to signify that protest would not avail, then slipped out the door and pulled it shut behind him.

Bing waited till he heard Father Mabbley get halfway down the stairs, then turned to Glandier and said, in a kind of stage whisper, "Well, that answers the question. You are invisible to everyone but me. Father Mabbley is the soul of courtesy, but even he could not have resisted noting the presence of a fat naked middle-aged man in a friend's bathroom."

"Go away," said Glandier in a voice hollowed out by hopelessness. "Just go away and leave me alone."

"Invisible, inaudible, and unable (as we well know) to go anywhere beyond the confines of this room. The prisoner, through all eternity, of the Oscar Wilde Memorial Bathroom. *I* think it's droll."

"I'll scream," Glandier threatened. "I can still do that."

Bing grinned. "And *I* . . . can *tweak* . . . your *nose!*"

Glandier backed into the corner of the bathroom. Bing often carried out this threat, or otherwise collided with, bumped into, or goosed Glandier's immaterial body. Each time Glandier would pop out of existence and instantly reappear on his back in the bathtub, or, if the bathtub had a corporeal occupant, seated on the toilet. It made him feel like a ping-pong ball caroming about in a shoebox.

"I thought you were going to scream," Bing taunted. "So, scream, I'm waiting. Your screams amuse me."

"Fucking queer," Glandier muttered.

"Nowadays the correct term of abuse is 'faggot,' I'm told." Bing turned to the mirror and affected to study his right eyebrow. "If you mean to be insulting. While for *fat* people 'pig' is generally considered most opprobrious. You do, in fact, look very porcine without your clothes."

"Do you know," said Glandier, in a tone of thoughtfulness, "if there were a hell, I think I'd really rather be there."

"Does my company get you down so terribly? Poor baby! I don't think that was Mother's intention when she billeted you here. Indeed, I understand from a young friend of mine, whose name is Puck, that she expects us to become *friends* in due course! I believe her hope is that some of my good manners may rub off on you, and some of your *manliness* will seep into my character. What are the odds, do you suppose, of *that* dream coming true?"

Glandier closed his eyes and threw his head back and screamed as loudly as he could.

"And *this* little pig," said Bing, stepping forward, "said wee-wee-wee-wee-wee all the way home." He tweaked Glandier's nose.

Instantly Glandier found himself lying on his back in the bathtub.

"Well, *I* must return to my duties as a host, and *you* must stay here and haunt the bathroom like a good ghost. One of these days I'll open a savings account and get a radio for in here so that you'll at least have a beat to help you while away the hours. And the days. And the years. Ta-ta."

Glandier did not stir from the bathtub when Bing left the room. He lay on his back staring at the ceiling, where ill-

289

drawn grotesques leered and winked and jubilated at his expense. Unheard even by Bing, who was in the kitchen helping Father Mabbley with the dishes, Glandier screamed at the jeering faces, and screamed again, and continued screaming until his throat was quite sore. Then he simply stared at the faucet of the tub and the folds of the plastic shower curtain. As so often before, he found that the best way to pass the time was by doing long division in his head. He had always excelled at arithmetic.

CHAPTER
60

The child in whose form Giselle was to have been reborn died in the third day of its embryonic life through the beneficence of a chemical abortifacient. Such was the gift of grace that she was at once free to leave Earth and old mortality for the blisses so long held in abeyance.

Without a name, without an aim, with no idea of before or after, no tears, no laughter, no clothes to wear, no forms to fill, what could be said of her soul now? That sometimes it moved, sometimes stood still. That there remained a core within, a kind of skin or shell without; and in the core a pulse, and on the skin a sense of something or of someone else, other templates and tempos, of opposing or concurrent wills.

But in such crass archetypal particulars as flowers, blue skies, sun's heat, or star's distance, what could she be said to know or feel? That flowers cry like children, demanding a doting adult attention; that the dome of the sky and the lens of the eye rhyme to each other, and both are real; that all heat is dissipated as a function of time; that distance is God's supreme fiction.

Yet can't something more *human* be said? Are souls so ethereal that all statements we attach to them must be abstract as Christmas tree ornaments? Even nameless, cannot Love, like Amor, shoot his arrows into our random hearts so they may bleed responsively? Indeed he can. Indeed, there are moments when a soul released from its cave of flesh will speed toward a mortal mind as it lies entranced in sleep, will curl across its surface, frothing, like waves across a beach, touching its tenderest parts and causing dreams to rise from its depths, like the bubbles of burrowing clams. And we awake, knowing we have been touched by something beautiful, whose beauty we shall never understand, knowing only that we have been witnesses of its inexpressible passing. We call her name, if we can still remember it, and ask her to remain a moment longer, only a moment. But already she is gone.